THE DEVOURER FROM BEYOND

RK JACK

PRAISE FOR "THE DEVOURER FROM BEYOND"

"RK Jack's *The Devourer From Beyond* turns the knob up to eleven then breaks it off. Nonstop action, chills, and a terrific storyline that sets a pace faster than *Raiders of the Lost Ark* and continues to deliver." —Mark Everett Stone, author of *Things to Do in Denver When You're Un-Dead*

"In *The Devourer From Beyond*, RK Jack combines various genres to create a gripping page-turner. The author adeptly conveys the law enforcement representatives' way of thinking and their perception of hazardous circumstances, increasing the psychological and emotional depth of the narration. An enthralling twist promises more breathtaking discoveries, and the conclusion does not disappoint." —*Readers' Favorite* 5-Star Review by Nino Lobiladze

CONTENTS

THE DEVOURER FROM BEYOND

Published by Horizon View Press LLC

Denver, CO

ISBN: 979-8-9900568-1-7

FIC015000 **FICTION** / Horror

Cover design by Shira Atakpu, copyright owned by Russell Jack (RK Jack).

To those who keep us safe from evil in the real world.
Thank you.

CHAPTER 1
FLIGHT 436

Agent Thomas

MY FEET HIT the planked wood floor next to my bed, even before my mind caught wind that I was fully awake. Years of training have conditioned me to get up when that alarm goes off.

I am Thomas Schmidt, a federal air marshal (FAM).

My wife, Grace, moaned and rolled away from me. She hated how I shot out of bed when the alarm went off. She seemed to hate many things about me lately. It was clear to me that we had grown apart for the last couple of years. Our kids, Rick and Jillian, complained that I wasn't there enough. And when I was, Grace said I wasn't fully "present." The reason? I am habitually sleep deprived and never have a regular schedule, so I am always exhausted.

And rarely even home.

I just returned yesterday from an international trip, where I slept at a hotel during my body's regular "daytime" hours and missed an entire night of sleep. I got home, had a pleasant dinner, and then spent some "quality" time that night with her and the kids. By the time I went to bed, I had about five hours of sleep and am now on my way to a Remain Overnight (RON.)

As usual, I went through my morning routine. I had coffee, showered, and put on my clothes and FAM gear. Then, I rechecked all my FAM gear. Lastly, I had a quick protein shake and cereal, filled a Thermos with more coffee, and was out the door in under thirty minutes, like always.

My flight to JFK departs at 0705, but I am required to be there early. I would show up early even if they didn't require it, because I hate rushing. I always have to do that in this job, but at least I can control when I first show up.

I set my cruise control and tried to relax—but not too much—on my drive to Denver International Airport (DIA); I didn't want the flatlands and urban sprawl to lull me to sleep. And yes, I was speeding, but only by the usual nine miles per hour over. Still, early in my drive, with few cars on the road, I passed a white Subaru with no hubcaps. That would be James, my partner for today. In what seemed like no time at all, I pulled into the employee parking lot and took a shuttle to the airport.

When I got into the sterile area, which is located just past security, I still had almost two hours until my flight—plenty of time to go to the United Club, a great little place in Concourse B for exclusive members like me.

I chuckled.

If by "exclusive," you mean willing to pay $650 a year. (I'm willing to pay it.) I spring for it every year, and although I cannot consume alcohol while on duty, having a spot to unwind when I arrive early is worth it—especially today, since I am flying on United.

There was nothing unusual about today. It was just an ordinary "routine" flight.

No one was in line as I walked up to the check-in desk. I could see the escalator heading up to the lounge behind the woman sitting at the counter.

"Hi, Thomas." That was Debbie.

She was a beautiful, tall, blonde woman who had worked exclusively at the United Club for over two decades. Her demeanor never failed to cheer me up, and although she was ten years older than me, she looked much younger. We had been friends for years and even saw each other on occasion for birthdays or social events. My wife had met her and her husband and found them quite friendly.

"Hi, Debbie. How's the club treating you?"

"Great as always. Welcome, Thomas." She smiled and winked.

That was our morning routine.

I went up the escalator, walked to the food bar, and got snacks. On the way to work, I had finished my coffee, so I refilled my Thermos for later, and then poured a fresh cup while relaxing in the club. Being an air marshal is both fatiguing and stressful, so sitting quietly and reading the paper with a cup of joe is nice. I sighed contentedly as I flipped through *The Wall Street Journal*, my usual relaxation before my workday really started. Time, as usual, went by too quickly, and I was off to my gate.

I thought this day was off to a good start, even as I checked for that messy newspaper ink on my fingers.

———

Agent James

My coffee was fresh and hot, and I watched the little wisps of steam. They were in no hurry and just took their time to reach into the air, unlike me, who snapped awake mere minutes ago and would soon have to go to work.

I envied my lazy coffee steam as my alarm went off.

As usual, I was up before my alarm, but the alarm meant it was time to hustle. Crossing the room, I hit the alarm icon on my iPhone. With a last longing look at my peaceful half-drunk coffee, I left it for a quick shower and started getting ready for work. My clothes and gear were already laid out. Last, I opened the safe to get my duty weapons and credentials.

I opened my credential case and looked at it—Federal Air Marshal James D. Grey.

I felt inside the inner part to ensure my government credit card and other items were still inside. They always were, but I checked every time I got ready anyway. The other agents and I often joked that our most important job was ensuring we had all our equipment and returned with it. The way they disciplined us with cut pay made that a high priority.

I am still having nightmares about the love of my life leaving me, only to wake up and realize she had been gone already. I didn't sulk anymore, but I was still mildly depressed. The combination of my terrible work/life balance and the intractable issues between us sealed my fate. My doctor had given me a regimen to follow, with an admonishment from me not to put down what I was there for. If I told my employer that I was depressed and needed help, they would "help" by having FAM medical pull me from flight status. I had annual leave to use, but that had to be planned. This was going into summer, so the leave calendar was mostly booked. Besides, I needed the routine of work.

With a final recheck of all my gear, I grabbed my bags and coffee and wandered to my car.

It was a white Subaru Impreza, the base model with the hubcaps removed. Not to make it look like a cop car, but just because they kept coming off while I was driving through the snow. I bought it because it was the only new car that was relatively cheap, highly reliable, and had all-wheel drive.

I got in and drove to work at the speed limit. People who knew me would know that that meant I was not OK. I never went the speed limit before the breakup, so I usually passed everyone else. Speed did nothing for me now, and I relished the slow drive to the airport on the toll road—E470. It was nice that you could set your cruise control and rarely pass anyone. The view was mostly wide open with majestic mountains to my left, but more importantly, it was a sharp contrast to the stop-and-go traffic hell of driving on I-25 and I-225. I enjoyed sipping my coffee and watching the world go by. The world, being all the cars to my left, going by me like I had come to a halt, including Thomas's Silver BMW.

I pulled into the employee lot to start my day and texted Thomas: "At the parking lot."

"Good morning, James; well rested, I hope."

"Bright-eyed and bushy-tailed," I said

He responded with a quick "Ha Ha" response.

As fun as this exchange was, I had to climb out of the car and carry on with my day.

I exited the comforts of bucket seats and went through all the checks an air marshal must do to enter the sterile area. Once there, I made my way to Concourse B, where United Airlines fly out of at DIA.

Before my flight, I had plenty of time to use the restroom and go to Starbucks. I ordered a refill for my Thermos and also splurged and got a chocolate scone.

Why not?

I usually eat very cleanly, but when I have a crazy urge to eat something terrible, I usually do. It doesn't happen often. Every day, I bring fruit to work and a Ziplock of spinach leaves. I like eating those on the plane because they are healthy, and people give me funny looks.

Arriving at my gate, I ate my scone, threw the wrapper away, and sat back down.

We were departing out of gate B24.

I read the news on my phone and casually looked around the gate area—no more often than anyone else would do. Only I was registering anything unusual, especially anything that could become a problem.

So far, so good.

I sipped my coffee. Starbucks had almond milk and raw sugar, so I added that. I should've stuck with black—too much sugar, blah.

Once boarding time got closer, I saw Thomas in the gate area. We did not acknowledge each other for obvious reasons. Eventually, they started boarding, and Thomas got up and went to the queue.

I decided to wait and keep watching.

Thomas walked down the jet bridge and out of sight. A few minutes after he boarded, what I saw emerging from the crowd into the gate area was *definitely* out of the ordinary and had the makings of a problem. The man was gigantic. He seemed almost inhuman at seven feet tall and 400 pounds of solid muscle.

Swell.

I sipped my coffee and watched.

———

DIA—United Check-In Counter

He said nothing as he checked in at the United Airlines check-in counter, only pointing to his throat and covering his neck to indicate he was suffering from a throat issue. He gave his driver's license and credit card to the ticketing agent at the counter but had no carry-on or checked luggage.

The ticket agent thought that was very weird and called ahead to the gate agent, who then told the captain of United Airlines flight 436 about it.

With only the clothes on his back, the man had passed through security without uttering a word.

People instinctively gave him space, sensing something sinister about him.

Upon reaching his gate, B24, he found two open seats at the end of a row. It was easy to find open seats, as he had deliberately waited (in one of the stalls) in the men's room until boarding started. Squeezing into the seat at the end, his size and demeanor starkly contrasted with the other people in the busy airport. Now that he was seated, other people were staring at him. He noticed them but paid them no mind. Sitting perfectly still, he was barely breathing and just stared straight ahead. Waiting. He was in first class, so he could have gotten on with the first group, but he had decided to wait a bit—to look more carefully at those around him. When he was done, he looked back straight again. He spoke to no one.

Eventually, they called the final group, and he got up and went to board the plane.

———

Agent Thomas

Detecting a potential threat or a criminal's subtle behaviors requires special training and years of experience. As a FAM, I have honed that training over the last five years.

Not that I needed it with the passenger who had just boarded, though; *everyone* noticed and was afraid of him. He never spoke and only glared at anyone who tried to talk to him. James had seen him in the gate area and texted me about him. He had sat at the end of a row of seats alone. Not that anyone could have sat in the seat next to him; He looked like he was about seven feet tall and damn near as wide; OK, not really that wide.

But, my God, is that guy enormous!

I knew James was concerned because he had already described the subject's weird behavior in texts from the gate area.

James had texted me the man's description and behavior. His last text was, "As people stopped to stare at him, he mostly just sat and stared straight ahead. Even when he turned his head to look around, it looked like his natural state was perfectly still and staring straight ahead. OK, this dude is bizarre. One to keep an eye on. He is boarding now."

The big man ignored the flight attendant's greeting as he entered the front left boarding door. He said nothing later when Nancy, the lead flight attendant, asked if he was feeling alright or wanted some water; he just gave his baleful stare. Finally, she left him to continue her duties.

I genuinely have never seen a man that big before. The older man seated next to him in the window seat was visibly shaken—and trapped —as the giant man's shoulders protruded into his space, even in a wider first-class seat. The poor older man had to lean toward the window. There was also a strange and rather unpleasant smell to the giant man. He did not quite have an unwashed smell, but it was not clean either—almost a rotting fish smell. Unfortunately, he was sitting close enough for me to catch whiffs of his body odor occasionally.

James came on shortly after and headed past us; he was sitting in coach.

We liked to switch out who got the best or worst seats for our "missions" (a.k.a. "flights"). We weren't supposed to, but everyone did it.

The crew had decided to continue the flight. After all, even though he was scary, not talking, and didn't smell too good, he had not done anything actionable to stop the flight. But the crew, James, and I were all watching him.

Dammit, this was supposed to be an easy day.

I have just two flights out to Dulles and then two more flights back tomorrow. Then I get to be with my wife and kids for a couple of regular days off (RDOs), a.k.a. my "weekend."

The unhappy moan of my wife this morning kept repeating over and over in my head; it sounded almost mournful. Was I that much of a burden to her? Was she dreaming of how bad our marriage was?

My kids have not seen much of me over the last five years, and missing their most important life events was hard for me. I can't count how many games and plays of theirs that I have missed. This also made it hard on Grace.

Jillian's first play, with her as a lead character, was at seven p.m. last Tuesday night. I was scheduled to land at 5:35 p.m. and would make it with time to spare. Unfortunately, thunderstorms made the flight land two and a half hours late, and I landed to a text from Grace:

"Congrats, you missed her first play. We are headed home, dinner is in the fridge. I'm going to bed."

When I took my position as a FAM, she knew it would be hard on us, but living that hardship was a totally different animal. I desperately needed to take a vacation and spend some time with them, or else my marriage probably would not last.

Luckily, I had gotten some days of annual leave off for a vacation with them. We were going to Orlando, Florida. The kids had never been to Disney World or Epcot Center, so they were excited. Our vacations seemed to be the only time we were happy as a family. Unfortunately, the only time I could get all the days off in a row was several months from now. Rick was now in the sixth grade, and Jillian was in the first grade. I realized that I had hardly gotten to raise them. That was what being a FAM was like in your home life. So many of us ended up divorced, and I might be one of them—

I sighed.

I could feel the airplane's acceleration as it started its takeoff run.

It looked like our flight was taking off on time.

After a few minutes, the flight was finally at cruising altitude, and the seat belt sign came off. It was time to take a closer look at our large friend.

I went to the front galley and got coffee, hot and black as always.

Plus, I wanted to chat with Nancy about our gigantic person of interest. I have flown several times with Nancy, and she is polite and competent. I have seen her respond to in-flight medical emergencies, and she is always precise and calm.

"What is the story with our large friend, Nancy?"

"Jesus," Nancy rolled her eyes. "I guess the ticketing agent said he is mute, but he is creeping everyone out. The captain knows about him but says there is nothing we can do except watch him. We can't cancel a flight just because someone is scary looking, huh?"

I laughed, but she had a severe look on her face.

"Thomas, what *is* his deal?"

"I don't know yet, but we will find out soon enough."

I took a sip of my coffee. It was bitter and terrible—just like usual.

Perfect.

I was casually observing him. There were many indicators that he was going to be a problem. He was wearing a loose, long-sleeved sweater and baggy sweatpants. His behavior, of course, was peculiar, but it was not dangerous. I did notice something wrong with his features. His arms, legs, and neck seemed too long, and he was not sweating.

Weird.

His head turned toward me, and he stared straight at me. It was still hot on board, so he should be sweating and blinking.

Why wasn't he blinking at all?

"Guess we can't do much for now but watch him," Nancy said.

I sipped my coffee. "Nope."

I glanced back at my partner, FAM Grey, in the cabin. James was indeed "the grey man."

The other air marshals had already given him the moniker.

James had a fantastic talent. Wearing nice clothes but not a suit, he looked like everyone else on board. Many of the FAMs were fit, muscular, and looked too much like ass-kickers, making it difficult to blend in. He, however, looked like a young "Mister Rogers."

Perfect for the job.

Like all of us, he was also exceptionally well trained to handle situations in the air. Being the law was very different when the flight crew, your team, and the passengers were your only backup. You had to be innovative. Luckily, James was. He had earned the respect of his fellow FAMs by being good at his job and caring about people. He was always even-keeled and thought ahead.

It was sad. James was a good man and always gushed about his love for his live-in girlfriend, Janice. He even mentioned asking her to marry him—a big deal from a guy who never wanted to get married. After she sat him down to say she was leaving him, his personality changed dramatically. He became cold and started talking less. He used to never shut up …

I could see that James was also secretly watching the big man.

Then the big man leapt up.

———

Agent James

I watched my partner, Thomas, go to the front galley to talk to the lead flight attendant.

He probably wanted to know more about the big guy. And he drinks way too much coffee, so for that, too. I saw him looking back calmly but knew he was also wary of the scary guy.

I only had a small paperback book out. It was just a prop. I pretended to read so I wouldn't have to talk to anyone, and so I could keep an eye out for trouble. The book, which was trendy, was about a young woman's search for love and happiness after getting divorced.

Just looking at it made me sad; I missed Janice.

I loved that woman so much, but there was nothing I could do. I told her I would do anything to stay together, and she made it worse by saying she loved me, but nothing was to be done. Two weeks later, she left for her new apartment. Being with her those days, without loving affection, left me a husk of apathy.

At least I was starting to get over it. I think.

I had talked to my doctor about the depression it had caused me. After I said I couldn't take anything FAM Medical could know about, we came to the same conclusion, which left me with aspirin and rubbing dirt on it.

And alcohol, of course.

There is a reason why so many FAMs are divorced or end up being put out because of alcohol. We aren't allowed any real solutions to our problems, or even to *say* we are having a problem—not if we want to keep our jobs.

Oh, well.

I stopped my reverie and thought about what could go wrong. Right now, the big guy presented my highest probability of something going wrong. I hated that I was a better hands-on fighter than Thomas. It meant he was overwatch (he watched over me while I made contact), and I had to confront this man if he started something directly. In the movies, we can just shoot someone bigger than us, but in the real world —you go to prison if you do that. Which meant I was going to have to go hands-on if he went all "emotionally disturbed" on us.

Lucky me.

Back to keeping an eye out for any trouble.

Trouble!

———

Agent Thomas

The man had shot up out of his seat, letting out a low but loud growl. It sounded more like a wolf than a man.

Oh crap. This is going to suck. So much for an easy day.

"Thomas!" Nancy started to warn me.

But I had already put my coffee cup down, and when Nancy saw my look, she immediately grabbed the phone to call the captain. The other flight attendant, named Scott, I think, was already yelling to the wolf-man, "Sir, are you alright?! I need you to sit back down. The seat belt sign is on!" (It wasn't.)

I have been in a lot of direct citizen contacts, even some violent arrests. But this guy was terrifying. Something was seriously wrong with his brain housing group; he was definitely mentally disturbed.

Most of the passengers were watching in fear as well—seeing a seven-foot tall, four-hundred-pound man leap into the aisle astonishingly fast—caused several people to let out cries of alarm. Scott approached behind him, reached *way* up, and touched the big guy's shoulder.

What happened next wasn't natural.

The man spun, faster than humanly possible, and his fist shot out into Scott's face.

CRACK!

The crack was almost like a gunshot, so much so that I reflexively drew my firearm and yelled out, "Police!"

Scott's face had imploded.

Blood sprayed out in every direction as the fist went *into* Scott's head, and his head snapped back.

And I mean snapped.

The fist hung in the air briefly before returning to a fighting stance. Scott's head was hanging backward at an impossible angle. Then, he fell lifeless into the aisle.

What, in the actual hell, just happened?

IT turned back toward me—

It had a look with no emotion, but with evident malice; I've never seen that look held so steadily in my life. This thing had no fear and no compassion of any kind.

Luckily, my brain had registered the lethality of my situation. As my weapon was pushing out to full extension, I was already shooting it—

BANG, BANG, BANG!

Many of us call this "combat mode." It happens when you suddenly fight for your life, and everything becomes surreal. Your field of vision narrows, fixating on your threat. You seem to think fast, but you feel you are moving very slowly—as are they.

In reality, you are both moving very fast.

They say you realize in a flash when your life is ending; I hate that mine was. This thing, whatever this "man" was, was moving way faster than humanly possible. It was charging me, and I had nowhere to go. So, I drilled round after round into it. It didn't even slow down. I was firing as fast as humanly possible—BANG, BANG, BANG!

It was on me.

———

Agent James

What the hell?!

Everything was OK, and then the big man stood out of his seat. Well, I shouldn't say stood up. He shot out from his seat way faster than any FAM could, and that is saying something.

Am I hallucinating?

I had just returned from an international mission the day before, just like Thomas had, so I was even more sleep deprived than usual. But it didn't seem possible that he could have stood and gotten into the aisle that fast. He was just standing there like his brain was off but letting out some weird growling noise.

The flight attendant, Scott, asked if he was OK and told him to sit down. It was clear that he was also visibly shaken by what he saw. The man did not respond, and I saw Thomas in the front galley put his coffee down.

Crud. Show time.

Looking around, I didn't see anyone else being weird, so I turned back to the big guy just as the screaming started. He had struck Scott, who was falling back toward me, hard.

Holy crap!

I could see Scott's dead eyes and mutilated face, looking toward me upside down, but his body was still facing forward. Then he dropped lifeless into the aisle.

The giant man turned back to Thomas and started running toward him.

"Police!"—BANG, BANG, BANG!

Thomas was shooting him!

My gun was instantly out, and I was already in the aisle when I realized my lack of luck. Murphy's Law had screwed me again.

Ever notice how cops stand at angles to each other when they talk to you? We do this so you can't easily engage us both simultaneously, and we aren't in each other's field of fire. It's called a combat "L." Have you ever noticed how linear a plane is? Well, I noticed that in that moment. We were in what police jokingly call the combat "I," which was not funny at that point. That is when your perp is directly between you and your partner. So my shots could over-penetrate and hit my partner, requiring me to move, or I couldn't shoot. You do not want to be in the combat "I."

This isn't possible.

Everything had slowed down as my adrenaline kicked into hyper-drive. I heard Thomas's gunshots, very loud, in the sealed metal tube that was our plane. Strangely, I barely registered the sound. The man had rushed forward and smashed into Thomas.

BANG, BANG, BANG! Crunch!—Crunch!

I heard the sound of crunching bones—twice. Once when IT hit him impossibly hard and again when he crashed into the Flight Deck door, denting it and leaving a giant splash of blood. I knew Thomas was dead.

BANG, BANG, BANG, BANG, BANG, BANG!

I fired at center mass on the giant man—half a dozen times, even as it turned on me. My bullets hit it in the back, the side, and the front.

It.

I could see the blood puffs where my rounds struck it and dark-red blood and tissue spray behind it, but they had no effect. I raised my aim as it turned to charge down the aisle to me—BANG!

As it finished turning, my next round hit its neck. It was starting to charge.

BANG!

One more shot in the face; it was almost to me.

BANG!

One more shot, right between its eyes.

WHUMP!

The pain was intense as it hit me, knocking me over—

Holy cow, I am alive! How?

Turns out I got back up pretty darn fast. My head hurt from where it thwacked the aircraft floor when I was knocked down, but I was still functional. There was screaming and crying; I hadn't heard all of it until now. I felt like I was hit by a truck and, lying at my feet, the big man was dead.

Jesus, I hope he was anyway.

My last shot must have killed him, or else I would be somewhere farther back in the plane and very dead. Still, his momentum, even lifeless, had knocked the wind out of me.

Somehow, I had held on to my weapon.

My training kicked in, and I reloaded my firearm—as most of the magazine was emptied on it. Still trying to breathe, I went to the front and checked on my partner. Thomas and Scott were dead, but Nancy and I checked them anyway.

I couldn't even remember all the details of what happened between then and when we landed, but I had much to do. Luckily, there was too much to do to get nervous. Everyone was counting on me to keep them safe. My badge was out, and everyone in earshot, at least those with eardrums still intact, could hear me yelling, "Police!"

I felt the plane slowly turning 180 degrees; We were heading back to DIA.

The flight deck must have been pretty freaked out; that was a lot of gunfire and screaming.

Once the turn was complete, they poured on the speed—I could hear the engines being pushed hard.

As we approached the airport, people pointed out the windows. It looked like the Air Force had decided to join us for a ride back in.

We got back to DIA much quicker than our pre-shootout flight time. We also descended and landed faster than usual. As we taxied to the "hot spot" for emergencies, I saw an army of official vehicles with emergency lights waiting for us. Usually, I would be nervous about protocol, but this wasn't my first time having an incident on a plane. But it was the first time I had ever had a gunfight ... Against an unarmed man.

Oh, crud.

I knew I was justified, but it would be hard to explain. This would go to court.

What was I even going to say?

CHAPTER 2
THE TOME

Mary

IT WAS *another glorious spring day in Colorado Springs,* I thought, as my children and I left the NER, or I should say, the New Era Revivalist Church since they hate it when I call it that.

I had never felt so alive!

Colorado was beautiful this time of year. Just starting to come out of winter, the birds were chirping, and perennial flowers were just starting to bloom. A lovely blue sky with fluffy white clouds reminded me of just how blessed I was.

The Reverend's sermon just made the day all the better.

Reverend Turner had delivered a passionate sermon as usual, reminding the congregation again that the Ascension would come, with the help of true believers, and that they would ascend to their heavenly reward when the rest of the world ended. Many in our church had lost friends and even family when they joined the church. We were considered "extremists," and other mainstream churches disagreed with our "fire and brimstone" philosophies. Beyond my beautiful offspring, my family refused to talk with me anymore. They accused me of being in a cult and of having "turned my back" on Christianity.

Well, the joke will be on them when the end days arrive.

Only the truly faithful will be spared an eternity of hellfire. Luckily, our Reverend has found a way to speed up that day's arrival. Just today, he told us about an expedition he was planning. A voyage that would bring everlasting peace to Earth and a beautiful surprise that would be unveiled in one of his future sermons. Something magnificent!

I can't wait, and I hope it is an ancient relic.

We all know the Reverend's love for the arcane and its rarity. It will be such a joy to see what they have found.

Reverend Turner, a brilliant leader and a beacon of hope, was more than just my pastor. He was a guide, a mentor, and a source of inspiration. His words resonated with me, instilling a sense of purpose and belonging.

During my walk home with my kids, I couldn't help but smile—I am so grateful for his guidance and wisdom.

––––––––

Clarence

Mary and the other parishioners left at the end of the service. As usual, the other members of the church's "enforcement arm" and I stayed after. The Reverend had something extraordinary for us, he said.

I watched as the other members took a seat: Margret Thompson, Devon Clark, Gerald Torrens, Henry Johnson, Roger Clemence, JoAnne Hawthorne, Tracy Codsworth, and Lawrence Stenbrook were there—all proud new "Wrath of God" team members.

Most of us think it is a bit of hubris and even a bit presumptive to call it that. However, no one questioned the Reverend's name choice for our group. The "WOG" members were all selected because the Reverend recognized our skill sets and what we could contribute to the mission. Everyone was surprised when the Reverend introduced a new church member, for he had not yet been at a service …

"Alright, everyone, I want to introduce you to Captain Sam Miles.

He'll be the captain of our vessel for the journey to come," the Reverend said.

"Hello," Sam said and smiled.

"Sam, you're the captain and in charge of the ship, but this is Margret. She'll be the mission leader and in charge of the team."

Margret nodded to him. She was intelligent and adaptable, and chaired almost every position in the church.

"This is Devon; he was an explosives specialist—EOD—in the Army. Gerald, over there, is a geologist, and Henry is a 'jack of all trades' and handy with almost anything," the Reverend said.

Smiles and nods came their way as the Reverend continued the introductions.

"Roger, Tracy, and Lawrence all work together as hunter guides and have extensive experience. Roger was even a sherpa guide years ago … And over there is former Staff Sergeant Clarence Briggs, he's also a former Army Ranger."

I nodded to Sam.

He was noticeably impressed, nodding and waving to us all.

"And last, but certainly not least, is JoAnne. She's a paramedic with AMS."

Everyone was smiling but had curious expressions. We all wanted to see what had the Reverend so excited; he did not excite easily.

"OK, everyone. Let's have a seat and get to work." Reverend Turner said and then paused before dropping the bombshell, "I want you all to know I have had a visitation."

Murmuring broke out. He stopped it quickly as he raised his hand for us to hush.

"The Angel had no face or form, but it told me what to do. It gave me a number and then was gone."

"A number?" That was Gerald.

"Yes. It's a number that I have checked out. The only thing that makes sense is that it matches GPS coordinates to where an ancient temple it spoke of holds what we seek—something called only the "Harbinger."

He paused to look at each of us before continuing,

"Your mission will be dangerous. I've procured a vessel and found our newest church member through my vast contacts to get you to where the Angel has decreed; It's in Antarctica."

There was more murmuring, not so quiet this time.

"Are you certain?" Lawrence asked.

He regretted saying it out loud as several severe looks shot his way.

"It's OK, everyone. He's just saying aloud what's on your minds and mine."

Looking at Lawrence, he said, "Yes, I am certain. The planning has already begun. Your skills and talents will be put to the test in this tribulation. It will be dangerous, and I would understand if any of you want to back out …"

The pause was unnecessary; he knew we were all in 100 percent.

The Reverend nodded at us all. "OK, then. Let's talk logistics and planning."

Margret

After a week of planning and training, we are ready to start our journey. The time for our voyage is finally upon us. It is the beginning of spring, and I am thankful we would return to what would most definitely be a warm early summer.

I am the team leader on this trip, so everyone now calls me "Ma'am." As proud New Era Revivalist Church members, we were all eager to succeed on this pilgrimage—ever since our church learned of an unearthed section of Antarctica.

Or I should say "un-iced."

Our Reverend, Doctor Gregory Turner, *the Third*, had learned of its location through extensive research of our religious and other ancient tomes. Until now, whatever we were after, it had been trapped in an ancient temple, too far under the ice.

Thanks to global warming, we will finally be able to reach it.

Most of us don't believe that people are the primary driver of climate change, as the climate is constantly changing, anyway.

Some may think that, but it is a moot point for us.

There was less ice for whatever reason, and we were thankful, mainly because it was going into winter there. The Ascension was coming soon anyway, long before climate changes could destroy humanity.

Before we could get to the temple under the ice, we had to navigate the Drake Passage—the most dangerous body of water on Earth. The passage spans from South America's Cape Horn to the South Shetland Islands of Antarctica. We would go through to the central part of Antarctica.

I had learned everything I could about it. Sir Francis Drake, whom the passage is named after, could not have completed our journey to this part of Antarctica. He would have needed an icebreaker ship, which he didn't have in 1525. With the help of our 1980s-built but thoroughly modernized icebreaker, "Will of Genesis," we made the crossing less dangerously than he did. Even though it was "small" for an icebreaker, that is relative. Ours measured thirty meters from stem to stern and had a long history of successful voyages on the ice.

Spring and summer are the best times to cross, but we were going into the Antarctic winter. It seemed strange since it was the opposite of the Northern Hemisphere. Antarctic winter starts in March and ends in October. However, the Angel's commandment did not say to wait, so we had to go as soon as possible. The wind was at Beaufort 11—on a scale of 1 to 12—so we were all getting pretty knocked about. You could see the icy mist coming off the waves, which reached up to forty feet or more. There are no land masses to slow down the wind and water as the currents circumnavigate the globe around Antarctica.

They call this the Arctic Circumpolar Current, and it makes for a *wild* sea journey.

Even in the twenty-first century, we are still discovering places in this land: a mass of ice, permafrost, and, lately, mud. Every year, there is less ice, though.

Thank the Lord!

Without it, we would never have been able to retrieve our artifact. That effect may be preordained. Maybe all this talk about climate change was just God's will to allow for the Ascension?

Yes, maybe, but there is no point in overthinking God's will. You obeyed the scripture and, now, the Angel's commands. Past that, God's plan is ineffable.

I thought about the Harbinger—

That was all we knew of it, just what it was called. But from the Reverend's visitation, we could see what it is for—it will bring the end days and the holy Ascension.

I know of God's true wrath; He is not a pushover. He smote Sodom and Gomorrah for their wickedness—destroying two cities! Not someone you want to go against; His will shall be followed! So, the heretics might have asked us why we are helping with God's will to bring about the End Times? Because he commands it, of course.

Why else?

My reverie was ended as I was jolted, hard, into the side of the kitchen galley.

"OW!" I yelled out—*That was going to leave a giant bruise.*

I heard a shout, "You OK down there?"

That was Miles, our ship's captain, and another devout member of our NER expedition team. He was a stout man with pug-like features and quite a pug-like body. Lots of beer and little exercise gave him that appearance. He was, however, a little fitter and stronger than before this assignment.

The Reverend insisted that we all follow a diet and exercise plan to be ready for our journey as soon as he learned about the existence of the coveted artifact. I wish we knew more about it, but we had established its location using the exact coordinates the Angel had given him.

I keep thinking about how lucky I am. The New Era Revivalist Church is the best thing that ever happened to me, and being part of its action arm—the WOG—was the most tremendous honor I could *ever* have.

I am a sixty-year-old woman, but I am fit for my age and not bad looking, if I say so myself. Regular hikes, a clean diet, and CrossFit make a difference—

"Ma'am! Are you OK?!" Captain Miles yelled down again.

I suddenly remembered where I was and that I had a job to do!

"Give me a SITREP!" I demanded a situation report from him. He was the ship's captain, but I was the Mission Leader.

"Yes, Ma'am!" he yelled back down.

I usually hate someone calling me "Ma'am." Still, we had learned from our glorious church leader, the Reverend Doctor Turner, that we must always be concise and professional on a mission.

After cleaning up the spill in the kitchen, I walked up to the bridge and met Captain Miles. He turned to me as I came in.

"Ma'am, the ship is 100 percent, but that last nasty bit injured Roger—sprained or broken ankle."

"Thank you, Captain Miles," I replied.

"Fiddlesticks," I grumbled as I walked away.

Roger was our trail leader and had the most experience; he used to be a sherpa guide.

This was going to get more complicated.

Luckily, we all have been trained—just like the military does—to be able to perform all roles in case something like this happens. And challenges always occur.

We may have been set back by one injury, but thanks to modern navigation equipment, satellites, and communication, we had no loss of life.

CRACKK!

The ship had just begun the final voyage to land, breaking through massive ice sheets. It was almost time! I went below again to assemble the team.

Roger was there, his leg iced with a giant bandage and propped on a bed with many blankets. He was white with pain and shock; the sea was not kind as it jostled his leg about.

I felt a surge of pride.

He briefed the team as if nothing was wrong with him. Luckily, the

Reverend gave us all the GPS coordinates, which we inputted into satnav-capable tracking devices.

As our ship headed into the land, nose first, we were ready—braced for the shock of its impact. Now, suited up, we began our six-mile journey overland. As we left the ship and reached the shore, we gasped.

We had all expected a *lot* more ice.

The brownish-white hillsides and small mountains shot into the sky in stark relief to the angry ocean below. The wind was frigid and unceasing. It howled and ripped at us, even through our Outdoor Research thermals and coats.

The trip was dangerous, I confirmed.

As we traveled, we groused about not having snowcats or snowmobiles. We all knew why, though. Each time we fell through a hole or into a newly opened chasm, we realized the futility of crossing with any serious weight. Even our bodies and drilling gear were too much for the freshly unfrozen land. The ice gave way to permafrost—and even mud. Thank the Lord we all were connected by a rope. It saved our lives. Our arduous trek took its toll from exertion, stress, and the occasional beating of falling into a hole and being pulled back out.

Finally, after what seemed an eternity, even if it was only a day's travel, we arrived at our destination. There was nothingness in all directions but, as our satnav devices all concurred, we were standing over the temple we sought.

Devon, our Explosive Ordnance Disposal (EOD) specialist, who had served in Afghanistan, unpacked and set the high-explosive demolition charges. The ice where we were was not as thick as it had been, but it was still thick enough that we had to get deeper than our hand tools could go. As Devon activated the explosives, we hunkered down, and the blast wave rippled over us—

BOOM!

In a panic, I looked around.

There were no hills nearby to bury us in an avalanche. I breathed a sigh of relief.

That was sloppy!

I should have looked before starting, but my fatigue had blunted my usual thoroughness. Taking a deep breath, I realized our explosives specialist, Devon, would have checked for that.

Then we dug.

Our drills made a racket. Between the electric whir of the rotary hammers with the ice drill attachments and the cracking of our shovels, my ears were painfully thumping from the noise. Those portable ice drills we brought allowed us to penetrate the ice much easier than by shoveling or picking. They were Milwaukee SDS Max Rotary hammers, each weighing just over twelve pounds. We had extra lithium batteries and several attachments to make sure we could dig through the ice and permafrost. In addition, we brought Garrett Wade Super Penetration Shovels, which were super strong and only weighed six pounds. With the rotary hammers and shovels, we were making good progress.

Finally, with a loud crack, we hit something very hard. We had dug through to a stone structure below, so I decided to set one more demo charge, and after backing away a safe distance—

BOOM!

Walking back over, I saw an area about four feet wide in the ice of what looked like concrete and some metal. The material was weird. It had cracked, and chunks had been blown out, leaving a small hole leading to the emptiness below, but we still didn't have a hole big enough to climb through. I shined my light into the hole but saw only yawning darkness.

"Devon, have you seen anything like this before?" I asked, looking at the strange substance we had uncovered. Its substance was mixed in a way I had never seen. The white stone had strange metals embedded in it. This was not something I expected from an ancient temple.

"No, Ma'am," he replied.

"Do you think we can safely set off another demo charge?"

He looked at the strange stone and metal at the hole's edge. I could tell he was thinking about the peculiar mixture as well. What kind of material is this? How is it going to be affected by more explosives?

"I wouldn't risk it. Without knowing what this is, or how the temple was constructed, I could cause a cave-in of the whole structure. For all we know, this is a capstone we are messing with," Devon finally said.

I had no idea what a "capstone" was, but Devon knew explosives, so I deferred to his judgment. He saw the befuddled look on my face.

"A capstone, or keystone, is just what we call the wedge-shaped or curved stone at the top of an arch. It is the final piece placed during construction and locks the other stones into position, allowing the arch to support weight," he explained.

I nodded. That made sense now.

"OK, you're right … I don't want to use another charge and risk a cave-in. Let's work around it with hand tools again," I said.

Devon nodded his head. "Yes, Ma'am."

No one spoke as we attacked the hole again. It was grueling work, and we were exhausted when we made a slightly bigger hole. We stopped for a water break.

Gerald was the first back, and we could hear his drill cutting away.

He started clearing more around the hole so we could get inside. I was the next person tethered to him, only twenty feet away.

CRACKK!

The ground in a ten-foot area around Gerald collapsed inward.

"HELP!" He screamed as a mountain of debris fell in with him.

The rope yanked me violently, and I let it pull me to the ground. We all laid flat to keep him from falling in further. His weight was much less than all of ours combined. I just had to stay calm and figure out how to get him safely back up. I could see where the rope strained against the hole's edge, mere feet away.

"HELP ME!" we could hear the panic and fear in his voice.

He was the last person tethered in our line and, as he fell, his rope bit hard into the sharp edge of the hole and cut back and forth as he swayed below.

"Stay still, and we'll get you out!" I yelled.

Without warning, there was a loud "SNAP!"

I felt the rope go slack in my hands, and a lump formed in my throat.

Gerald screamed as he fell into the hole.

We heard his screams as he fell and then a distant thump deep below. There was no more screaming …

Gerald was a good, kind, and decent man who would be sorely missed by many, not just our crew. But glorious salvation was close at hand! If only we could return with our prize, the Ascension could begin!

We went down the rope with our headlamps on, careful to put things between the sharp edge of the hole and our ropes so as not to have another lethal accident. As we descended, we shined lights around the giant chamber of stone and metal all around us. Strange carvings and symbols were everywhere. None looked like anything I had ever seen. Deep inside, we reached the floor and assembled.

The crumpled and crushed body of Gerald gravely greeted us. His body was flattened, and blood was splattered around him from the impact. There was no doubt he was dead. We all had tears in our eyes.

"Oh, my God! Please watch over him, dear Lord." That was JoAnne Hawthorne, our medical specialist.

"Yes," I responded. "Let's take a moment to pray …"

"Dear Lord, please watch over our team and let Gerald look down upon his contribution to Your holy will. Let his final resting be here, in the temple of our salvation, until he shall be resurrected, if that be Your will, for his death in our holy quest. In your glorious name, oh Lord. Amen."

The team said, "Amen." Each pair of eyes looked at me severely as if to say, "Now what." We knew we could not get his body back to the ship. Besides, we knew he would not be here long if we succeeded. The resurrection of the true believers would be part of the restoration. This would come after God poured forth his wrath upon the world. Damnation would be upon those opposed to his rule or those who failed to follow His commandments. I know that He does not need our help. He tests our resolve, allowing us to prove our dedication to Him.

I turned my flashlight on to see the temple in full—

"Oh, my Lord!" I gasped.

All of us looked on in awe.

The temple under the ice was a giant chamber. Ornate drawings and writing were carved into the strange stone everywhere we looked. At least I think it is writing, as it looked like no language I had ever seen. After a long moment, Staff Sergeant Clarence Briggs spoke first.

"What *is* this place?" Even he was awestruck.

"The temple of salvation, as far as I'm concerned," I replied.

Clarence was everything that Captain Miles was not. Young, fit, and strong, he was the one you wanted on your side when something called for the physical work of implementing God's will. Clarence was not someone you wanted to tangle with. He had survived multiple combat engagements in both Afghanistan and the Horn of Africa.

"Do we know where the Harbinger is?" That was Tracy.

She was one of the most devout among us.

I looked at my GPS and then back up again. I gestured to a small alcove in the corner of the giant room. "It should be in there."

Sure enough, in a very anticlimactic way, there it was.

That must be an altar.

In the center of the alcove, a significant altar of white alabaster stone was surrounded by strange runes and carvings of impossible atrocities. Alien creatures were intermixed with scenes of masses of people praying to them. In others, scenes of alien creatures were among the people. I couldn't tell if they were protectors or wardens. Then there were all the alien writings. Everything swirled together and made my head hurt just trying to understand what I was looking at.

On top of the altar was a giant tome.

It must weigh a hundred pounds, I thought.

I was the leader and would not ask a subordinate to take a risk I wouldn't take. I went forward and opened the book. As I opened it, I felt an incredible sensation—

The room suddenly took on an impossibly silver hue.

It was not extreme; it was more like the clarity you see when the sun is just right and everything has an intense and precise color. Every-thing emanated this beautiful and calming hue. I could feel the energy of everything I looked at. It felt like something marvelous had awak-ened in me!

Everyone had come into the room to see what was going on.

The tome was covered in indescribable runes and was faintly glowing with an otherworldly silver aura. It was like the air around it had suddenly taken on an unearthly silver sheen.

"Isn't it beautiful?" I said with a blessed smile.

My hands were covered in the same silver aura now, and I could see it climbing up my arms very quickly. My smile disappeared when I saw what came through to our world.

"No … NO!" I screamed.

I looked everywhere in a panic and screamed nonstop. A horrible scream of unfathomable terror … then everything went black as I went unconscious from fear.

The Reverend

I had received word from the team.

All of them had made it back except Gerald, who had died in a fall.

Gerald was a good man, and it's hard to imagine a congregation without him. Also, Roger Clemence had hurt his ankle and was at the emergency room. He might have broken some bones.

All around, I am pleased.

I am glad I trusted Margret to lead the team. She had proven to be both intelligent and capable.

Everything was going according to God's plan. The Angel had a straightforward message—retrieve the Harbinger and summon the Ancient One—to bring forth the end days and the Ascension. How come I never saw or could even define its gender? Because it was just a blurred vision with a message commanding me to find and return with the Harbinger. Those numbers are seared into my mind even now —those exact coordinates to a place in the Antarctic, in a temple just below the ice. I did not question His will; I obeyed, for I am the chosen vessel of His divine plan!

After months of planning, our heroes had returned—with the tome!

As I gazed upon the tome, I couldn't help but voice what was on everyone's mind:

"My goodness. It's colossal!"

The tome, an enormous book weighing nearly 60 pounds, was a sight to behold.

It measured a staggering 38 inches tall and 23 inches wide and was a formidable 11 inches thick. Its pages, over 600 (614 to be precise), were all adorned with incomprehensible alien language, intricate diagrams, and enigmatic pictures. The sheer magnitude and weight of the tome and its otherworldly contents were a testament to its profound significance in our mission. Deciphering this tome would be a Herculean task, demanding an immense amount of time and effort.

We had gathered in the church's basement rectory, and most of the WOG team was present.

Everyone stood a little apart from Margret, who was emitting an almost invisible but palpable silver aura. She had regained consciousness shortly after this strange phenomenon had occurred.

The others had wrapped the book, seemingly unaffected by its presence. When Margret awoke on the vessel the following morning, the silver sheen that now enveloped her had vanished entirely from the tome, leaving the expedition team in wonder and confusion.

I was excited to begin my research.

Days went by as others brought me food and drink, and I seldom bathed, but I could not stop. Impossible creatures were just a simple incantation away!

Our world, our universe, is not alone. As many physicists have predicted, a parallel one inhabits the same space as ours.

The Harbinger was not the book, not really. As I researched, it became clear that the book was an instruction manual on bringing *them* forth. They would be the Harbingers. And Margret was now the conduit.

"Ashta'goth, In'hukula, Shart'um ..."

These cryptic "words" and many more were scattered throughout the tome. It was inscribed in some alien language, but with modern technology and my linguistic prowess, I could finally unravel its meanings after weeks of relentless study. The book revealed the path to our salvation! The end days were nigh, and I eagerly anticipated the love and adoration of the pious after God's wrath was unleashed.

The silver aura that now enveloped Margret was the key.

The first person to find and touch the book would become the conduit, summoning forth the other universe and its unfathomable creatures. Each time, it would require willing sacrifices of life. I longed for it to be me, but I must lead the operation.

Mary

As I approached Margret, I saw her features were abject with horror. She tried hard to be beatific, but I could see her terror.

"Margret," I said softly.

"Yes, Mary?" She turned and smiled a beautiful but horrible smile. She was starting to scare me.

"Does it hurt?" I asked.

"No, Mary. I am blessed. It's scary, but it's God's will, and I'm his instrument. I could not wish for more."

"Can you tell me what it's like?"

I didn't want to know, but I had to. Nothing like this has ever been seen or recorded in history. Despite no dry eye after Gerald's service, I was overjoyed at the team's return.

Margret responded, "I cannot. Not really. I can see the creatures from the other side, whatever that is. I can feel them. They move around with no physical law. They crawl, fly, swim, or all of it at once! And they're moving through everything: the trees, me, … and you …"

The smile faded, and she abruptly said goodbye and walked away.

I watched her go and am not relieved at God's plan. I know it is blasphemy, but I feel a numbing terror at the idea of what Margret just told me. The regular parishioners were to be kept unaware of the "grand plan" in motion. But, since we all believed in the Ascension and our Reverend, it was the worst-kept secret in the history of our church.

No one would tell anyone outside of our church, however.

A breeze blew, and I could hear the leaves moving. It reminded me of something. What Margret said came back to me—

I looked around in a panic, but I saw nothing …

———

The Reverend

The time had come.

After many weeks of research, I had found the key.

An altar had been built for the tome, made of the purest white alabaster stone and painstakingly carved with the required runes. The tome was instrumental in making the altar correctly, as the runes had to be done perfectly, or the summoning would not occur.

Next to it was a massive platform of the same white stone, large enough for several people to lie upon. At the head of the platform, the pedestal sloped up to a smaller area where the summoned creatures would form.

We had built it in the basement rectory, where I was first shown the tome. It was also out of the view of any regular parishioners when they came to services.

"Reverend, we are ready."

That was Henry Johnson, and he was the first church member to volunteer enthusiastically.

He had lost his wife and only son in a car wreck with a drunk driver. The driver was serving, concurrently, a five-year sentence for each of them.

Only five years.

That's all the time this man would spend in prison. This man lost his entire family, and the man who did it was only getting "vehicular manslaughter" charges. Because somehow a car made it a different kind of murder … We knew Henry was eager to rejoin them, which would assure his ascension, no matter how it turned out.

The other man was Lawrence Stenbrook. He had also volunteered.

His only family was the church. His prior family and friends wanted nothing to do with him. He had lost them all due to his addictions to hard drugs and alcohol. He was homeless when he came to the church. But now, he had a new family and wanted to repay the church for everything they had done for him.

Henry and Lawrence lay on the platform naked, as directed by the tome, as the WOG members assembled around the altar. The New Era Revivalists were all very pious, but the WOG was the "enforcement" arm of our beloved church. All who volunteered had vowed to put God's will above all else, to bring forth the Ascension. And to obey me, the Reverend, as His holy Messiah.

Our group was new.

I approached each of them and asked them to join, telling them of my visitation by an Angel and what must be done. None of them doubted me or even considered not being a part of it. No one shall turn their back on God!

All the chamber was lit by candlelight from the nearby altar.

Well, that and the overhead lights.

I knew the summoning would draw energy from everything around it, especially from Margret, to complete our first attempt at bringing the *Others* to our world. The things needed bodies to attach to the moment they came through, or else they would die. We knew they would create what we decided to call "Deathwalkers."

The first summoning would bring two of them. They would make each of them into the version of a "man" that it chose to protect itself.

Not a zombie, but something else.

The Deathwalker would be a symbiosis of human and *Other*. Henry and Lawrence both lay naked and shivering next to the pedestal as we all began to chant alien words to bring them forth. Their shivering was not just from the cold.

They were scared.

It was dusk, and the sun's last light was waning from the windows.

As we finished, all was quiet. Everything. No birds, no wind, no insects.

Then we heard a soft, squelching sound, growing louder. Something was forming on the small part of the pedestal next to the altar.

We all looked at Margret.

She was glowing brightly with that strange silver color, and we all had to shut our eyes as the intensity grew to the power of what felt like the sun. My eyes, even closed, were on fire, and my skin burned! I could hear the cries of the other acolytes as they felt what I felt.

Everyone lay still—unconscious with a mild "sunburn" on all their exposed skin.

The *Others*

The *Others* were here.

There were two of them. A strange mix of hundreds of tiny tentacles and cilia, they sensed their new hosts nearby. Their skin was flush with the heat of their arrival. Both slithered and flipped their way from the top of the pedestal. They sensed the *conduit*, the strange silver woman who brought them forth, nearby. Each of them fish-plopped down the pedestal and onto the naked men. Sliding and probing with a hundred tentacles, they found the mouths and slid inside.

Henry was the first …

It shredded his vocal cords and ate its way through until it reached his brain. Somehow, it knew where to go, and it began connecting to its new host.

An alien intelligence was now in control and probing through Henry's thoughts and memories. Tendrils began to run through thousands of miles of blood, muscle, viscera, and bone. It was making his body more robust and rigid. Now, it also controlled the hormones and cells, and began to change its vessel into the creature it was always meant to be, not the puny human it once was, but …

———

The Reverend

As we awoke, we all stared in amazement.

Henry was no more.

What stood silently in his place was much taller and inhumanly sized—like a six-foot-nine, overly juiced pro bodybuilder. His muscles were impossibly large and full. He gave each of us, in turn, a malevolent look.

"Are you able to understand us?" I asked.

It nodded Henry's head up and down once. *A yes!*

"What do you wish from us to help bring forth the Ascension?"

I knew, as the Angel had told me, that the Deathwalkers had specific targets in mind. But the Angel never told me the targets. I wanted to see if this creature knew and could tell us.

It did not answer. It turned and walked out of the church and into the night without a word, just as Lawrence, the other man on the altar, must have, as he was gone when we awoke.

We did not know what we had unleashed …

CHAPTER 3
FBI—OST DIVISION

Denver Field Office
SAC Robert

"THIS IS Special Agent in Charge Robert Cho, report," I said.

"Sir, an incident onboard UA flight 436 DEN to JFK. It isn't good. There were lots of witnesses and an air marshal team on board. Fatalities. Reports indicate a huge, unarmed man killed several people barehanded. FAMs shot him multiple times. The flight has returned to DEN. FBI agents are with them now."

I thanked the agent and hung up.

Great.

Another simulant, I'm sure of it—first the one in the Springs and now this one.

How did I become SAC, or Special Agent in Charge, of the Overwatch Surveillance Team (OST)?

I wasn't promoted to this obscure "secret" division of OST. It was never founded to take on actual occult entities—we never thought those were real. Merely, it was to brush under the rug anything that would give the media something to sensationalize.

Especially anything that could cause my bosses' blood pressures to rise.

My bosses like easy nine-to-five weekdays, with holidays and vacations off. They like "easy wins." What they do not like: headaches. And this was a headache, both literally and figuratively. Absent-mindedly, I was already chewing an antacid after swallowing a couple of ibuprofen pills.

It was time to get to work again.

The original and relatively new teams are called Overwatch Surveillance Teams, a part of the Federal Bureau of Investigation under the Department of Justice. This was a "pilot program" to see if allocating resources and agents to OST was worthwhile.

Even though the FAM Service was under the Department of Homeland Security, we had used their agents in the Joint Terrorism Task Force (JTTF) before. After seeing the success of the FAMs with Southwest border security and hurricane responses, the FBI decided it needed its own teams to respond and assist with surveillance and countersurveillance quickly. Then, the agents would pursue whatever the FBI wanted without being specifically assigned to a "case." Clearly, some incidents were not terrorism but something much darker …

So, the Occult Strike Team was born.

It was ostensibly just another Overwatch Surveillance Team, but that one team exists to stop these "what the hell?" events. Thus, the Occult Strike Team was created to deal with these "problems."

Like now with the newest simulant attack.

There had already been another Occult Incident (OI) in Colorado Springs, Colorado, that we had "hushed up." Colorado Springs PD was not too happy about the Feds stepping in. They had lost officers fighting this thing, so we would have to forge some goodwill to get their help. Since I am in charge of the OST division, based out of the Denver FBI Field Office, I also get to oversee this.

Hooray! Lucky me.

It's not like any of this information can be shared, or we can get help outside of our group. Who would believe it?

"Hey, we have a superhuman monster getting on your plane that looks human, and we thought you should know." Or—"Hey, can you enter a monster into the federal databases and put out an 'unarmed and extremely dangerous' flag?"

I sighed deeply.

Part of me realized that many men were selected for higher positions partially because they were tall. There have been many studies showing this. Sure, my education and experience mattered, but I subconsciously believe that being tall didn't hurt any.

I knew I was an imposing figure.

Standing six feet, three inches and a fit 200 pounds, I was everything you would expect of someone of Polish descent with a former last name of Kowalski. So, how is a big Polish man like me named Cho?

Well, I met my wife fifteen years ago. Amanda Cho is Vietnamese and the most wonderful and lovely woman I have ever met. She is also the direct descendant of the Cho family—a family heavily involved in commerce and influential in both social and political circles. Young Alex Cho, the fourth, would not be Alex Kowalski, the first.

Fine by me.

A beautiful, well-connected wife who loves me wants a name change—Done. Robert Cho it is. The voluminous a.k.a. name change forms were worth it, even if Amanda and Alex hardly ever see me nowadays.

Anyway, I am off to the FAM's Denver Field Office to "brief" the air marshals. It sucks to be them.

FAM's DENFO—Denver Field Office
Agent James

So now I am sitting in the conference room waiting for some bigwig from the Denver FBI Office. My SAC at DENFO looked at me like a soon-to-be former air marshal. Not that I blamed her. I felt that way too. Soon, it would be just James Grey, a civilian and ex-federal air marshal, possibly even convict James Grey. I respected our SAC; she genuinely cared about the well-being of our FAMs. That's why the look on her face did not help my feelings.

OK, something is up.

I had already given my full report, factual and exact. I had reported everything as it happened, but I had thought long and hard about whether I should embellish specific details of my report—especially the fifteen shots it took to take him, or it, down. I also knew ballistics were going to show every one of those bullets, and the eyewitness testimony had already said that Thomas and I were the only ones with guns.

Sucks to be me.

Oh well, the truth will set me free. Or at least that is what we tell suspects—right before they spill their guts in grief on a one-way ticket to jail. The looks I got when I gave my report to my FAM supervisor and the responding FBI agents let me know that I was in for more than a few days off with my gun taken away.

I love all those TV shows where the detectives fire at the bad guys, and then afterward, they are glibly having coffee and talking about where to go next. Nope. Your life after a shooting is all about the incident that just happened. They take your gun away, and you get a mandatory period off where you talk to the Office of Chief Counsel (OCC.) You give the basics of what happened in your initial report and then have a "cooling-off period" before providing a complete, written report. They then decide if you are "scoped" or "acted in the scope of your duties." If you were, you might be OK. If not, you were screwed.

I was feeling very screwed.

Now you worry about whether you will still have a job and if you might be going to jail. Unlike what people watch on criminal investigation shows, you aren't running down the next lead. Under the best of circumstances, it is incredibly stressful.

And this is not the best of circumstances.

Now I am going to have to explain how eff'ing Superman killed two people, including my partner, and then justify why I shot him nine times while he was unarmed after my partner had hit him with a full six to center mass. Maybe a lovely stay in a white room with Thorazine is in my future? That may be for the best—

"FAM James D. Grey?" I heard a man say.

I turned to see a tall, fit, Polish man in his mid-forties, dressed in a very nice suit and tie and looking very VIP. He came in and shut the door behind him. We were alone in the room.

"Yes, sir," I replied.

"I am Special Agent in Charge Robert Cho from the FBI, OST Division. I need to ask you some questions ..."

With a gulp, I nodded.

"I read your report. You took this *thing* out and lived. Not easy."

Hold up! Red flag!

"Excuse me, sir. You said thing, not man."

"That is correct. We're calling them simulants." He frowned but did not look like he was joking.

I could hear the buzzing sound that fluorescent lights make but, for a while, no one spoke. I couldn't tell if he was messing with me or waiting for the truth to sink in.

"I would laugh or say something smart, but Thomas is dead. This isn't funny." I was pissed at this wise-ass, SAC or not. I have had enough of people mocking me for telling the truth.

"I'm not laughing," Robert replied.

I looked closely at him. His face was set in stone, and he gave off no indicators he was lying.

"OK. What happened then? How could he have lived through all of that?" I asked.

"*He* couldn't. He, from what we can tell, was probably dead from parasitic infection, anyway. *It*, however, maybe just had to live long enough to get to a new host or ... Hell, we don't know ..." There was a quiet pause. "From what we can tell, which isn't much, it attaches to the brain stem. Then, it transforms that person into the most muscular and bone-dense version of a human you can imagine, with adrenaline and hormones at maximum, lethal levels. We don't know a lot. We have no idea why it can't talk. Maybe it has something to do with the unnatural mutations it causes?"

Robert took a seat and popped an antacid. After chewing it up and swallowing, he continued.

"If you hadn't hit it with that last shot, it would have killed you and everyone else on the plane probably, and then moved to a new host. I don't know; we are guessing at this point. They found some purplish and grey thing attached to his … *its* … brain. With a hole in it from your bullet, obviously."

OK. That explains everything. It all makes sense now.

"What?!" I said.

I felt fuzzy and wanted to wake up—or throw up. This could not be real.

"Do you care what happened? Are you sure you really want to know?" Robert asked.

"Hell no, but I haven't got a choice. It killed Thomas and Scott. If these … things … are out there, they need to be stopped."

"Oh, they are. There was already one other incident in Colorado Springs. We are praying this is some weird one-off. However, as you well know, once is an anomaly—" he started.

"Twice is a pattern," I finished.

A long silence.

"Do you still want to stop them? Your dossier says that you are unmarried with no kids. This is a one-way trip. We fight them until the end, or at least until your initial year assignment is complete. It can be happily extended after that if you are still alive, of course. Are you sure you want in?"

"No choice, like I said. It has to be done," I replied.

Robert and I sat quietly, watching each other for a long time.

Finally, he sighed and said, "Welcome to the Occult Strike Team. Your assignment starts immediately."

———

So, was I headed to a shadowy recruitment, where my former life would be erased, my fingerprints seared off, and my pay bumped to astronomical levels? Nope, this is still the federal government; it is just a weird clandestine group within it. I am still Federal Air Marshal James D. Grey, but now I'm assigned and attached to the FBI's OST Division for at least one year—same pay, still in Denver.

OST doesn't need FAM's help with quick-response surveillance and countersurveillance. However, they like our ability to get on planes quickly with weapons without raising suspicion—a specialty of ours. Yes, the FBI can get on planes, too, but their movements could become suspicious to higher management or other agencies. We could be assigned a "mission" on the aircraft through the FAM Service, and nothing would seem unusual.

After talking with SAC Cho, it was decided, by him, that my FAM credentials could have that unique application. I already had everything necessary to go into any US airport or US-flagged airplane with a gun and not arouse suspicion from any stakeholder, like the airlines, or any other agency. They told me I was assigned a FAM partner for those missions when needed: Patricia Levingston.

She was now also assigned to the OST.

I knew her well, and we had worked together often. She was also from DENFO. The other agents were not FAMs but FBI agents. I quickly learned they were picked for their exceptional abilities and lack of familial connections. Usually, that would violate the Civil Service Reform Act, but we had to live long enough for someone to find out and complain about it.

So, this is weird, but my new job description only mentions people and Known and Suspected Terrorists (KSTs). It does not mention simulants or other creatures.

I'm not sure why that surprised me.

It's not like you can put that in writing. This was OST's first time having an Occult Incident on board an aircraft. I had found my niche, or it was found for me. It's too bad Thomas Schmidt wasn't here to see this; he would have loved this new role.

I had to lie to his wife and kids at the funeral. Luckily, I had years of experience lying to people. To the point that it is natural now, and it doesn't even bother me to lie anymore. But lying to Thomas's family still hurt somewhere deep inside. The official story had changed. Now it was, "An Emotionally Disturbed Person had gotten a weapon on board and was shot by the air marshals." But he had killed two people, including FAM Schmidt, before being neutralized. The other people on the plane were gaslighted and told he had a knife and was on drugs. Those nearby *it* knew it was BS, but what would they say? The truth? No one would believe them, and we knew it. Hell, I was there, and I find it unbelievable.

Except it happened.

After the fact, the passengers took a lot of cell phone videos, but the shooting was over before anyone could film it. Besides, the incident was already being spun by the pro-hackers who worked for OST, so it was "just" a shooting incident. Still, this was going to be a problematic cover-up.

The FBI hadn't been beating down my door to join them. Until now, anyway.

I honestly don't have what it takes to be an FBI agent. We did laugh about them as FAMs (no agency beats us at pistol shooting or airplane tactics), but you needed stellar experience and education to join the FBI. I never even finished college. While in the army, I was studying for a BA in Economics online and thought about becoming an economist—I should say, until I found out what they *got* paid, or *didn't*.

Our new team had been flown to the Federal Law Enforcement Training Center (FLETC) in Glynn County, Georgia. I was surprised they chose FLETC over the FBI's training center in Quantico, Virginia, but it was the fastest way to give us a training "refresher" for our new opponents. We will only be here for four days while the other OST teams (and CSPD, to be sure) investigate where the "SIMs" came from. I had guessed that they had finally abbreviated simulants.

I guessed wrong.

Of course, they made a three-letter acronym for them: Simulant Infected Monster (a.k.a. a SIM.) Leave it to them to make a longer name for an acronym instead of a simple abbreviation.

The other OSTs were still under the impression that they were hunting whoever was behind the attacks, sending out two "killers."

Nothing supernatural about it was mentioned to them. Things were still "under wraps," for now anyway.

We were already told we would receive extensive training after this OI investigation. Luckily, we were all used to long duty days.

We did not work nine to five like the bosses.

Training days started at 0500 with physical training and went until 1700, followed by dinner and homework.

There were no days off.

When we get back, I will be going straight into the mission. Is that what the FBI calls them?

So, now I am learning all about—or how little we know about—the real occult. I never expected to take classes in a government training center on things like this: "Myths, Legends, and History of the Occult." I knew my career as a Federal Agent would take some interesting turns, but I never imagined this! The class was labeled "Constitutional Law: History and Applications." But when the door was shut, the actual classes started.

They also taught us an abbreviated version of the Multiple Weapons Training Program so we could effectively use submachine guns (SMGs), rifles, and shotguns. Almost all of us, I would guess, have already been trained on and used those weapons, but we needed a refresher. That makes sense to me. Being a FAM, it's not like I carried a full-sized rifle or a shotgun on planes while undercover.

I can't tell you how strange it is to take courses of instruction in the occult, in an official federal training facility, from calm and rational instructors. We had all the usual learning objectives, hands-on applications, written tests, etc.—just like any other courses I had in my federal career. I am now learning what weapons, or shot placement, work on which creature. Our live fire was practiced mostly on fast-moving human silhouette targets; they drew on the crazy creatures with a sharpie. Most targets are for the things we never want to see again in real life. Only I am probably going to see them ... again.

We also learned how they blend in, or don't, and their known abilities or weaknesses. The terrible news? The number of classes on real creatures encountered was limited to the SIMs. Everything else seems to be theoretical.

Great.

And there have only been two incidents with them so far.

The good news is that, for once, the government was being proactive. They decided that other occult-spawned creatures might be real if SIMs are real. *They definitely are!* It's time to find out if garlic or silver bullets work. God, I hope not. I don't want to know if vampires, werewolves, or other creatures that go bump in the night are real, too.

I know I don't sound like a hero. The reason is that "heroes" are mainly just dedicated people willing to go on the firing line against bad people, or monsters, I guess. We are just as human as anyone. Am I scared? Hell yeah! I would be worthless otherwise. No fear equals no adrenaline, which means no "combat mode." That means I don't react or move fast—which means I die.

We had settled in for a classified briefing on the SIMs. Our instructor's name was Daniel Histon. It still amazed me. There must have been some serious pull to make this happen, both in terms of the courses we were taking and the speed at which they were set up. Usually, it takes months to get a training slot at FLETC—

"OK, everybody. I thought this was a bad joke or something until I got a top secret briefing on what happened and saw this …" Daniel said.

The projector cut to a vivisected body lying in a morgue, and it wasn't my SIM from the plane. It was on its stomach and was split from its skull down to its back. Ugly grayish, purple tentacles ran throughout its body, and its darker-than-normal red blood was evident.

I remember, at the time, I thought the blood from the giant on the plane looked strange.

"The tentacles, or whatever they are, have run through every inch of its body," he continued.

The projector zoomed in on a leg. "You can see these tentacles have augmented all of the muscles, and here …"

Another change to a close-up of its torso, which was shredded by SWAT's bullets. "These bullets did almost nothing to it. Sure, it wrecked organs and even caused some damage to the tentacles, but it looks like the body is a husk for the tentacles to move. And the tentacles are super strong. Several bullets bounced off …"

From another angle, we could see on the screen where some tentacles had been damaged, but none had been severed.

"This f—ing thing is real …" he trailed off.

We could see his ashen face. No one spoke for a bit as he played picture after picture of how the entire body had been filled with these tentacles. The last picture was the worst.

"This is it, naked from the front. You can see the inhuman elongation of its neck and limbs. And those seem to have the most tentacles."

On close inspection, we could see now how to spot it as inhuman.

"The length of the limbs and neck will give them away from here on out … Plus, a close look will reveal that the bone structure is off," he said.

"Yeah, that and being ten feet tall." That was Greg Morris, one of the FBI Agents.

There was some chuckling, even from the instructor.

"Yeah, being shredded and huge will also be a big giveaway," Daniel replied, turning back to the screen.

Another close-up of a mutilated face with an eye hanging out, with most of the top of its head missing, was next on the screen. The structure of the bones looked enlarged, like someone with gigantism. We all looked at each other.

"Any questions?"

FAM Levingston started, "I know the headshot hit the creature and killed it, but did any other damage affect it?"

"From what we could see, it appears minimal. So, no. Your reports from the field tell us it is swift and strong. The bones also have a rigidity that must be from the tentacles. We had to use more than one bone saw; they kept breaking on it."

I felt sick, and I wasn't alone.

"Did the bullets still break bones?" Chayton asked.

There was a long pause.

"No. The bullets just left scratches on the large bones. The only ones that 'broke' were some fingers in the left hand when it was hit, but the tentacles make the skeletal structure redundant. The blood was livor mortis; meaning the blood was not oxygenated. The heart must have been pumping just enough to keep it from pooling. Which means … it … was trying to blend in. But the blood and organs were not functioning as normal. There was some oxygenation, so it used the lungs like the heart. Just enough to "look normal." Whoever this man was, he had probably been dead for many hours or maybe days."

"Are you guys going to experiment on it?" I asked.

A couple of people chuckled, and then they realized I meant it.

"Yes. We want to know what makes it tick and how to stop it ticking …"

I nodded.

The briefing was over, and we headed out to the driving range. Everything was way more compressed than usual. Instead of a few blocks of instruction, we were going almost nonstop. Meals were done quickly, and we were back at it.

So, this next instruction block was the Emergency Response Driving Course. Years ago, I attended performance driving schools on my own in my old 2010 Jeep SRT8 and did great on the autocross, even beating the instructor.

Well, the win only lasted for the three minutes it took him to beat me on his next run.

Still, winning was great while it lasted. I already had done the Emergency Response Driving course, but they wanted everyone to take or retake it.

We got pretty good at all the different driving courses, and it was fun until I realized I would need this training to save my life and the lives of my fellow agents. The State Department course drove that fact home, as it covered driving into unexpected contact. That was a buzzkill for the fun. I noticed the same look on the other agents' faces, except for Chayton's.

He is an inscrutable, scary dude.

Chayton is in charge and the team leader for our little group. Our OST team, the only one informally called the "Occult Strike Team," consisted of six people, including the Team Leader, Chayton Blackwell—a Supervisory Special Agent (SSA).

Why were no additional layers of management mentioned?

Because we report directly to SSA Blackwell, who reports directly to SAC Cho, there are no other levels of middle management. This is incredibly unusual. Chayton was in charge of the team, and Robert was in charge of us and the OST Division, which was probably about to get one hell of a change in their job titles soon.

Keeps it simple.

So now it is time to talk about SSA Chayton Blackwell, a.k.a. scary dude.

He only talks when necessary and is surprisingly eloquent and intelligent, definitely not what you expect looking at him. Making him even scarier is his six feet, two inches, 220-pound fighting physique.

In a regular fistfight, we all could last as long as it took him to get to us.

Greg Morris was probably the only one who could hold his own against him in hands-on fighting. It didn't hurt that Greg was also an amateur Mixed Martial Arts (MMA) fighter and had forty pounds on him, but Chayton had fought as a pro. I guess we will find out tomorrow in the Defensive Measures class. Chayton, so far, did well with every weapon we used at the range and calmly eliminated every threat. It was like watching an artist of death.

I love watching good shooters; I like the challenge of competition. The only place I could take him was on that firing range, but it was a close fight. If we were using pistols, it would be no contest. FAMs are that good. We are the undisputed best shots of any federal agency when using handguns—no room for error on a metal tube in the air—but I feel outclassed here in hand-to-hand combat. And I am a good fighter. Oh well, at least I blend in.

Chayton, however, does not blend in as well. He has the ears of a pro MMA fighter and the scars of battle from his many combat tours as a US Marine in Force Reconnaissance—not that he talks about them. Violence is the same as breathing for him.

I wish we could clone him to kill these things.

We only knew about his past because we had all read each other's dossiers. It was mandatory. All knowledge, skills, and abilities were laid bare. A strategic tactic so we knew who was best at what. Knowing each other's strengths and weaknesses can mean the difference between life and death for team members. And the success of our missions. Being shy was not an option.

The long day of instruction came to an end.

Most of the team headed off to dinner, but I went back to my little dorm room. I wanted some time alone to digest what I had learned and just relax.

Finally, I headed down to the Dining Hall for dinner. Most of the team had already eaten when I arrived, so it was just Chayton and me. I guess he wasn't in a hurry to eat, either.

"Hey, Chayton," I said,

"Hey, what's up, new guy?" he said with a smile.

I laughed.

"Yeah. Everything, I guess." I shrugged.

"Don't sweat it. You have more experience with this thing than anyone here. Remember that."

"True, I guess … I just wish I had more experience like you and the other team members. All I want to do is pull my own weight; I feel like an anchor compared to the skill set of the rest of the team. I still wonder if I had been faster, or better, if Thomas would have lived …"

"James, I've been in combat and have killed. Most soldiers and cops have never fired their gun in anger, much less in deadly close combat. They aren't less because of it. That is an experience we can both agree that no one wants."

Chayton had a point.

I nodded, and we went back to eating. Not much more needed to be said. After finishing my food, I said bye to Chayton and headed to my dorm room. I hoped I wouldn't dream.

———

The following day, I awoke and had a quick cup of coffee.

As an air marshal, I was used to being awake at all hours of the day, so it wasn't "early" for me. Breakfast would be after PT. I strolled from my little dorm room to the training building. We all filtered in, and the last of us, Skaggs, showed up just before 0500.

"Good morning, team," Chayton said.

It was morning, alright.

"Five a.m. is as morning as it gets," said Greg Morris, a special agent with the FBI. He was a huge man, standing at six feet six inches and 260 pounds, and his MMA record was excellent—five wins, two losses, and no "draws or no contests."

"We use military time from here on out, so you may as well get used to it," Chayton said.

"Got it, boss. 0500," Morris replied.

We were assembled in the training department. A full gym, mat room, and simulator rooms were all in the building, along with many classrooms.

Today, we were in the mat room.

Chayton had decided PT would be incorporated into a whole morning of Defensive Measures work. DM is any hand-to-hand fighting, whether armed or unarmed. A bunch of varied blue weapons were on the walls. They were inert but identical in size and weight to the real thing.

Red guns could fire "marking cartridges." Think paintball, but faster and more painful. Those, and the actual weapons, were always kept in the armory.

Everything in the mat room was "inert, non-firing" blue: the guns on one wall and the hand-to-hand weapons on the others.

"So, who wants to go first?" That was scary Chayton again.

We were assembled to practice some light sparring to assess our abilities. No one was eager to start with Chayton.

"I'll go," said Larry Skaggs, an FBI special agent.

Chayton nodded, and they started to spar.

We were all wearing full MMA gear to avoid getting too banged up. Chayton and Larry circled on the mat. Larry had some MMA background and was also an excellent pugilist, a.k.a. boxer. But we all knew he was no match for Chayton. So did he.

It happened fast.

Chayton shot in for a takedown, and Larry sprawled to defend. Then Chayton knife-handed Larry's neck. Luckily, he just cupped his hand, but if it had been the ugly version, Larry would not be getting back up.

"Owww …" Larry was still face down, holding his neck. As he got to his feet, Chayton said, "What I just did would get me banned from Mixed Martial Arts. That's the point. If you fight fair against a trained MMA fighter, you will lose. Imagine if it was something worse than *a person* you were fighting?"

We had all reviewed the report of my ill-fated last mission as a regular "flying" FAM. The only other known occult incident was where CSPD had fired a ridiculous number of rounds before taking that one out, also with several casualties. Luckily, people weren't hard to convince with the "real story." The people witnessing it were upset, of course, but they found the fake story much more palatable than the real one. Helping our cause, the "news" agencies that were the most sensational and untrustworthy went to run something close to the real story, but our hackers criticized them on social media. So, the public figured they were trying to make up ridiculous stories of "aliens attacking Earth." It wasn't hard to convince people it wasn't a supernatural attack. That isn't something people want to believe anyway.

We practiced many more techniques from Chayton and other professional fighters that would never be considered an appropriate use of force in any US court.

But dang, if they weren't highly effective!

I heard rumors that the "legacy" FAMs—who started right after 9/11—had been taught stuff like this. Before the lawyers freaked out and management stopped bringing in Spec Ops people to teach them to kill. I'm sure these were the same type of guys training us now. Friendly enough, but they had that dead look in their eyes that told us they had seen combat up close.

As good as many of us were, we were no match for those who lived and breathed violence daily. We all gave them a good fight, anyway. After an entire morning of DM, and some ice packs and ibuprofen for various bruises, we headed to the Dining Hall for lunch.

"I think I could take Chayton," said between big bites of food. That was Larry Skaggs, now known as "Skag."

He did not like his moniker, but that is the point. You don't get to pick your nickname or call sign. Your team picks it for you. I chuckled. He hated it.

FAM Levingston, who went by Lev, responded first. "In what world, Skag?"

"The one where I surprised him while he was asleep, of course," Larry said.

We all laughed. He could then—maybe.

I must hand it to the Dining Hall at FLETC. There was a lot of variety, and we didn't have to cook or do dishes. You gotta love that! Alan was the only one bummed about it; he liked to cook. So, all full and sleepy, we were off to an afternoon of academics on the occult.

Or so we thought.

Chayton walked into the classroom and said, "Change of plans. The mat room, in full HIT gear, and ready to go. Ten minutes from *click* (he hit his stopwatch) NOW!"

Everyone looked at each other and ran to the mat room. HIT gear is high-intensity training gear. This is also called the "REDMAN Defensive Tactics Training Suit." However, RDTTS is hard to say. Plus, and I agree with the government on this one, using the term "Redman" could be understandably offensive to Native Americans. Plus, HIT gear is more accurate. It is the big black or red armored suit you see police wear when training to get hit hard by simulated weapons or big and very tough instructors. We knew Chayton well enough to know that whatever gear we didn't get on in time would be where he hit us. So, we hurried to help each other into the gear. Surprisingly, we all got it on with only a minute to spare.

"Very good." Chayton was in the mat room with us.

He was not wearing any HIT gear, just MMA gloves and a mouth guard—probably for our benefit, not his. "Wall one, whatever you want. One minute."

Wall one was the small hand-to-hand weapons. All "small" ones included knives, brass knuckles, and batons. Again, they are blue ones designed to hurt but not injure.

"Pair off," Chayton said.

We did.

No one wanted to "pick on" Lev, as she was smaller than the rest of us, although she seemed more challenging than Alan and Larry, to be honest. Compared to Greg Morris, she was tiny. Standing five feet, six inches and weighing only 160 pounds, Lev didn't even look that heavy until you saw her muscles in gym clothes. She immediately picked Greg Morris, even though he was the biggest of us all. He blends in like a bull elephant and kinda resembles one, too—a bit of fat weight, but still very strong and fit. Greg was also a pretty good fighter, having won several bouts as an MMA expert. He smiled when she immediately said, "Morris!"

We all looked at her incredulously.

Alan paired off with Chayton. Larry turned to me, shrugged, and said, "Grey." It was settled. Skag it was. Skag had picked a single knife. So, not to be outdone, I grabbed two brass knuckles and a baton.

Lev and Greg's first bout was beauty and the beast, though. We debated calling him "beast," but all agreed it was just too cliche.

They squared off and started circling.

Lev had two wicked-looking Karambit knives. Karambits are unique because the grip has a thumb ring, making it hard to drop. It was just under nine inches long with a five-inch curved blade.

They reminded me of Velociraptor claws.

Our training ones didn't have that ring because that would cause students to lose thumbs; otherwise, they were identical. Morris had picked a pair of brass knuckles.

It was comical to watch—the fight was very one-sided.

Morris had an unfair advantage. He was a foot taller and one hundred pounds heavier, an experienced MMA fighter, and had reach, size, and strength on his side. He smiled as he circled Lev, who was also smiling, but hers was an icy smile. It was a little scary to see.

She seemed relaxed and eager.

Weird.

Morris faked a kick and threw a hard, fast leading-hand punch at Lev's face. There was a collective gasp. We expected him to hold back, but he didn't.

Agent Greg

I was surprised when Lev immediately picked me to spar with, as I had a whole foot of height and a hundred pounds of weight on her. This meant I had a significant reach and strength advantage over her. Seeing my size and knowing I was a fighter, most people thought I was of limited intellect. It's understandable but incorrect. I have a Bachelor's in Criminology and a Master's in Forensic Accounting. Using intelligence to figure out your opponents is always an advantage. I knew my strength was not an advantage against those knives she held. We all knew she had some knife training, so I needed to hit her quickly in a way that would end the fight. I didn't want to hurt her, but I had to be lightning-quick with my strikes. If I held back, she would cut me apart. This was fun but also serious training to survive real encounters.

As we circled, we both smiled. She moved gracefully and was comfortable using those wicked knives. My advantage was that I had more MMA experience than her, so a quick fake and strike was the answer. I flinched at her a few times to see her reactions, but there were none. Crud, she was good; there were no amateur flinches.

Impressive.

I deliberately threw my strikes softer, showing I was holding back to not hurt her. Not because I *would* hold back—I just wanted her to *think* I would.

I couldn't hold back if I wanted to hit her fast, so I faked a kick and shot a fast jab into her head. I was pleased with the combo; I threw it as fast as possible.

Only her head slipped just out of the way, and she shot in.

———

Agent Lev

The weight of the Karambits felt good, like natural extensions of my body. They made me smile. The monster that was Morris was circling me, his every move a calculated step toward a strike. The tension in the air was palpable. He faked some punches and kicks to gauge my reactions, but I had experienced that many times before and did not over-react to them. He unconsciously nodded approval when I didn't fall for them, a silent acknowledgment of my skill.

We kept circling, and I could tell he was not underestimating me. He was holding back from full-speed strikes, but I knew he wouldn't when the actual strike came.

When it came, he threw his whole power and speed into his strike, but not in an off-balancing way. I had to admit it was skillful, but I had practiced my counter-move countless times.

As his strike came in, I didn't block it. Instead, I slipped just outside and moved in with lightning speed. He almost had me, but I was just a *little* bit faster. My left Karambit struck with full force, slamming hard into his rib cage—

"Oof!" He let out a grunt.

Shooting past him, I executed a swift, precise spin, and the other Karambit found its mark in his kidney—"Oof!"

I retreated out of his reach as swiftly as I had entered.

———

Agent James

Have you ever had that moment when something happens, and everyone is so shocked you could hear a pin drop?

This was that moment.

We all gasped when Morris went one hundred percent on Lev. It was a fabulous fake and punch combo. Those brass knuckles with 260 pounds of MMA fighter behind them would have destroyed Lev's head in real life. And even with the soft "blue" version, he may have hurt her with how hard he hit. Kudos to him for not underestimating his opponent.

But it didn't matter.

The human blender that was Lev hit him twice, so hard that he grunted even with the armor on. It was unreal. She then moved out of range again in what seemed like only a second or two.

There was a long moment of silence.

Morris just stood there looking at her with eyes the size of half-dollars. He didn't move on her again. He knew he had just been killed. So much for the "some knife fighting training" she listed on her intake sheet. She had neglected to mention she was an expert in Pencak silat and other Indonesian martial arts.

Chayton started slowly clapping, and we all joined in.

Wow. Just wow.

The training devolved into us all taking turns getting cut to shreds by Lev.

Unbelievable.

She had earned a new nickname and call sign—"Blender." The worst part was that the more she sparred, the more she seemed to be enjoying herself! She was like a cat with mice that just kept coming. Word always gets out, and by the time she sparred with Chayton—She even took out Chayton after a much longer session—it seemed half the training staff was there to watch.

After that, everyone looked at Lev—I mean, Blender—differently. We all had talents in different areas, but she was a goddess with knives.

Well, a goddess, period.

She had the body of a powerful CrossFit woman combined with looks that belonged on the cover of magazines. The only giveaway, besides her effortless pull-ups, was her trapezius muscles. Those are the ones you see that slope up from the shoulders to the neck. No one can hide their neck with regular clothes. But you must know what you are looking for to notice that. She seemed twenty pounds lighter in everyday clothes.

Even the instructors, who hadn't seen the match, wanted to try their luck. They thought for sure we were making it up. After each of us lost, we had decided to try pairing up two against one. We sometimes got her with two, but it turned out the magic number was three of us. We could always get her then, but at least one would never return home. And she smiled the whole time.

It was unnerving.

CHAPTER 4
THE OFFICE

Agent James

WE FINISHED our four days of training at FLETC, with the FBI promising a lot more training to come. The next day, today, is our travel day, so now we get to enjoy a leisurely trip back to Denver …

After going through everything we did to enter the sterile area past security, Lev and I strolled along like a happy couple. There was no PDA or anything, but we had worked our "husband and wife" schtick as FAMs before. Our cover story was rock solid. We had one kid at home, and we would bicker about our differences in child-rearing. No one ever thought we were FAMs. We even had some excellent tiffs in the gate area and on board, but we always stayed civil. We were settled on board our flight back to Denver.

"Do you want to sit beside your wife, young man?" The grey-haired, quite nice lady next to me asked.

"No thanks. She needs to take some alone time to think about what she said to me this morning," I replied, deliberately loud enough for Lev to hear. An angry look from Lev shot my way.

"Oh, oh." The old lady sat down beside me, clearly concerned about our tiff.

Again—for about the dozenth time on a plane. The man sitting next to her started chatting her up. He had the sleazy look of a man who knew the beautiful woman beside him was mad at her "husband." It was time for him to make his move …

"How are you today?" he said with clearly his best smile. Lev deliberately waited, then turned on him.

"How the f—k do you think I am? You just heard what happened."

She said it just loud enough to shut him down without making a scene. We were left alone by the passengers next to us for the rest of the flight. Another beautifully executed plan to shut them up and get some peace and quiet. I know that it is mean, but it is effective. More talking equals more chances to blow your cover. And more distractions from the job.

I was still "reading" that same book from before, and Lev had out a romance book. It had a handsome, bare-chested man with flowing blonde hair on the cover. He had a beautiful woman bent over in his arms, longingly looking up at him.

Oh my god, she is *not* the kind of woman to read something like that! She definitely one-upped me.

Lev was a gorgeous woman. Tall, with long, beautiful blonde hair and mesmerizing light blue eyes. She would be a great wife for someone if they wanted to be told what to do and didn't mind dying by a thousand cuts if they made her mad. She saw me looking at her and seemed to know what I was thinking—then she scowled.

I glared back, then went back to my "book."

The rest of the flight was "routine." I try never to use this term until the flight is over. Assuming it will be routine is a huge mistake.

One I know for a fact after my flight with the SIM.

Thankfully, this one *was* routine—no disturbances or disquieting activity. No one argued loudly or even used the bathroom when the seatbelt sign was on. Even rule followers break that rule nearly every flight. I never thought I would be *so* happy to have a "normal" flight again. So, after our uneventful and joyous flight, we were well rested and ready to go—except for the joy and rest part …

———

Agent Lev

Our little escapades as husband and wife were always fun for me.

It was a great cover story and a lot of fun. Our son, Andrew, always caused trouble for us, even though he didn't exist. We could freely look around at people, see if anyone may become a problem, and look out for Known or Suspected Terrorists or BOLOs, which we would know by their photos and descriptors.

No one suspected we were air marshals.

After settling into my seat, not far from James this time, I heard an older woman ask if he wanted to switch seats to be near me. He said no and something about me needing to think about what I said to him.

I chuckled inwardly.

I liked James—I would want to date him if he weren't a fellow FAM. But, in this line of work, I didn't need the headache of being in a relationship with a co-worker, nor did I want a reputation as a "slut."

It's weird.

If a guy sleeps with many women, he is a cool dude. But if a woman does it, she is a slut. It was so messed up. Hell, maybe I didn't want to "fit in" that way—even if it *was* OK. Military and law enforcement cultures were still more "old-school" than many other professions.

My reverie was broken by the man next to me.

He was not unattractive but had a bit of a sleazy look to him. He was clearly about to hit on me, and I didn't want to spend the next half hour talking to him. Plus, I still needed to be "mad at my husband." Usually, I would be more polite, but I was working and needed to shut him down fast. I gave my response some thought.

It worked. He sheepishly turned away from me.

I felt terrible for him, but I had work to do. Seizing the moment, I took out my book. I knew James would see what I was reading, so I bought the steamiest romance novel I could find. I hated the crap, and James knew it, but I wanted to "one-up" him.

It's just a little game we like to play.

I saw him looking over, and it unnerved me a bit—he was admiring me.

And it felt good.

Dammit, if I didn't like that man, but I had to stay "in role"—as the angry wife.

––––––

Agent James

Lev and I landed at 4:20 p.m.—ugh, I mean 1620—and were met by a blacked-out Chevy Suburban once we finally got to the passenger drop-off at the top level at DIA. (Police play by different rules when on duty). Our driver was a gruff guy—he said his name was Baker—and had no personality whatsoever. He drove us to our new field office in silence. We pulled up to a garage door and went inside. That was new. I had expected just to park and walk in. We drove around some barricades as we entered and pulled around to a parking space. Baker backed it in like we always do as police.

We parked and exited the SUV, and I suddenly turned back.

"It's Baker, right?"

"Yeah," he replied.

"Here you go; thank you for the ride!" I was holding out a dollar bill.

He grunted and made a sour face before walking off.

"I've never seen such a grumpy Uber driver. He didn't even take your tip," Lev said, even though she was smiling.

I don't know if I read too many books or watched too many movies, but I had been expecting to go into a library or tailor shop and then be ushered to a back room (that was secretly an elevator) leading to an underground super-complex.

Of course, that was not the case.

It was a typical, bland office building. There were no signs out front saying what it was—just Units 200, 210, and 220. What *was* unusual was that all the units belonged to OST—the entirety of the office building. Once inside, it was clear that the interior was starting to be completely remodeled, and some serious security work was being done. Unit 220 used to be a shop that worked on cars, 210 was a catering company, and 200 was office space. So, it was an ideal fit.

The agency had built into the garage bay a sally port (a kind of "airlock" for a car to come in before being allowed through into the main garage.) At the moment, it was just a blockade. You had to swerve around concrete barriers to drive through, and men with submachine guns guarded it. Eventually, it would be a sealed room with two garage doors. That was our standard method of entering and departing while on duty.

Building things to new, ever-changing specs takes time, especially in the government.

So, it wouldn't be fully operational for quite a while. They had leased this place sometime earlier, probably slotted to be something else. There were some seriously bad-ass security teams already here. I found out later that they were Nuclear Materials Couriers (NMCs) from the Department of Energy (DOE) on permanent assignments like us. They have the most training of pretty much any federal agent. I also discovered that we now have the same training budget as they did—almost unlimited.

Well, unlimited as long as we could lay on the BS to get the funds anyway. I'm glad that was the director and SAC's job. I am not a fan of politics.

Once we were allowed through the sally port, we saw how immense the garage was. It housed all our government-owned vehicles (GOVs). Every vehicle had a specific spot to park, and all preventive maintenance, checks, and services (PMCS) would eventually be done in-house. Those sexy Suburbans would be getting replaced or modified soon. The average car dealership would have a heart attack if they looked at what our vehicles would become. Our technicians also dealt with vehicle features for the unusual array of security, communications, disguised emergency lights and sirens, weapons and equipment storage, armor/protection, etc.

Every person in "the office" was going to have their own "studio" apartment for when we were on quick reaction force (QRF) status. We still had our cars and homes, but sometimes we would stay full time at the office while operations were ongoing.

Ever see those furniture showrooms that have sample displays with dorm sizes, like "150 square foot efficiency apartment for one, fully stocked and furnished?" The quarters were kind of like that. There was a simple galley kitchenette, a restroom with a shower, a desk and chair, and a very comfortable-looking full-sized bed. Where it didn't look like a dorm, there was a regular closet and a biometric locked safe. The safe was for our firearm, other "police" equipment, credentials, passports, etc.

Quite cool. It's too bad it was just a brochure at this point.

Most of the dining would occur in the Mess Hall, and serious weaponry was to be stored securely in the Armory, neither of which were ready yet.

A makeshift Mission Control Center (MCC) was set up in a large room. Alan's computer specialists were already here, and this is where all our operations would be run out of. The wires and cables were still visible, snaked all over the room.

Besides all of that—and the sally port entrances—it was mostly a recently leased government office building.

I was impressed they had even gotten that far, and I was a little concerned at the urgency they were moving forward with. They must know something that they were not sharing with us. There was no point in asking; if it wasn't shared, it was because it was classified above us (unlikely as we have top secret clearances), or we didn't have a "need to know." That bothered me because I felt we had that now. But when I brought it up to Chayton anyway, he just smiled at me. That told me what I "needed to know." So yes, something was up, and no, it wouldn't be shared with us. At least not yet.

After a brief orientation, we walked to our hotel to check in—for one night. We were to report at 0500, and breakfast would be catered (delivered prior and reheated in the morning).

Well, it was time to get some shut-eye. The day would start early. I was exhausted and laid down to sleep.

The nightmare began again.

———

Thomas was there at my bedside, his torso caved in, and his head smashed at the back. He was standing next to Scott, whose head hung on his neck at a weird and dead angle.

"Why didn't you stop it faster? All you had to do was shoot it once in the head. Was that so hard?!" Thomas scolded me.

Scott tried to nod in the affirmative next to him, but his head just wobbled grotesquely ... I could see Thomas's caved-in torso and knew the back of him did not look any better. And it was clear that Scott would have been decapitated if his skin wasn't holding his head like a grotesque balloon. They both stared at me wickedly.

Suddenly, I was somewhere else.

I was standing at the funeral again. Grace is still crying, her face swollen from the anguish. Her kids looked confused still, not sure why Dad was never coming home. Grace turned to me—

"You did this! You were supposed to look out for each other! He trusted you!"

I looked around in a panic. Everyone gathered had elongated necks and limbs. They all sat perfectly still and looked straight ahead. Then, as one, they all turned to stare at me at the sound of her screaming voice.

They leaped up and came at me and then ...

———

I slammed awake with a start, not sure of where I was. I was reaching for my waistband to grab my gun by the time I realized I had only been dreaming. My surroundings didn't make sense at first. This was common, as half my life was spent in ever-changing hotel rooms.

At least I didn't dream about Janice anymore; I had new nightmares now.

Oh well, it was time for a cup of coffee. It was 4:12 a.m. Ugh, military time—0412. All the flights we went on still used the silly a.m./p.m., so we all had to get used to that as FAMs. But for our operations everything is in the military 24-hour time. My alarm was set for 0430, so I just stayed up.

"Go get 'em, tiger," I grumbled into my coffee cup.

Great, now I am talking to myself.

The little hotel coffeemaker made the usual terrible cup of coffee, but its bitterness woke me up. I showered, got ready, checked out, and walked to my new field office.

We were all assembled in the break room. It was a lovely summer morning in Denver—the kind of day when everything just seemed alive and happy. The birds outside were chirping and flitting about. I sat contentedly watching them.

Of course, Chayton had to ruin it.

"OK, team, report to the briefing room," Chayton said over the intercom.

Off I go, coffee still in hand, tossing the remnants of my catered breakfast in the trash.

The briefing room looks like a typical government conference room. I can see a projector and screen, a long table with chairs, and an STU-3 (Secure Terminal Unit) phone in the middle. An STU phone is part of the secure terminal equipment used to have secure conversations with other offices or agencies. Without it, we could not discuss sensitive or classified information.

Once we were all settled, Chayton hit the button and said hello.

"Hello, SSA Blackwell." It was SAC Cho. This was going to be good.

He was calling from the Denver FBI Field Office. Although the "new" Denver OST office was under his jurisdiction, the building was a secret and existed only for the "Strike Team."

"Everyone is assembled, sir. The team is ready," Chayton said.

"Alright, we have received word from the other OST teams that there is a convergence of where the two simulants originated from. They have narrowed down the possible locations and the most likely area is in the mountains west of Colorado Springs. While you were all on vacation at FLETC, *they* were working. Traffic cams, ATMs, and bank records show that both simulants lived in the area. So, we are starting your team off there first. The GOVs stick out too much, so it's rental cars for the team this time."

Everyone except the two FAMs groaned.

Lev and I are used to sitting in coach, so a road trip was a joy for us. While everyone else groused, we looked at each other and smiled.

There is a misconception about where air marshals sit on planes. We are OK with that. We will not tell anyone (without the proper clearance and need to know) how many of us there are, where we sit, or what planes we are on. Suffice to say we aren't always stretching out and enjoying delicious in-flight meals. And we are used to traveling on planes. The advantage of having us on the team is that we were experts if something happens on board.

I felt cold and started remembering my last flight as a "regular" air marshal—

"You OK, James?" Chayton said.

Crap.

Everyone was staring at me as I was having my day-nightmare. The look on my face showed what I was thinking.

"Sorry," I said.

"No need. We know what you went through," Chayton said with actual empathy.

SAC Cho spoke again on the intercom. "Alright. Team Leader, you know what to do. Logistics are already being handled. SSA Blackwell has all the details for everyone. Good luck." With that, SAC Cho hung up the call.

"Wonderful," I said aloud—I knew this would be fun.

Chayton assigned us "battle buddies" (BBs).

A BB is another person who is responsible for you, and you for them. If you stop to take a leak, they cover you. If they are going to check on something, you go with them. Remember all those movies where one guy wanders off and gets killed?

That's why.

"There should always be two bodies, not one," my drill sergeant told us during basic training in the army. Good advice.

Chayton decided that Lev and I would be battle buddies and head to the Colorado Springs Police Department (CSPD) for their morning briefing to try to recruit them for help. Meanwhile, he and the others would look for more leads on the simulants and assist as needed.

Besides, SAC Cho also said if we didn't make it back, he wanted to have the other members of the OST still alive. I didn't think it was funny—but he may not have been joking.

At least I had Lev, the Blender, as my BB.

She was a new hire as a FAM, fresh out of training with less than a year of flight status. Some agents forget that we all came from other backgrounds. Most of us were military or police—and all are fighters. So, she may be a newer FAM, but she has skills and experience. Having been a former border patrol agent on the Southwest border, she was hardly a newbie.

There was no doubt that she could have any modeling gig she wanted but, as she had the temperament of He-Man and a Rottweiler mixed, she had less interest in modeling than a Rottweiler.

It made sense that we were BBs since we had already worked together as FAMs.

Getting a rental car was easy enough since it was already there.

I could get used to this, I thought.

As FAMs with no admin staff—that was usually only for the bigwigs—we had to book everything, except flights, ourselves.

Our vehicle was a late-model Toyota Prius—sexy.

"You want to drive?" I asked Lev.

"*That*? No thanks."

"You are such a diva."

"I know!" she said with the cutest shit-eating grin. She helped herself into the passenger side.

Alright, it was time to put on our game faces again. I adjusted the seat and mirrors and then pulled out of the parking lot.

"I have the address in the CarPlay; good to go," she said, after entering the address at the speed of light. She could type as fast as she could use a knife, and I was glad she was on my team.

I nodded, and we took off at full speed. I kept thinking of the guy in *The Fast and the Furious* who said, "I live my life ten seconds at a time." It's very accurate in this car.

Except it's ten seconds to 60 mph, not to the end of the quarter-mile.

Oh well.

It was comfortable, though; I am glad we had the "Persona" model. It had fake leather seats and a decent sound system, which we left off.

"OK, we have about an hour or so on the road ahead of us. Stop for donuts?" I asked.

She just smiled. We both tried to eat clean and stay in shape. She didn't even drink alcohol—so no donuts for us.

"OK, coffee it is," I said.

I know, it's almost unbelievable, but there was a Starbucks on our route. We decided to make a quick stop for coffee: two black Americanos. While she went to the bathroom, I placed the order, and she picked up the drinks while I took my turn. We managed to get back on the road in under ten minutes.

The view kept getting better the closer we got to Colorado Springs. Looking out the windows, we could see the majestic mountains to our right as we headed south. Pikes Peak steals the best view, rising over 14,000 feet into the clear sky. The sun rising to our left made the windows of homes and offices glint like diamonds embedded into the verdant mountainsides.

The view of Lev was good, too.

I tried not to make it weird, though; we were co-workers, after all. In what seemed like no time at all, we arrived.

We pulled into the Colorado Springs Police Department.

CHAPTER 5

COLORADO SPRINGS PD

Sergeant Donaldson

AS USUAL, I was early and looked out at the assembled briefing room. It was time for the morning roll call and shift briefing. The morning shift of patrol officers, detectives, supervisors, and SWAT were all present. After the usual formalities, the lieutenant got to the main briefing.

"Sergeant Donaldson, your SWAT team will be on standby as needed for the OST team," Lieutenant Harris told me.

"Yes, sir."

There were audible groans; many here were not pleased with the Feds.

Everyone knew what had happened at that truck stop, how a giant man had gone crazy, killing people barehanded. A concealed weapon holder was the first to shoot it.

She wasn't the last.

After it killed her, the first CSPD unit arrived—with two patrol officers. Shortly after, the Special Weapons and Tactics (SWAT) team arrived. According to the official report, the perp wore armor and had a gun. Except everyone in this room knew that was BS. Even the media was calling foul on our official report. This was a serious mess; we could see it on upper management's faces.

The SWAT team members and I, now assigned to help the Feds, were the same ones who directly engaged the suspect at the truck stop. That is probably why the lieutenant picked us.

I thought back on what just happened.

———

"Dispatch to Sam One—"

"Go for Sam One," I said.

"SWAT is requested for an active shooter at Perry's truck stop, 1330 Wilcox Road. Shots fired, officers down. Unknown number of assailants; additional units are en route."

I never wanted to hear those words again. Officers—plural.

We were already on our way to serve a warrant, so we had a quicker-than-normal response time. It was pure luck, but when luck was on my side, I would take it. We arrived a very short drive later, with the lights and siren going and driving faster than usual, even for running code. Ominously, we could hear the distant "pop, pop … pop, pop, pop" of sporadic gunfire. We deployed out of the back as we had hundreds of times before.

Lewis and Channing took overwatch on the front (A and B sides) of the building while Krieger and I moved forward—only one of us moving while the other covered, known as "bounding overwatch" in the army. Channing was our sniper, so he and Lewis stayed back and got a good angle on the glass wall at the front of the truck stop. Lewis stayed with him to be his guard. The reason snipers always have an assistant gunner (A-gunner) is because you can't look through a scope and watch your ass at the same time. You have a limited field of view, so the spotter also watches the larger area and relays critical real-time data to the sniper.

The other sniper team was DeFontes and Edwards. They had a lock on the two rear (C and D) sides of the building. That put rifle scopes on all sides, just as we normally do. Usually, the regular patrol officers would beat us there, but as luck would have it, we were there first—as we were already on our way to serve that no-knock warrant.

That warrant would have to wait.

Police no longer just set a perimeter and wait for SWAT during an active threat (a.k.a. active shooter) event. Whoever gets there first forms teams and goes in.

Luckily, SWAT is the ultimate "team."

SWAT officers Nealy and Maloney came in through the back to clear that part of the truck stop. Once the suspect was neutralized, we would meet in the middle.

As Krieger and I entered the truck stop, we could see dead bodies, some with crushed heads, some at impossible angles on top of the aisles of goods; some had been, what—*thrown*?—into the ceiling first. I could hear the crunching of my boots as I walked, but there was something else—

I spun.

After years of experience, you sense attacks as much as you see them. Maybe it was a quick shuffling or a shadow, but the move saved my life. As I stepped sideways and turned, a blur of a gigantic man rushed past me. He collided with the soda machine, smashing it to the floor. I noticed blood spray out of him as he hit it.

CRASH!

What in the hell?

"Contact!" I yelled, but it wasn't needed.

Krieger had his MP5 submachine gun up, and when the man turned, it was all we could do not to freak out; luckily, our training had kicked in.

The man stood with one eye dangling out, dark-red blood all over him from impacting the soda machine and from multiple gunshot wounds (GSWs). He clearly should be dead.

But he wasn't.

He made an inhuman growl and started to charge Krieger, who had deliberately backed up to the glass windows. The thing rushed him twice as fast as any living person could. Krieger and I acted in unison.

Both of us pushed out our MP5s. And straight in front, we pushed tight on the slings—with both eyes open—looking through the round front sight.

Unlike the TV shows where SWAT puts MP5s to their shoulders, you don't do that when you have helmets and other gear that gets in the way. This technique is called the SAS sling technique. Using this method, a trained fighter with an MP5 can hold the trigger down and put thirty shots nonstop into a dinner plate at fifteen yards. I know this, as we all could do it, at least on a target that doesn't move. We were doing that now but on a *very* fast-moving target.

BRRAP!—BRRAP!—BRRAP!

I had to fire bursts because it was moving so fast and at an angle. However, no one was alive behind it while it was running toward Krieger—so even though some of my shots missed—I put quite a few in it.

BRRRRRRRRRRRRAP!

Krieger, on the other hand, had one significant advantage. It was coming straight at him, which is what you want with an MP5. He fired nonstop on full auto and was shredding its upper torso. Blood and internal matter were spraying behind it as it ran.

Suddenly, a massive explosion of bone and brain shot out behind its skull—its head snapped forward. A lot of people don't know this, but the pressure of the exit wound, from a rifle round to the head, pushes the head *toward* the rifle that shot it—not away. A split second later, we heard the CRACK! And saw where a rifle round came through the glass—as the glass shards started to settle.

The *thing* fell lifeless to the ground.

It joined the other bodies strewn around the store, including two of our own. The patrol officers who had responded on scene first—and the civilian with the concealed weapon—had all engaged it. And all had been smashed or ripped apart.

Blood, guts, excrement, and lots of bullet casings were strewn about the floor.

I looked up at the lieutenant and knew I had been zoning out and reliving the shooting. I am not easily spooked; I am only thinking about my performance and my team.

Could we have done better? Was there something I needed to add to our training?

I have been in charge of the SWAT team for going on five years, so they all knew me well. I never let them see me as anything but calm and unflappable. I have a wife and kids at home, but they know the job comes first. Angie is a teacher and our three kids—Vivian, Trevor, and Billy—know that when Daddy is working, he is not to be bothered. We have a good family, and my job was always getting myself and my officers home at the end of each shift. Now, I must figure out how to fight things that aren't even human.

The horror of that day was still in my mind; I saw that some officers were staring at me. Usually, they would say something witty like, "Have a nice trip, Donaldson?"

But nobody was in a joking mood.

Two officers were killed, along with eight civilians. I shudder to think what would have happened if Channing hadn't been overwatch with the sniper rifle. We never got back ballistics, but he—or *it*—had been hit dozens of times with 9mm rounds from SMGs (with a higher velocity and more terminal damage than a pistol round) and was still going. We saw the spray of blood and tissue; it was no bullet-resistant vest or armor that had saved it.

My God, what the hell was it?

So, we were all a little—OK, more than a little—pissed when the FBI stepped in and took the body before our coroner could look at it. There was no need for an autopsy report, though: We all knew that whatever it was, it wasn't human.

I looked around the briefing room.

Those that had been there that day were ashen-faced with anger. Those that weren't just looked furious. No one kills one of our own, much less two, and gets away with it. No overtime had to be offered, as none of us would rest until everyone involved in this was behind bars or six feet under. Usually, the other officers would call BS on our story, but we had all seen what remained of that thing's body—

We stood around, like in that movie with the alien creature in the block of ice, staring in horror at what we saw. No one could even speak at first.

The SWAT team and I looked at each other. The SWAT officers on the other teams not selected were miffed, but we all knew we would work together to catch everyone involved. Plus, we would use the full strength of the SWAT teams and CSPD once we found the perps. Everyone, including the rest of SWAT, was still on duty or on call. We all would be helping in any way we could. No matter what.

The briefing would be long this morning. There is no point in leaving yet; the FBI should arrive soon, so we took a break until the Feds arrived. It was time to get coffee, use the bathroom … and wait.

I hope these Feds can help figure this out and not get in our way.

Agent James

Lev and I parked our ten-second car in the visitor space and entered the vestibule of the Colorado Springs Police Department.

"Agents Levingston and Grey. We are here to meet with SWAT."

I had never heard myself say that before; it sounded strange. The desk officer checked our credentials, looking up to verify that our faces matched.

"Come on in," the officer at the desk replied.

A short while later, we met a hard-looking SWAT officer with sergeant stripes; his name tag read "DONALDSON."

"Sergeant Donaldson, I am FAM James Grey, and this is FAM Patri —" I stopped mid-sentence as Levingston glared at me. She *hated* the name Patricia. "—this is FAM Levingston; she goes by Lev."

He nodded to us both. "I'm Graham Donaldson," he said, and shook our hands.

I was glad he had a firm, no-nonsense handshake with Lev and me. It showed his professionalism.

"Let's go to our shift briefing, and you can fill us all in on what, in the actual hell, is happening." His friendly demeanor had changed, and he gave me a fierce, questioning look. Luckily for us all, I am not one to mince words or play coy with a team that depends on my life and me on theirs.

"I'll tell you and your team everything I know, clearances be damned."

He relaxed a little and nodded. We followed him to the briefing room, where the SWAT team and at least a dozen patrol officers were assembled.

"OK, listen up. Agents Grey and Levingston are going to brief us on the OP," he said.

I took the lead, as Levingston and I had agreed. (We are both the same "rank.")

"So, I don't have to tell you the cover story is BS," I said.

There were appreciative nods all around.

"What we know about them, so far, is that the two of them, both neutralized, are supersized and juiced-up versions of their former selves," I said.

Levingston was controlling the laptop to show what we had on the projector.

"Both were real people who had lives before being transformed into the *things* we dealt with."

The slide showed the one that the CSPD had "neutralized."

"This is the one you all killed. Henry Johnson was a forty-four-year-old Caucasian male, five feet, eight inches, and 180 pounds. He lived in Colorado Springs." The screen showed an average man with a little potbelly and average muscle.

"As you can see, he looks nothing like—I paused for effect—*whatever that is.*"

A vast, six-foot-nine, 360-pound horror of his former self was now on the screen. Replete with fifty-three bullet wounds. The following pictures showed the head cut open and the body in stark vivisection from Quantico's coroner. I knew they were angry that the FBI had taken the body before they could look at it, but our coroners were better, and we had to keep things "under wraps" as best we could.

"You can see *he* should not have been able to continue functioning with the damage it sustained. We found these strange, grayish/purple tendrils throughout his body. They made him bigger and stronger; some were strong enough to stop bullets. The main creature has a grayish/purple mass of microscopic tentacles from which all the others seemed to be 'sprouted,'" I said.

Lying there naked on the screen, the elongation of his body and limbs was apparent.

"Because of what we learned, we know they cannot 'hide' indefinitely. Now that we know what to look for."

I looked around. I wasn't the only one who was queasy after seeing it. The room was deathly quiet as I showed picture after picture of the autopsy and its notes.

"Now here is the one I … well … Thomas and I … killed."

I cringed when I said Thomas's name as an even larger specimen filled the screen, splayed open on the autopsy table.

"This was Mr. Lawrence Stenbrook from Monument, Colorado. He was a thirty-eight-year-old Caucasian male, and his driver's license (DL) lists him as six-foot even and 200 pounds. What he was turned into was a hair over seven feet tall and 400 pounds …"

The look of horror on their faces matched mine.

"The one you guys killed weighed 348 pounds, but we estimate you gave it a twelve-pound bullet diet," I said.

Laughter from everyone.

God, did we need that!

As the projector switched off, I turned to the room.

"OK. Do you have any questions about what we are facing? Any I can answer, anyway. You know as much as we do now."

I could see the wheels turning. These guys were pros—no BS questions or joking around now.

"Is killing the main creature the only way to kill the tentacles?" asked Officer O'Donnell.

"As far as we can tell, yes. My team," I gulped, "and yours took them out only with a headshot to the lower part of the brain where both creatures resided."

This was almost a "normal" briefing for them. Everyone there already knew we were dealing with something unprecedented and horrible.

"So, what was the final cause of death? Was it my rifle shot? Since we were denied an autopsy, inquiring minds want to know."

That was a SWAT member named Channing. He had a little edge when he said it. But they were, so far, taking what I said about full disclosure to heart. I knew I would lose their trust forever if I didn't fully come clean with them.

"Yes. We don't know much from the autopsy, but we know that. They are running every test they can, but it will take time to learn more about it. We know that whatever it is, it is attached to the brain-stem area and causes its host to grow unnaturally large, strong, and fast, as you know all too well."

The SWAT team nodded in agreement.

"Is that the only way to kill it?" The man's name tag read "Lewis."

"We only have your OI, sorry, 'Occult Incident' and ours to look at. But, yes, both were killed by a headshot that hit the creature attached to the brain stem. It appears that it sends tentacles everywhere throughout the body. Maybe before, during, or after 'enlargement.' Not sure how else to destroy it … If there is enough damage to destroy its ability to move, maybe?"

I paused to think.

"We know that the creature has those greyish-purple tentacles throughout its body. They are solid and tough. So, we are guessing—I won't lie—the thing can probably continue to move, even with incredible amounts of damage … Well, we all *do* know that, actually …"

I leaned against the wall.

"I told you I would tell you everything we know, and I am. All of our lives will be on the line against these things, and anyone who may be helping them. Let's work together and share all information."

"Wow!" That was Channing. "I never thought in a million years I would hear a Fed say that and actually mean it."

Some chuckling and nodding from all around.

I was done and motioned to Sergeant Donaldson to take over.

"All right, thank you, Agents Grey and Levingston. Now, let's talk about everyone's assignment ..."

CHAPTER 6
IT IS RELEASED

New Era Revivalist Church

The Reverend

THE MOMENT I had been dreaming about for so long had arrived.

I finished the second—and last—incantation. This would bring the Ancient One to our physical plane. There was a more potent and much longer incantation that could be done afterward to free it from the altar, but we did not have time for it. I knew the Ancient One would bring forth the end days and the Ascension. I only hoped it could do it without being fully released into our world.

The third and last *Other* appeared on the altar as I finished the incantation. It was the same as the others—small and feeble. I looked at it as it flopped off the pedestal to the platform and then flopped onto the floor. Sprouting what looked like little caterpillar feet—it ran off and out of the room.

Where was it going?

Curious, I followed it.

It went out the rectory door as I calmly walked behind it. Although it was running, it was small enough that my brisk walk could match its pace. It turned and went up the stairs—then down the hall and out to the main vestibule of the church. It got to the front doors and waited patiently—it was clear what it wanted. Without another thought, I opened the main doors to the church—it ran forward and disappeared into the brush of the forest.

So weird.

The Ancient One was supposed to arrive after this *Other* was summoned. Perhaps it was already downstairs? I briskly walked back through the front vestibule, down the hall, then down the stairs, and turned and went into the rectory.

I saw a flicker of movement—something going down the heat register vent.

And it was not of this world, but rather …

———

Ashta'goth—the Devourer

Finally, the long-awaited moment had arrived: Ashta'goth, the Devourer, emerged from its parallel plane.

The second summoning drew the last of the *Numil'e*, the enigmatic creatures the priest had cryptically called *the Others*. Once they had subsumed their prey, the humans dubbed them "Deathwalkers." As the third *Other* was summoned, a minuscule fragment of Ashta'goth also materialized on the platform's pedestal, too tiny to be discerned. Only Ashta'goth dictated the path of the summoned creatures, a mastermind orchestrating a plan beyond human comprehension.

Ashta'goth commanded the last *Other* to find the most enormous creature possible. The creature scuttled off to look for its prey. The priest followed it, unknowing of Ashta'goth's arrival.

This minuscule part of Ashta'goth also looked for prey in the new world. Luckily, the creature's scent brought its prey to it.

What materialized was alien to it.

Dozens, if not hundreds, of these creatures swarmed in, their six-legged bodies armed with fearsome mandibles. As they clambered onto it, they began to bite and tear chunks out of it. Each bite was a death sentence, as the creatures could not release their grip. Slowly, Ashta'goth drew each one in, absorbing them. Now slightly more prominent, with a thousand legs and hundreds of eyes, mandibles, and antennae, it scurried down the side of the platform, heading for a hole it sensed on the floor. There was life below; it could feel it beckoning …

No human would possibly understand how it thinks.

In its universe, it was all a giant food chain. The bigger eats the smaller, absorbs it, and becomes even larger and more dangerous. Shedding parts of themselves to become new creatures as they grow. This is how things are where it comes from. It lives in an ocean of a galaxy with the same worlds, but nothing except the creatures exist. No plants or other animals were like the ones on Earth, only the many strange and terrible creatures from their plane of existence.

They are always searching for new food and to grow.

They are always watching for even bigger predators.

As an Ancient One, it has lived for millennia on end. The larger it can get, the safer it becomes. That is the way. A few mighty creatures did not grow this way, but they were the exception, not the rule.

Now, it has found refuge. By migrating to this parallel Earth, it could have a whole universe of creatures to grow itself—and no predators!

Humans would possibly be a problem, but by comparison, an easy one.

It just had to control the priest, and then it could force him to complete the final summoning. Then, it would be free to leave the area around the altar. It noticed that the further it moved from the altar, the more it could feel its connection to this world starting to break—so it could not travel far. It could also feel the resistance of this new reality.

Gravity! A strange feeling!

It had already gotten bigger … and curious, squeaking creatures with long tails were already heading toward *it*.

Like these creatures, it knew more humans would come for it soon also, and it looked forward to their joining *it*.

Forever.

The Reverend

My heart sank as I realized things were not unfolding as planned.

My operation to retrieve the tome and create the Deathwalkers was a meticulously crafted plan. I chose the name "Deathwalker" to add an air of mystery. Given their enigmatic nature, it felt fitting.

However, for some ineffable reason, the two Deathwalkers had been killed!

I do not question His reasons, but I was unprepared for this outcome. I had thought they would succeed at whatever task they were sent to do—

Maybe they failed because of how much hubris I had?

Hmm … so the grand plan was for them to fail. But why? This would lead the police back to the church, and they would try to stop the true Harbinger from rising.

I alone knew the grand plan in full.

I was to raise the two Deathwalkers, I did that, and then summon one more "*Other*" creature and leave it on the pedestal—but it ran off as soon as it was summoned! And our new Messenger of the Ascension?

It also ran off!

I knew I must be patient, but oh, the clock ticks. The police would be coming soon, and I must prepare. I hoped—and yes, prayed!—that the Ancient One would be willing to help protect us from them.

Part of the difficulty in doing God's will on Earth is that He is an enigma. No mere human could understand His plans. But I always remember the saying, "Put your faith in God, but keep your powder dry." It just means that people must still do their part to make His will happen. Following God's will has never been easy or without sacrifice. That is how we show our commitment to our faith. Many nonbelievers have mocked us for this and called us an extremist cult.

There was even an article about us in the magazine *Christianity*

Weekly News, entitled "Devout Christians or Insane Cultists?" by the famous theologian Phillis McDonell.

The article did not show us in a good light.

She said in the article that an all-powerful being doesn't need our help and that our beliefs were based on a strict but flawed interpretation of select quotes and passages in the Bible.

How trite!

Of course, He doesn't need *our* help, but we need *His*! What they don't understand, but will soon, for eternity, is that humanity was expected to *earn* its way into Heaven; it is an active process. Heaven did not have Angels because *God* needed help. They were there to help *us* in our efforts to get accepted into Heaven. It was all part of His grand plan to weed out the unworthy and the unrepentant here on Earth —and we were expected to do our part.

From our inside source at Colorado Springs PD, we have received intel that they are coming at us with full force. They haven't pieced together all the connections yet, but they will. The silver lining is that Henry, at least, took longer to be identified. The downside is that the Feds have taken the body. That will slow CSPD's investigation, but the knowledge of the federal government's involvement is unsettling. The Feds may not be as swift-acting as the locals, but once they set their wheels in motion …

Hmm … with that in mind, I think Sunday's service would be a good time to tell everyone.

Of course, the WOG already knew, but perhaps it was time to let all my flock know of the grand plan for Ascension and that we must prepare to defend our church when the enemy comes.

———

Sunday arrived, and I was ready to speak to my congregation. Would the Ancient One have anything more for me if I visited it?

I didn't know; as it had disappeared two days prior, and I had not seen it since. I was terrified but knew it must have its reasons.

I put on my finest raiment and prepared to give the sermon I had memorized. There would be no other topic for today …

The parishioners had already gathered in the pews. Two of them, he could see, were happily chatting.

"Hello, Mary."

"Hi, Sam, how are you?"

"Good. I'm excited to hear today's sermon. Since the Reverend said today was special—even a new holiday—I haven't been able to sleep!"

"Me too!"

They smiled as the Reverend took to the podium, quiet filling the room.

"I want to talk about our 'secret' that most of you already know—"

A few chuckled from the congregation.

"I've had a visitation from an Angel."

Murmuring broke out in the crowd.

"This Angel—I know not what it is, except a messenger of God's will—came to me in a vision. It was not a dream. It happened in the middle of the day. I could only make out a warm, contented feeling of divine blessing. And I could feel it speak to me, straight into my mind, and I could hear its words. When the vision ended, I remembered everything communicated to me—" I paused before continuing.

"The Angel told me that the end days are upon us!"

Yells and clapping! People turned to hug each other, and everyone was smiling.

"God be praised!" and "Hallelujah!" sprang, unbidden, from many mouths.

Another long pause to let them enjoy the moment. Anyone not of our faith would be devastated to learn our world would be ending—but to the pious, it was glorious news!

"I know what I'm asking each of you to do now is going to be hard, but your everlasting soul is going to go to Heaven no matter how this plays out for each of us," I reassured them.

There were fewer smiling faces now.

"We have risen two Deathwalkers according to His will."

Gasps from the pews and some questioning looks from the few who didn't already know.

"Deathwalkers are people who have been transformed into Messengers of God," I explained. "Both Henry Johnson and Lawrence Stenbrook volunteered to become these Messengers. They failed in what I thought was their mission … Perhaps it was a warning for my hubris in thinking I could know exactly what God's plan is. Yes, perhaps. Or perhaps something we could not possibly understand—it matters not. We do as He commands and give with all our bodies and minds in pursuit of His will. We all miss Henry and Lawrence but will be reunited with them in Heaven. We will give them a service tonight; no one outside the church may know any of this."

All was quiet, and the people were looking scared but resolute.

"The police will be coming for us all, and we must prepare for their eventual arrival here at our church. We must resist them long enough for whatever the Great Plan entails. I know as much as you do now."

Lying is OK if it is in the pursuit of a greater cause.

"Go now, tell no one, and return to the church immediately with food, water, weapons, and medical supplies—anything you need for a long siege and to fortify our church to defend against those who would try to stop us."

I ended the sermon and watched them briskly leave. Many conversations were going on simultaneously, and I could see their tight expressions as the enormity of what was to be done sank in.

––––––––

It was midafternoon that day, and I was sitting outside the church on the steps. I watched as the parking lot filled in like a giant jigsaw puzzle. They had returned with pickup trucks full of boards, metal sheeting, and power tools. Many had brought guns and lots of ammunition. We all worked through the evening to board up windows from the inside and bolt shut and reinforce all the doors—except for the large main one (we needed one, for now, to get in and out.)

Sergeant Clarence Briggs was overseeing the preparations. As a former Army ranger, he knew more than anyone how to mount a defense. Plus, we had Officer Vincent (Vinny) O'Donnell. He was an active-duty Colorado Springs police officer. And he was the source of our valuable intel on how close they were to finding us.

They were close now.

After the service for our fallen members, Vinny told me about the briefing that SWAT and the other patrol officers had gotten from the Feds. Plus, when he and dozens of church members didn't show up to work tomorrow, their chances of finding us were almost assured.

I am eternally thankful for Vinny and Clarence.

Clarence had taught us all about concentric circles of defense (being able to quickly "fall back" to another interior place to continue the fight). He made sure the barricades were strong and even put booby traps in place for the first intruders to activate. He ensured all shooters were in position and set up a "fire-watch" of persons (to always be up and guarding the perimeter.) Even though we would know, he also set tripwires to sound an alarm on all the windows and doors. It would activate the church's PA system to play a loud, squelching sound for several seconds. He carried a remote to activate it as well. Plus, he had set up some demo charges as entry traps in a few key areas that he marked with red spray paint "EXPLOSIVE!!"

The first guards were in place, and the rest of us ate and settled into sleep. Every adult and some of the children were armed. They were all in full clothes with their weapons by their sides. Clarence even gave me an H&K USP 40 pistol with three full magazines. I had used pistols and rifles once or twice before but had never owned a weapon. He quickly showed me how to use it properly and carry it on my person. We never would have known what to do without him.

Bless you, Clarence!

———

Clarence

I think the defenses look good.

Of course, I only had what was available to work with—one cop, one other veteran, and me; that was it for combatants—everyone else was a civilian. Luckily, most of the congregation is familiar with firearms, as many are hunters. We were set up as best as time allowed. In a perfect world, we would have more time, but this Monday morning was going to leave a lot of businesses in a lurch since dozens of workers were not showing up today.

Or probably ever.

As a former army ranger, I knew we would not be coming home. There was no chance that law enforcement was going to let us walk away after shots were fired. Everyone was either going to jail or heaven today. I was planning on heaven. But only after I took out as many of them as possible to buy us the needed time. I took no joy in killing police, but God's will is paramount.

I had taken the first shift to sleep. I knew the conflict would be sometime today, but I needed them all to have a combat mentality from day one. Waking early at 0500, I walked the perimeter. I caught a few asleep or inattentive—they would not do that again. After ensuring everyone was ready, I ate a quick breakfast and found the Reverend in the central vestibule.

"Good morning, Reverend," I said.

"Good morning, Clarence. How does it all look?" he replied, sipping tea.

"Good. The perimeter is wired, most of our guards are now awake and alert, and all weapons are prepped and ready. Reserves of food, water, ammunition, and first aid supplies are in the basement rectory, along with the demo charges from the expedition. Well, the ones we didn't use on the perimeter anyway. There is a hidden generator set up for power outside. We cut a hole for the power cables running in, but it is not big enough for a person to get in. It has plenty of fuel … Glad us common folk are the most resourceful and prepared." I smiled.

"Yes. Thank you for all you have done, Clarence. You *are* a Godsend, to be sure."

"Thank you, Reverend. I need to go. I want to make sure every-thing and everyone is ready."

"Of course," he replied.

Walking away, I knew it was time to oversee the final preparations; the police would be here soon—I'd bet money on it.

I had used our resources as efficiently as possible.

Everyone had at least one gun, but no one was as well prepared as me. I had body armor, several different weapons, and even an illegal full-auto AR-15. I had changed the civilian version's sear, so mine could now fire fully automatic. It would be totally legal if I had the Federal Firearms License (FFL) and the required permits. But those cost a fortune, and I didn't have the time.

Besides, I was planning to commit *a lot* more felonies very soon …

Most of the people here had a mix of rifles, shotguns, and pistols, and many also had knives.

And all would be ready for our unwanted guests.

———

The New Era Revivalist Church—The Gatehouse
Samuel

A short while later, as the sun was still low in the sky, a solitary police car, its siren muted, made its way up the winding rural road that led to the church. The car's tires crunched on the gravel, breaking the early morning silence. Ahead, a gatehouse stood sentinel, its windows reflecting the golden light of dawn, casting a warm glow on the scene. It was on the very edge of the land the church sat on, but the church was visible in the distance.

A tall, gangly man came out as the cop car approached the gatehouse.

Samuel Hobbs was the product of his actions. Having been very Libertarian, he had joined the Sovereign Citizens group. After getting pulled over and arrested for not having paid his extortion fees—to register and insure the car *he* owned or to have a license just *to drive*—he had a bad opinion of law enforcement and a criminal record.

"Good morning. Officers Brice and Johnson, we are here to see the minister of your church, Mister Turner," the police car driver said.

"Sorry there, officers (he pronounced it "Offy-Surs"), but the church is closed 'til next Sunday. I'm gonna have to ask y'all to git," the man said.

The officers saw that he was armed, but he was on private property, which was not illegal. However, his immediate and brusque response told them what they needed to know.

"We have questions that need answers; if he doesn't speak with us, it will be *very* suspicious on his part," Officer Brice said, his voice tinged with a hint of foreboding.

"Welp, I guess y'all be needin' a warrant then," the man replied in his thick Southern accent. A sly smile played at the corners of his lips, hinting at a secret he was not yet ready to reveal. Then he spat chewing tobacco between him and the squad car and gave them a look of utter contempt.

The two officers looked at each other, turned the car around, and drove off without another word. The judge had already approved the emergency no-knock warrant, so they radioed to dispatch that it would be needed.

The man in the gatehouse watched the cops go.

"Yup, y'all best run," Samuel said to their retreating taillights. Then he picked up the phone and called the church number, telling them he had sent the cops packing.

CHAPTER 7
SOMETHING WICKED

Monday, 5 p.m.—Skyway Area—West of Colorado Springs
Agent James

CSPD AND OST had determined that the best connection between the two perps, the SIM things, was that they both belonged to the same church. When a church guard, armed no less, unceremoniously turned away the CSPD, we had our confirmation for the warrant. The fact that the entire congregation of the New Era Revivalist Church had not shown up for their jobs this morning, at least the ones who worked for someone else, was the final nail in their crucifix. We had a target now with 100 percent certainty.

The New Era Revivalist Church was up a newly improved trail, now a passable dirt road. It didn't even have a formal name—just Section 16 Trail. Most of the congregation probably came up Gold Camp Road from the Skyway area west of Colorado Springs to get to the trail. Our preplanning had found a small building supply company, CTX Building Supplies, just a bit further up Gold Camp. It had a single security officer on duty during the week after it closed at four p.m. We could get to the church in under an hour on foot from there.

That was where we were headed.

Our SWAT-OST team pulled off the road near our staging area at CTX. We didn't want to drive up to the church and lose any element of surprise, including being shot by rifles as we drove up—lots of incentive not to do it that way. Everyone on the SWAT team was using their personally owned vehicles (POVs) to avoid drawing suspicion before getting out. The situation was far from ideal, but we had limited options.

We pulled up to CTX Building Supplies in our cars and saw the security officer in his white Ford F-150 pickup truck. He looked bored as Donaldson's vehicle pulled alongside him. The security officer's expression changed to one of shock as a dozen officers and agents piled out of the other cars.

"Hey! I'm Sergeant Donaldson, Colorado Springs PD. We are conducting an operation. Do not tell anyone we are here," he said to the security officer.

"Yeah, uh … sure," he stuttered.

OST's two NMC guys walked over to join Donaldson. We knew they were there to watch the security officer and our vehicles, as planned.

Luckily, we were obviously police; the security officer didn't even ask for our credentials. All of us were in full tactical gear with POLICE displayed. We had armor: helmets with night vision goggles (NVGs) and both long arms (rifles and SMGs) and small arms (pistols), with way more rounds and magazines than usual. Plus, flashbang grenades, first aid gear, and water canteens. We were all on the same tactical channel on our radios with ear mics. Unlike the SWAT team, the FAM's bullet-resistant vests said "Department of Homeland Security" and were "borrowed" from the FAM's VIPR team. Lev and I didn't have helmets either and had to borrow a couple from them. That was the only difference. No one would question whether we were the real deal.

We wanted to get to the church before dusk. That way, we would have the advantage of daylight maneuvering through the forest and then surveilling the church.

A much larger perimeter of marked CSPD units was already set up around all the roads and access ways to the church property. We didn't want anyone getting away. After a final comms and equipment check, we were prepared to enter the forest.

In the movies, the police or soldiers always pull back their slides and load a round right before going into battle. In real life, the loading, press-check, and reloading of a new full mag—and topping off the mag missing a bullet—are all done before even leaving the office. And our guns don't "click" every time they are moved. Only complete amateurs load their weapons at the last moment.

Without a word, Donaldson used hand signals to start us into the forest and up the hill. Each fire team moved in a modified diamond formation, with our SMGs facing outward. Each team was within visual range but separate so that one grenade wouldn't kill us all.

I really hope they don't have those ...

I was on fire team Bravo in the middle of their diamond formation.

Why the middle?

Because SWAT had done hundreds of training and real-world missions together—I was an "add-on." So, my job was to stay out of their way and provide additional support to any engaged flank.

Lev was on fire team Alpha, which was the same deal.

On my team, Nealy was on point (in the front). Krieger and Maloney followed him on his right and left. The rear guard was a man named Robertson.

We were halfway to our target now.

I suddenly noticed it was eerily quiet as we went through the forest —too quiet.

All the birds had stopped chirping. Even the insects had stopped trilling. The outdoorsmen among us knew that only happened when a predator was nearby.

"Yeah, I don't hear it either." Came through my earpiece.

That was Donaldson.

He was the mission leader and was on fire team Alpha. Even though OST was technically the "lead," his SWAT team had far more experience in combat missions than we did. So, it was wise to let his SWAT team lead combat patrolling, and we were along to get results for the Feds. I am a big fan of doing things smartly, so we don't all end up dead.

Donaldson called a halt.

"Eyes open," he said.

We all stopped and formed a makeshift circle—360-degree security.

Everything was quiet.

The last of the insects stopped making noise. Whatever it was, it was close by. After a few minutes, we could hear something big moving through the bushes and trees.

"Movement at three o'clock." I heard in my ear.

That was Channing on Charlie team, which had four officers. It consisted of our two two-person sniper teams, which would deploy as overwatch when we got to our assault position for the church raid.

A couple more SWAT officers joined us to reinforce the right flank —the one I was on.

That's when we saw it over a low rise, about a hundred feet away.

A real black bear was no more.

In its place, standing the height of a man while still on all fours, was an 800-pound mass of black fur and impossible muscles with elongated neck and legs. The head was enormous and misshapen. I can see its foot-long claws, teeth, and strange eyes looking at me. It reared up to its full height, almost ten feet.

RROAR-CHIK-CHIK!

It let out an earsplitting roar that sounded like a mix of something alien, wolf-like, and a bear. I peed my pants a little, I won't lie.

Sprinting at us like a cheetah, it is running well over forty miles per hour.

Straight at us, straight at me.

No one needed to say, "There it is!" or "Open fire!"

BRRAPP! BRRAPP! BRRAPP!

Our MP5s all fired at once. They are not suppressed, so the noise is deafening.

The H&K MP5 submachine gun fires 9mm rounds at a rate of 800 rounds per minute, emptying its 30-round magazine in just over two seconds on full auto. Thanks to its roller-delayed blowback operating system, it is known for its reliability and reduced recoil. I appreciated this fact at this very moment.

We were all either on burst mode (a three-round burst setting, besides the single shot and full-auto switch locations on the side) or were firing short bursts on full auto. All of us knew to aim at the head. We also had a combination of slung rifles—M4a1 Carbines (firing 5.56mm rounds) for the non-snipers and the M24 Sniper Weapon System for the Snipers. The M24 is a police version of the Remington Model 700 rifle and fires 7.62mm rounds using a bolt-action system. Unfortunately, we only had MP-5s in our hands. The MP5 is an excellent weapon for targets at close to medium range. Out to 100 meters, it is as good as, or better than, a rifle and much easier to move quickly—at least against people.

We were not expecting a bear SIM.

It made it to us far too quickly. I could see its eyes clearly now. They were an unnatural shade of blue and looked right at me. Its head was as big as my torso, letting out an eerie hissing growl. I could see its open maw with dozens of foot-long teeth. When it hit, there was no chance even to scream …

WHACK!

Adams, a SWAT officer on the Alpha team, was the first to go; he was just to my left. The bear hit him at full speed, literally like a truck. I could feel the gust of air as the enormous thing passed by within feet of me. One moment, Adams was firing next to me, and the next—he was just gone …

He was dead on impact.

Eight hundred pounds going over forty miles per hour does that. His body flew thirty feet before hitting a tree.

And now the thing was inside our perimeter.

We split apart our teams so we could keep firing from new flanks and not hit each other.

It turned to go after another person—me.

BRRRRRRRRAPP!

I was firing on full auto into its head as it started to close distance.

Its bright blue eyes locked onto mine, and its giant muscles bulged and flexed as it sprinted at me.

Crack! Crack! Crack!

Several loud shots from some quickly unlimbered rifles joined me, and one finally caught its head in the right spot. It let out a final sickening roar as blood and brain matter hit the tree next to me. Then, it fell at my feet with an earthshaking thud.

In the sudden silence, we could hear the cooling hot barrels clicking, the team members reloading, and multiple "clear" calls.

And—as a bonus—I no longer needed to worry about peeing myself …

The thing was terrifying to behold.

It still had red blood on it from hitting Adams, and now darker red blood pooling around its head. Its body was grotesquely enlarged and had unnaturally long limbs and claws. Its long teeth hung out of its mouth in death, with those startlingly all-blue eyes open to the sky.

The other officers created a new perimeter and hunkered down as I dragged Adams into the center. Our medic, Robertson, looked at him, checked his pulse, and shook his head. No words were needed; he was dead.

We quietly waited.

No more things came at us. We redistributed ammo, including the gear from Adams. After we finished our post-engagement tasks, we set off again. A couple of guys grabbed Officer Adams' corpse and carried it. They went in the middle when we moved out again. We were all walking a little slower now, both from carrying the body and from caution.

———

It was just after six p.m. when we got to the church.

We stopped to do an initial survey. It was quiet, and there was no sign of activity. We could see the windows had been boarded up from the inside, so they knew we were coming. There were a couple dozen vehicles in the parking lot. Our snipers and spotters could find no signs of people or movement. The snipers could see shooting slits had been built in on all sides, but none had anyone behind them. There was no movement anywhere inside. Ideally, we would have all of CSPD here to surround the building, but it was a hike to get here, and we would have to make do. Their superiors and mine thought a twelve-man SWAT team and two FAMs were sufficient. We had asked for more, again, anyway. But with no luck. Any extra task force units were cordoning off every egress route away from the church.

We decided to risk exposure—and possibly lose the element of surprise—by sending a drone. Officer Lewis piloted the drone to survey the compound. There was a cleared area around the church with forest on every side, and we were well concealed on the edge of the forest.

After the drone came back, we watched the footage. There was nothing. It was just a boarded-up church, ready for invaders. But there was no sign of anyone inside watching.

This is not what we had been expecting …

Donaldson made the decision: "OK, we're going in now. Team leaders, let's move to assault positions."

The assault position is where you prepare for your attack and conduct any final pre-operational surveillance. We moved into our places.

Charlie team stayed back to oversee security while Alpha and Bravo moved on to the church. Alpha would breach the front, Bravo the rear. Charlie was overwatch and split into two sniper/A-gunner (spotter) teams. We had left Adam's body with the front (front of the building) sniper team. They were watching walls A & B (Charlie One), while the other team had the rear of the building and was watching walls C & D (Charlie Two). So they could see all four sides of the building.

Now we waited.

Charlie and the rest of us were conducting pre-operational surveillance. The spotter/sniper teams had priority on comms right now, so we watched quietly for several minutes.

"Charlie One. There are twenty-one cars parked in the lot directly out front. The gatehouse appears to be empty also. There is no sign of any occupants or movement from inside. They are either having dinner or a church service, but they are not watching the perimeter. Zero visual contacts."

"Charlie Two, no movement. No vehicles or people visible."

"I copy. Stand by," Sergeant Donaldson said. After a minute or two, he came back on.

"Charlie teams, keep visuals as we go in. Let us know if there are any signs of movement."

"Check" and "Check," Charlie One and Two responded.

"Bravo and Alpha, move in and prepare to breach."

We quietly got up and moved in simultaneously to breach entry on both sides. It was showtime.

I was wondering, though … where *were* the cultists?

———

Monday, 8 a.m.—the New Era Revivalist Church
Frank

Frank was on the prowl.

As always, his breakfast was delicious, and now he was wandering the church. This new place was so different—there were so many new people and smells!

Frank was a Xolo (pronounced "Show-Low") and was all black with no fur—just taut skin over a muscular body. Even though he was only two feet tall at the top of his shoulders, two and a half to the top of his head, and fifty-five pounds—he could clear a six-foot fence with a good run. He was an intelligent breed and very friendly—but also protective of his pack, including his humans.

His tongue hung out as he walked freely around the church. Many people smiled and petted him as he explored this new place. He liked that! There was an open door that led to a hallway. Something was down there—a scent he had never smelled before …

After finding another open door down the hallway, he descended the steps into the rectory.

Carefully creeping into the room, he tensed—something unusual was in the middle of it. Approaching slowly, he sniffed the large white altar. No one had marked it as their territory yet—he could fix that …

Finishing a quick pee, he wandered around the room. There was a strange smell coming from the platform near the altar. His ears were up, and his bulging eyes peered up at it.

Something above him was moving.

He was getting scared, and another dribble of pee came out as Frank made a little whining sound.

WHAP!

Suddenly—a tentacle lunged out and hit him!

A frightened, terrified yelp came out of him as he felt a sharp pain from *its* attack, and he tried to run, but …

———

The Harbinger—The Ancient One—Ashta'goth, The Devourer

I couldn't quite grab whatever that strange creature was that came up and *sniffed*.

The creatures of this plane were decidedly amusing—so different from what it was used to. Many of these creatures acted in unpredictable ways. At least the priest was well under control at this point, so things were still going as planned.

Making the connection with the priest was easy, it thought.

The mental connection to him was strong, and it knew what he desired most. Although the others called him "Reverend," it only knew him as "priest"—the one who controls the other simple beings. Somehow, in one of the ancient texts the priest had foolishly read aloud, he had broken the barrier just enough to communicate. Convincing him that he was talking to an "Angel of God" had been easy. The summoning of the two minions, what the humans called "the *Others*," had given it the connection to the world it needed. The second summoning, which also brought the third and final *other*, provided enough power for Ashta'goth to come through finally.

It did find one thing peculiar—the longer these humans were around extra-planar beings, the more insane they became.

It knew seeing it in person would fully unhinge even the sanest among them. And so, the conduit, the Margret creature, was starting to lose clarity and would not work for more summoning in the future. Soon, it would be time for her to join with it. She had served her purpose and got it into this world, even if just a tiny part.

Now, it just needed to gather enough mass to venture into this brand-new world!

Once it had the priest under its complete thrall, he could finish the final incantation required to be free from this altar. For now, it could not move far from the altar and pedestal, which connected its plane of existence to this one. Its mass had to come from living things in this new world.

In its universe, it was already massive. It was the size of a small moon and wandered the galaxy in its parallel universe, looking for things to absorb and grow larger. Now, it could do the same in this universe as it had in others. It had already absorbed many creatures from below the rectory, as well as a few cultists …

It was growing, and its hunger was insatiable.

———

Monday, 12 p.m.—the New Era Revivalist Church
Samuel

Samuel was ready.

Before they sealed and booby-trapped the main door, he was the last man to enter the church. It was going to make his day to cap some of these cops. He hoped that the two cops he sent away were coming as well, those arrogant bastards. Through the tiny slit in the exterior wall of the church, he was watching the tree line on his section of the perimeter. The sun was high in the sky, so he had clear visibility. As he scanned the forest's edge with his rifle scope, nothing outside would go unseen. His rifle was ready, and so was he.

———

The creature behind Samuel could sense the life-forms near it in its alien way. Very slowly, it quietly came up behind its prey. It had chosen him, like the others before, because they were not visible to the others. This one was watching outside through a slit in the wall.

AHHkkk!—

His short scream was cut off by the tentacle that encircled his neck and crushed it. The power it had was vastly more potent than a python. Everything inside its grasp was crushed to the diameter of a finger, and the dead man's head "popped" up.

It began to drag him to the rectory, as it had the others, and …

———

Clarence

Something is wrong.

A few members of the church had suddenly gone missing since breakfast. Could we already have deserters?

No way.

Everyone here was all in on this. Besides, I had just walked the perimeter prior, and all doors and windows were still barricaded, and, at that time, all persons were accounted for. Trying to piece it all together was challenging—

"I can't find Frank," the young boy, Timothy, I think his name was, said to me as he walked up.

I knew he would be crestfallen, but I could not help him.

"Well, Timothy, I'm sorry to say we can't afford to go look for Frank right now. If you want to keep looking, please do. But do not go near the outer doors and windows; it is dangerous to do so now. OK?"

"Yes, Mr. Briggs." Timothy sulked off to keep looking for his dog.

I felt terrible for him, but finding a dog was not a priority. Everything about combat follows the order of priorities. At the top was 360-degree security, so I needed every man and woman. Especially now that the law coming was a certainty. Nobody was going to get in here without one heck of a fight.

Something else struck him now as well. Everything outside was suddenly quiet. The birds, even the insects, had gone silent. And there was an unpleasant smell. One he couldn't place but had smelled before—

I heard a man's yelp quickly cut off, and I knew that sound. I had heard it during the Somalia conflict. Someone had just been stealth-killed—I sounded the alarm.

"WE ARE UNDER ATTACK!" I yelled in my parade-ground voice. "THEY ARE INSIDE!"

I hit the remote, and the squelching noise came over the church PA system.

Right then, *I saw it.*

Ben had just entered the room to check on me, and we saw movement from the doorway. The thing pushing through the door—and breaking the frame around it—was seven feet tall and, with its mass of swirling tentacles, was almost as wide. It smelled like a rotting fish and moved on tentacle "feet." It wasn't humanoid, and its form was ever-shifting …

I must have been frozen from the initial appearance for just a moment. Now, I knew I was in danger. Ben must have done the same, but he was closer to it.

From only ten feet away from it, he raised his rifle.

Crack!

As the tentacles lashed out, he fired off one round before it grabbed him. Screaming in terror, it caught all his limbs *and pulled.* Blood shot out of severed arteries as his limbs and head were thrown in random directions.

I lifted my modified AR-15 and hit it on full auto.

BRRRRRRRRAP! Click!

The entire full-auto fusillade from my illegally modified AR-15 worked. I watched it fall—as my rifle clicked empty. I had used a full 30-round mag, bringing it down. And it was clear—from all the screaming, running, and gunfire—that there were more of them.

I reloaded reflexively and moved on.

I wish I knew where I had hit it to take it down. Would that spot even be the same? Looking down at the dead one, I saw *nothing but tentacles*. A giant pile of them. Each tentacle had wicked-looking barbs, suckers, and stingers all over them. The smell was too much—they smelled even worse on the inside! I puked up a little and forced myself to run. I had been to Somalia and Afghanistan but never saw anything like this! The reserves were going to be needed in this fight. I turned and headed down the hall to the stairs.

That would take me down to the rectory …

————

Margret

"Oh My God! They are everywhere!" Margret screamed.

She saw one charging toward her.

I guess I am not protected after all, she thought.

She lifted her pump-action shotgun and fired.

Chick, chick—BOOM! Chick, chick—BOOM!

Giant gouts of purplish slime shot out from each hit with the shotgun pellets, and it turned to go after someone else. Everywhere were screams and gunshots. She could see limbs and blood strewn all over and knew this was not what was intended by the Reverend. Could this be the beginning of the end already? Another one headed her way while she was reloading the shotgun. She fired and fired.

Chick, chick—BOOM! Chick, chick—BOOM! Chick, chick—BOOM!

The red shotgun shell casings clashed with the spilled blood that was everywhere.

She started laughing as it fell, lifeless.

The thing must have gotten hit somewhere that mattered.

God knows where that was, as it had no form she could recognize! She couldn't stop laughing. Everything was so wrong now. She could still see all the immaterial creatures moving about through the air like an ocean. But now, real creatures were mixed in with them—

Real ones that are killing us, she thought.

All hope seemed lost, and she tried to pray.

Please, God, forgive my sins and save me—

She never saw the tentacles reaching for her.

————

The Reverend

Something was wrong. There were gunshots and screaming, but it was all being directed inwardly, not outwardly.

What was happening?!

I saw Keith Johan and stopped him. His family was inside, as were many others.

"Keith, what is going on?" I asked.

"I don't know, Reverend, but we are being attacked from inside the church!" With that, he ran off, rifle in hand.

How did they get in?

The church is only accessible through the doors and windows; and we had sealed them all.

I knew I needed to go to the top of the church to see what was happening.

The gunshots and screaming below became more sporadic, and I knew we were losing the battle. But what of the war? Did the grand plan have an end that was not shared with us?

It was all too much.

I struggled as I ascended the narrow stairs to the bell tower, carrying nothing but the tome. Once up there, I was finally able to see out. What I saw chilled me to the bone—

I saw nothing.

No police, no human presence of any kind. Just the forest in all directions. I knew, somehow, that I must flee.

It was like an unconscious will was forcing me to run.

Without a second thought to my parishioners, I climbed out. Walking on the roof, I looked for a way down. The way the church was constructed, there were flying buttresses and downspouts, so I carefully made my way down to the ground.

All had gone quiet behind me in the church.

All was quiet outside, too.

It was like all of nature knew something unnatural was happening … but I could not dally to ponder. With the giant tome in both hands, tucked to my chest, I ran to the forest's edge as fast as possible. I must get out and continue God's work …

CHAPTER 8
THE SIEGE

Monday, 6:30 p.m.—New Era Revivalist Church
Agent James

GRENADES.

I wish I had some.

Sure, I have flash-bangs like everyone else on our team. Why no explosive grenades, though?

Because, as law enforcement officers (LEOs), we are responsible for every bullet we fire and any "collateral" damage we cause.

Weird, huh?

The M67 grenade, that I had trained with in the army, only weighed 14 ounces, but it contained 6.5 ounces of Composition B explosive and had a cast iron serrated surface. It's a weapon that explodes with enough force to kill out to 15 meters and spews shrapnel designed to maim and kill up to 200-plus meters in all directions.

So, it might not be the best weapon to avoid collateral damage.

And for that reason, they didn't give us any. Even our flash-bang grenades are signed out and tracked by the Bureau of Alcohol, Tobacco, Firearms and Explosives (BATFE).

Well, I guess it is time to use my SEAL training to the fullest. Dang, I was never in the Navy or Special Operations. That's a bummer.

Oh well, use what you have, I guess.

I am still on fire team Bravo, making entry with SWAT at the rear entrance. They set the breaching charges, and we backed away. All is quiet as we wait on TL Donaldson.

He got on the radio, "5 … 4 … 3 … 2 …1 …"

BA-BOOM! BA-BOOM!

Back-to-back explosions from each side.

I am glad we were hunkered down. The blast was *way* bigger than expected! Judging by the giant hole in the building, they must have left us a nasty surprise.

"SITREP!" Yelled Donaldson.

"Charlie One green"

"Bravo green"

"Charlie Two green."

"Alpha is green. Make entry!" Donaldson commanded.

Our ears were still ringing from the explosions, but at least entering was easy. As we came in, we saw the horror of the explosions. Blood and body parts were everywhere in the room. We cleared our areas and made a new hasty fighting position inside the church. We found an inner door that had been barricaded but now hung open. We heard movement from that doorway, and Lewis threw a flash-bang in.

One of *them* lumbered out.

Disoriented by the flash-bang and spinning wildly, this new creature was a ten-foot diameter of flailing tentacles. It destroyed the doorway it came through, throwing wood shards everywhere.

At this point, we were no longer stunned by seeing horrible, crazy monsters.

BRRAPP! BRRAPP! BRRAPP! …

Grrr-EEK!

There was another volley of gunfire, and after a few seconds and probably over a hundred bullets, it fell. We looked down at the creature. It looked like a giant pile of tentacles with unspeakable things in them. Somehow, it was clear that it was dead.

It was time to move on.

"Bravo team. The rear vestibule is clear," Krieger, our team leader, said.

"Also, be advised that a new *tentacle thing* has been encountered and neutralized. Grenades do disorient. There is no head to shoot, just lots of bullets."

"Alpha copies."

"Charlie one, copy."

"Charlie two, copy."

We took a closer look at the blood splatters and body parts. We all realized what we were looking at.

"Has anyone else noticed they are only heads, limbs, and limbless torsos?" Krieger said. "No intact bodies?"

Krieger looked over at me, as did a couple of others.

"Beats me; these things are new," I answered the unasked question.

"The cultists were fighting something here. Probably our new best friends," said Maloney.

The various weapons were strewn near the bodies. Shell casings were everywhere. This had been one hell of a firefight. I could see the torso of an older woman, her shotgun discarded, and her limbs and head tossed in different directions.

"Bravo here; these body parts were not from the explosion. The cultists are probably vics of our new pals," I said.

"Copy," replied all teams. We had secured the entire first floor. Our team, Bravo, was moving up to the upper balcony pews while Alpha went down to the basement—as planned.

———

Agent Lev

Sergeant Donaldson was leading the Alpha team.

He was highly competent, as were the other SWAT members, and I am glad they are on our side. Even though I had earned the call sign "Blender," the idea of knife fighting a tentacled creature did not sound good to me. Bravo team told us how many bullets they had just fired to kill one: a hundred total—give or take.

So, sticking to guns for now ...

Going through a door, we went down a hallway—all was quiet.

The church would be clear once we cleared the rectory and Bravo finished sweeping the upper pews.

We had not seen a single cultist alive.

The exterior doors and windows had all been booby-trapped with demolition charges, thus the gaping holes now on two sides of the church. Everything had been reinforced for an attack from the outside —by us. However, it looks like it did not go according to plan. We had reached the last open doorway leading into the rectory in the basement.

How did we know that was what was down here?

Because we had memorized the schematics of the church when we made our battle plans.

We quickly descended the steps to the last doorway—the one going into the rectory. It had also been ripped off its hinges and stood open.

"Alpha, cover the door."

"Copy," we all replied.

"Throwing grenade!" Donaldson said.

Everyone waited in a stack-formation as Donaldson threw in a grenade. Officer Hollister was point, or first, in the stack.

BANG!

Immediately after the grenade went off, Hollister went deep (going straight) into the room. Wilcox was second and button-hooked left around the open door (going left) directly behind him. Donaldson was third, and I was fourth. He and I also went deep.

Or at least we tried to.

Sergeant Donaldson and I had headed in right behind them—and I mean *right behind* them—to "fill" the room.

That is when we immediately saw what had frozen them in place.

The space was limited; a giant creature filled most of the area, overflowing from the pedestal. I cannot remember everything that happened after that, but I knew I would not be OK—

Not ever again.

The gigantic monstrosity was grey and purple—a grotesque amalgamation of eyes, tongues, teeth, and unnamable orifices—a pulsating mass that seemed to defy all logic. Its parts would shift and vanish within the mass, only to reappear in a different location. Tentacles would emerge and retract, adding to the creature's unsettling nature. Everywhere in sight was a mass of moving mouths with thousands of teeth. Its eyes were all alien and of varying sizes and floated—then dipped under and bobbed up—everywhere. Massive tentacles—covered with sharp barbs, suckers, and stingers, came out of the giant blob of gore in all directions. A few mutilated human heads popped out of it to look at us, too. Red human blood and purple slime were all over it.

I was reloading my MP5 mechanically; I had already fired it dry, even though I don't remember doing it. A considerable-sized tentacle hit next to my head and ricocheted.

WHAP!

I saw it as it slapped across my face—and I felt a horrible pain.

Dozens of barbs and more than one stinger slashed my face open and flung me back out the door.

I scrambled back up.

OMG—this hurts!

I couldn't see out of my right eye—and blood was everywhere. I am hoping it is just because head wounds bleed a lot. I knew I was badly hurt, though. My neck felt broken, and I couldn't turn my head. My MP5 was gone, so I unslung the M4 rifle that was previously cutting into my back. That *thing* had knocked me clean out of the room

…

BRRAPP! AAHH! BRRAPP! BANG!

I could hear the horrible screams of the SWAT members in the room with it. Automatic fire was going on, and I listened to another flash-bang going off. Donaldson dashed out of the room, lobbing yet another grenade behind him.

As he was leaving, a tentacle flashed out at him from behind—

BANG! WHAP!

The grenade's explosion luckily knocked it off course, and it demolished the doorframe instead of him.

No words had to be spoken.

We were "tactically withdrawing."

This is how cops and the military say, "running the f—k away."

The other team was radioing us—

"SITREP!" they demanded.

They wanted a situation report—but there was no time to respond.

We were running for our lives, going up the steps, down the hallway, and entering the central vestibule at full speed.

"Coming down!" Bravo team yelled.

We lowered our weapons as they came down the stairs from the balcony. We now controlled the vestibule and set up 360-degree security again. Donaldson and I were watching the door we had come from—

Grr-AKH, AKH, GHAA!

We all could hear a new and deafening sound—the horrible screeching, babbling, and roaring from the hall leading to the stairs and the rectory.

It must not be able to move from its spot—thank God!

Unfortunately, its sound stopped suddenly, and we could hear low growling and alien sounds all around—the same ones the SIMs and tentacle things made.

I guess the Big One was calling for reinforcements.

"We are about to have contact … again." That was Donaldson.

I saw James's stern look at me and knew I was pretty f—ed up.

"I know. No kisses right now," I said.

Jesus, it hurt so bad! I felt light-headed and sick.

James chuckled—and I could tell it was forced. I must be really messed up.

"Is upstairs clear?" Donaldson asked.

"Yes, sir." That was Nealy from the Bravo team.

"OK. All teams, let's get out of here and set a perimeter around the church. Call for reinforcements," Donaldson yelled.

At that moment, things went from bad to worse—

"Charlie One here, you have multiple … *tentacle things* … inbound to your location, from all directions. Count is eight out front."

"Charlie Two—" Loud booms came from rifles outside the church. "You have one down, six inbound rear."

Donaldson didn't hesitate to decide.

"OK—I guess we are staying. Up the stairs, now!" Donaldson demanded.

We all scrambled up the stairs to the balcony. Five guns—including mine—were covering down the stairs. The stairs were the only way up or down. The other two guns faced out in case they could jump up twenty feet to the balcony.

That would suck.

We waited …

We could hear them moving about, and they were heavy. They might be stealthy if they moved slowly, but nothing that big can move fast quietly. And they were moving fast. Some were near the stairs now.

I looked down the stairs—someone had been bleeding profusely coming up the stairs.

I knew who that "someone" was.

Nealy let his rifle drop on his sling and took out a grenade. We all nodded our silent agreement.

It happened fast.

The first one came around the corner in a flurry of whipping, deadly tentacles. The grenade flew as we fired full auto on it.

BRRAPP! BRRAPP! BRRAPP!

As the grenade hit beside it at the bottom of the stairs, we all turned away, covered our ears, and opened our mouths.

BANG!

The blast was intense in the narrow stairway. As we swung back around the edges, we saw it spinning even more wildly and ripping the drywall around it apart. We shot it mercilessly until it dropped.

BRRAPP! BRRAPP! BRRAPP!—

We can't keep this up, I thought.

We didn't have enough bullets or grenades to kill them all, much less that thing in the basement. My face hurt terribly, and my vision in my good eye was starting to grey out and close in at the edges.

I fumbled a magazine reload and dropped it—that never happens. I could feel the impending doom.

Crap, I am going into shock.

"I'm going into … I'm sorry," I stammered.

I leaned hard against the wall, slid down, and the world went black.

———

Agent James

"Is she going to make it?" Donaldson asked.

Luckily, they had stopped the bleeding. Mostly. But she had lost *a lot* of blood—along with half her face. It didn't look good.

"Yeah, I don't know," said Robertson. He was busy giving her first aid to save her life.

We all heard many more sniper rifle booms, followed by full-auto rifle fire from outside on both sides of the church.

"Heavy contact!" Charlie One yelled out.

We could all hear the panic and fear in his voice, but there was nothing we could do to help. The rifle fire decreased. We could hear flash-bangs going off as well—

Then it all stopped.

Donaldson called in on the two fire teams.

"Charlie One, report." Silence …

"Charlie Two, report." More silence …

We all looked at each other, and we knew what silence meant. They had done their job to try to protect us six: Donaldson, Nealy, Robertson, Krieger, Maloney, and me.

Donaldson switched channels on his police radio and tried to reach dispatch—to no avail. We were too far out from the repeater to get a signal. Next, he took out his cell phone and noticed there was no service out here—I smiled at him.

"Something funny, Grey?" he growled.

"Look behind you," I replied.

He turned to look, and attached to the wall was an anachronism—an honest-to-God landline phone.

"Huh … Welcome to the dark ages," he said.

He went over and picked up the receiver. After punching in three numbers, I could hear the speaker on the phone say, "911—what is your emergency?"

"This is SWAT at the church. We are in contact and have three to seven officers down and one critically wounded. We need reinforcements and medical ASAP. We are in contact with multiple monsters and one huge one. This is Sergeant Donaldson. I say again, we have three confirmed dead SWAT officers and four more probable. We are losing. Send F—king everyone!"

"Yes, sir. Notifying … F—king everyone," the dispatcher responded.

Donaldson dropped the receiver on its cord. We knew 911 was recording whatever the phone could hear.

"Any ideas?" Donaldson said to us.

There was a long pause. We had already divvied up the weapons and ammo from Adams and Lev. I insisted we leave her pistol and pistol ammo on her in case she miraculously woke up. The rest of the extra ammo would be needed.

"Well, if we leave, we'll be in the forest going into nightfall," Krieger said.

He didn't have to finish the statement. None of us wanted to be out in the open forest with those tentacle things after us, especially at night.

"Hmm … well, that is out," Donaldson said.

"We need to kill the big one," Robertson said.

All of us shot incredulous looks his way, including me.

"OK. I can buy that. Thoughts on how?" Donaldson replied.

"I saw all the demo charges we didn't blow on the way in," I offered.

Everyone nodded at my suggestion.

"Good plan," Donaldson said.

"But how do we get them to the … creature's *lair* from here?" Maloney asked.

Usually, I would laugh at such a thing, but "lair" fit.

We could hear them moving below us. They were doing something. We could hear them shuffling off. Quietly, Donaldson put a finger to his lips and walked to the balcony's edge to look down. I joined him while the other four guarded the stairway. We peered down just in time to see them all shuffling into the hall to the rectory stairs. Quickly, we retreated to the rest of the team.

Donaldson reorganized our team and ordered an organized rally point.

"Listen up. Grey, you're with me now on Alpha. Maloney, Krieger, and Nealy, you're still Bravo. Sorry, Robertson, you're the new Delta. You'll stay at the top of these stairs and give us an ORP to fall back to, along with taking care of Levingston," Donaldson ordered. "Check?"

"Check," replied Robertson.

"OK, let's go get us some bombs …"

Passing by the tentacled mass at the bottom of the stairs meant walking on it.

I was ready at any moment for it to spring back to life. It didn't, though. Donaldson and I went right; Bravo went left. We were to get as many as we could. I would overwatch while Donaldson disarmed the booby traps and retrieved the explosives.

I am so glad they are here.

I have no idea how to disarm commercial explosives. I messed with Claymore mines in the army and learned more about bombs as an air marshal, but very few of us knew how to set up demolition charges or disarm them appropriately.

SWAT had clearly done this before.

We operated quickly and reasonably quietly. Once we had several of them, we went back up the stairs to the balcony. There, we assembled them all into one giant bomb.

Assembly was simply duct-taping them all to the one with the blasting cap.

"OK, I want to get it as close to that door at the top of the rectory stairs as possible. Then we retreat out where the front door used to be and blow it. Alternate is the balcony if we can't get outside for any reason.

"Robertson, you stay here again; it's the same drill. You're taking care of Lev and guarding our alternate rally point. But when I call "EVAC," you grab her and come down the stairs. Once we have you two, we'll head out the front and detonate it. Then pop a few beers and wait for the cavalry." He looked around at us. We all nodded in agreement.

"If the bomb plan fails, and we can't detonate the bomb, the last stand is back up to the balcony. We'll hold them off there, in that narrow stairway, until reinforcements arrive," Donaldson added.

We knew if that happened, we were probably all going to die.

"Alpha. Hmph—I guess that's just Grey and me—we'll go down and plant the charges, unspooling the det cord as we go. Bravo, you'll cover our six as we exit that hallway. We'll break to the sides so you can light up anything following us. Krieger, you have the box. If we don't make it, ensure that big bastard doesn't either."

"Will do, boss," Krieger replied.

With that, we went down the steps. At the bottom, Krieger and Maloney set up the box at the base of the stairs to the balcony while Nealy covered for them and us with his rifle. Without another word, Donaldson and I started walking and laying the det cord as we went. Donaldson had his rifle up, and I was the one unspooling the det cord and carrying the bomb. We slowly and quietly walked down the hallway to the downstairs rectory. As we got closer, we could hear the creatures shuffling in the stairwell to the rectory. We crept down the hallway, as close as we dared, and I quietly set down the bundle of explosive charges close to the doorframe leading down to the rectory.

We started to back out—

The first one came hurtling around the corner at us.

BRRAPP!

I had just started to bring up my MP5 as Donaldson began to give it new holes. Donaldson and I both fired behind us, on full auto, as we ran away. Unless we wanted to die, we couldn't throw a grenade. Donaldson was just behind me and to my right.

AAHH!

He yelled out in pain and terror just as I cleared the doorway.

I had dived to the side as soon as I cleared the hallway door—

BRRAPP, BRRAPP! BRRAPP!

A fantastic number of bullets filled the air I had just been in.

Bravo team fired their rifles on full auto into the creature following me. I got up and turned to see it fall into a lifeless mass of tentacles.

I also saw pieces of Donaldson near that doorway.

Bravo team was still firing, though, so there were more of them. I sprinted for the stairs to help Robertson bring Lev down.

I yelled out "EVAC, EVAC!" into my radio.

BRRAPP, BRRAPP! BRRAPP! Grrr-EEK! BANG!

The shooting continued. I heard flash-bangs going off and "reloading" and "covering" over the din of automatic fire and the monsters' ominous sounds.

BRRAPP, BRRAPP! Grrr-EEK! Grrr-EEK!

Robertson and I got Lev down the steps in time to see several tentacle things tearing through Bravo team.

Krieger was the only one still standing.

The rest of the team was spread all over the floor in pieces; they had been ripped apart. We dropped Lev and started shooting, too. One of the creatures rolled quickly past me, and I saw it grab Robertson with dozens of tentacles and rip off his limbs and head. The creature's cries and his merged into a cacophony of shrieking.

I am beyond just being terrified.

There were just too many of them—I knew my end was near …

Leaping forward as Krieger was picked up by two of them and ripped apart in a shower of blood, I grabbed the detonator box and activated the explosives …

CHAPTER 9
THE FOREST

Frank

FRANK WAS SCARED.

Running, he went to look for help. He was limping from where he had damaged his left hind leg after landing from the tentacle impact. Everywhere he went, everyone was too busy to help him. He looked for Timothy.

The pain in his side grew worse.

Twisting his head around, he chewed on his side, above his left rear leg. A thorn was stuck in it, and he was trying to get it out. He had done this lots of times before—especially when he got those little round burrs stuck in his paws at the dog park—it was a lot of work. Panting with exhaustion, he felt woozy. It seemed to take forever, but he finally found a place to hide and fell into a deep sleep.

———

Frank awoke with a start!

Something had entered the room.

He recognized the smell—it was the same as the thing that had hit him. Lifting his head, he saw a giant ball of evil-looking tentacles, each with barbs and suckers all over it.

Grrr-EEK! Thwap, thwap, thwap …

It saw him!

And now it was rolling in his direction—he had to escape!

He leaped up and ran out of the room.

From sneaking off before, he knew where there was a small opening they had crudely cut the day before, just big enough to squeeze his lean body through. He wriggled into the hole. The thorn made a sharp pain in his side, and he yelped!

The thing heard him and was *thwapping* its tentacles his way.

It was almost to him!

"Grrr-EEK! Grrr-EEK!" it screamed as it entered the room and saw him.

With a fresh boost of terror, Frank popped through the hole and ran as best he could toward the edge of the woods. Pouring on the speed, he made it to the forest's edge. The pain in his side was incredible. So, he lay down near a tree and started chewing on his side again.

He was alone in the wilderness, having never ventured beyond a leashed walk to a dog park. None of his favorite humans were present to shower him with affection, and he missed Timothy.

Finally, the thorn was out (a three-inch-long stinger was what it was.) Panting from the exertion and filthy—his furless skin and mouth were covered in blood—he looked for a place to hide. This was more activity than he usually had in a week, much less a few hours. After a short search, he found what he was looking for—a pine tree with a thick base of leaves going all the way to the ground. He crawled inside and felt safer, just knowing he was out of sight. Giving in to the over-powering urge, he fell asleep to the smell of pine …

He snapped awake—he could smell them!

The sun had dropped low in the sky, casting a strange hue through the forest as the light fought to penetrate the trees. The pine tree he hid in obscured most of his view, but he could see the giant things moving out there.

They were in the forest, looking for him.

Frank hunched down lower in the little burrow he had found. With terror in his eyes, he stayed perfectly still.

One of them was nearby.

It was not quiet as it moved on its tentacles, which thrashed and crunched the foliage under its heavy weight. Thankfully, it could not smell as well as he could. It passed by within twenty feet of him and kept going. It was gone, but Frank was too scared to move.

BA-BOOM! BA-BOOM!

Two loud explosions came from the church, and Frank shuddered.

Carefully walking back to the forest edge, Frank wondered if it was OK to go back.

He had missed his second meal in a row and was hungry and thirsty, so very thirsty. He saw a bunch of strangers—dressed in strange clothes—entering the church.

Maybe they had food!

Steeling himself, Frank made his way out to the forest's edge. There, he waited a long time, watching and thinking about what to do. Finally, he made a run for it and dashed into the clearing. As he ran to the church, he noticed his leg was feeling much better. He was glad he took the time to get that thorn out!

He was even a little energetic after his long nap.

It started all over again as he was halfway to the hole to go back in. Hearing loud crashing and foliage and tree limbs snapping, he turned to look. He saw the things that had been looking for him were now at the forest's edge, heading toward the church. Toward him!

There were so many of them!

He had frozen in place for a moment when he saw them. Turning back around, he sprinted again for the hole in the wall.

BANG! Grrr-EEK! BRRAPP, BRRAPP! Grrr-EEK!

Now, loud bangs and alien shrieks were coming from inside the church.

He stopped just before he got to the hole at the church and didn't know what to do.

CRACK! CRACK! CRACK!

He could hear some loud rifle shots from a different area of the forest. Looking that way, then back toward the forest, he could see the tentacle things had changed course. They had turned to head toward whatever had made those sounds.

And they were moving quickly, rolling like giant tumbleweeds of death.

Seeing his moment, Frank made a beeline back to the forest again. He felt like he was playing a deadly game of fetch, going back and forth, but it wasn't fun like it was with Timothy.

———

Charlie One Team—Overwatch at the Front of the Church
Nelson

I heard the entry team explosives going off, and it was a *way* more powerful explosion than what they had put on the door—I was glad they didn't breach with a ram.

Nice booby-trap, cultists. I thought.

I watched as our SWAT entry team went inside. A few moments later, I heard a flash-bang go off and then automatic gunfire deep inside the church.

Then silence.

"Bravo team. The rear vestibule is clear," Krieger said on the comms. "Also, be advised that a new *tentacle thing* has been encountered and neutralized. Grenades do disorient. There is no head to shoot, just lots of bullets."

"Alpha copies."

"Charlie one, copy," I said.

"Charlie two, copy."

Great, now something called a "tentacle thing" exists.

Our job now was to ensure nothing went in to hurt the entry teams and to provide cover if they exfiltrated out the front of the church. We were at the edge of the tree line, with a sizeable open area between us and the church.

I am looking through my sniper scope while Lewis uses a spotting scope.

A few minutes passed, and then I saw movement. Something was moving toward the church quickly—a funny-looking, medium-sized dog.

God, this is getting weird.

Gunfire and grenades started going off in the church again, and the radio was alive, with both teams reporting on multiple contacts.

Now, there is motion behind that weird dog, back at the tree line. I can see several giant balls of tentacles coming out of the forest and heading for the church—or, I should say, rolling.

These must be the "tentacle things" Krieger spoke of.

Lewis got on the radio. "Charlie One here, you have multiple … *tentacle things* … inbound to your location, from all directions. Count is eight out front."

The radio came on again.

"Charlie Two—" Several loud rifle booms. "You have one down, six inbound rear."

So, the rear sniper team was engaging the creatures as well.

That is just wonderful, I thought.

"Engaging," I said.

CRACK!

My first shot took one down. It was center mass, but I had no idea what to shoot at. I had been watching them through my rifle scope. They appeared to be nothing but tentacles; I couldn't find a weak spot to aim at. No feet, no heads, nothing. It's just a big blob of frightening tentacles. And I mean *big*. Probably a good seven feet in all directions of spinning tentacles.

And now they are headed our way.

We could see them turn toward us as we started shooting them— the eight we had spotted were no longer the entry team's problem. They had spotted us, and they were headed our way now. And quickly.

Grrr-EEK! Grrr-EEK! CRACK! CRACK! Grrr-EEK! Grrr-EEK!

My next shots did not take them down.

"Weapons free!" I yelled.

I knew Lewis was probably already engaging them, but I wanted him to know that his role as an additional gunner, no longer just a spotter, was needed.

They were still too far away from us for full-auto fire. By the time we brought down two more of them, they covered half the distance to us. I fired the last round from my sniper rifle (there would be no time to reload it) and dropped it. I picked up my slung MP-5. Lewis had emptied several magazines from his M4 and was now firing on full auto as I joined him.

BRRRRRRAP! Grrr-EEK!

BRRRRRRAP! Grrr-EEK! Grrr-EEK!

Two more creatures went down under our combined, now fully automatic, fire. Empty magazines and bullet casings were everywhere.

I yelled, "Heavy Contact!" into my mic.

But they had reached us—

Grrr-EEK! Grrr-EEK! Grrr-EEK!

The first one grabbed Lewis. He dropped his gun and tried to grab a flash-bang grenade. It picked him up before he could use it. One moment, many tentacles encircled him. The next, he was flying apart in pieces, in all directions.

—Click—

I had emptied the last of my MP5's mag into it, and it fell into a lifeless mass of tentacles.

I knew I couldn't reload it in time. Dropping my SMG on its sling, I quickly drew my pistol as another one closed in front of me, mere feet away. I felt hard grips all over me from behind as I fired three rounds into the one in front of me—a tentacle wrapped over my face.

BANG! BANG! BANG! GRRR-EEK!

This is it, I thought.

Horrible pain, then nothing.

Charlie Two Team—Overwatch at the Rear of the Church
Kelly

The creatures were coming from different areas of the forest.

We know this because Charlie One radioed seeing the creatures on the church's front side.

Mike DeFontes was our sniper—and I was his A-gunner/spotter.

My job was to count the numbers and locations of hostiles. There were six—no, wait, now seven—tentacle things visible in our Area of Responsibility. I relayed their numbers and locations to DeFontes.

"Copy," he growled.

This did not look good.

There was no choice, however; it was "GO" time.

I wasn't happy with our chances, but we couldn't let them get to the church and our team inside. Our team members in the church had already contacted these new monsters and relayed just how hard they were to kill. And now, the entry teams were in a full battle with the monsters that must have already been inside.

"Engaging" is all DeFontes said.

"Charlie One here, you have multiple … *tentacle things* … inbound to your location, from all directions. Count is eight out front," came over the radio.

"Charlie Two—" I said.

CRACK! CRACK! CRACK!

John's sniper rifle interrupted me, and I saw the one he hit drop.

"You have one down, six inbound rear," I finished.

Our mission of protecting the entry team was a success. They were all coming our way now …

I added my M4 to the party. Our combined fire took down two more as they came across the clearing toward us. I was too busy to let my terror stop me, plus DeFontes and the whole team were counting on me.

Four of them were now almost to us—

Grrr-EEK! Grrr-EEK! Grrr-EEK! Grrr-EEK!

DeFontes was using his MP5 now, and we were both firing on full auto—

BRRRRRRAP! BRRRRRRAP! Grrr-EEK!

Another monster went down.

I switched out another mag as they reached Mike. He was firing full auto into them and screaming as he plunged his MP5 into the one in front of him, one-handed, fire still streaming out the end of his SMG into it. Another grabbed him from behind. With his other hand, he yanked the pin on a flash-bang grenade, and I saw the spoon fly off. A moment later, the tentacle things ripped him apart. His body parts flew for several yards in random directions.

But his torso fell right in their midst.

He didn't even take the grenade out—he had just pulled the pin. So, I knew the other grenades on his chest were also close enough to go off. Diving for the ground, weapon still held tight, I waited for the blast.

B-B-BANG!

Several flash-bangs detonated at once.

Although I was disoriented and my vision was blurry from the blast, I staggered up and continued firing at the monsters. They were spinning like dervishes of death as I fired mercilessly into them—

BRRRRRRRRAP!

Another fell.

Click. Click—

My M4's mag clicked empty, and I slapped in another hard enough to release the slide.

I continued firing.

BRRRRRAP!—

"Heavy contact!" was screamed into the radio.

I could hear the terror in Channing's voice—it mirrored my own.

The last two monsters had stopped spinning.

Crud, they did not stay disoriented long.

I knew this was the end as I pulled the pin on one of my grenades and continued firing my M4 into them as they closed—

BRRRAP! GRRR-EEK! GRRR-EEK!

B-B-BANG!

I felt the pain of my grenades exploding as they reached out to grab me. Through the pain, I felt myself starting to lose consciousness ... and everything went black.

CHAPTER 10
BECOMING

UCHealth Memorial Hospital
Colorado Springs
Agent James

I SNAPPED AWAKE, and all of me hurt.

This was a pain I am familiar with.

I have been knocked out by explosives before—from an artillery simulator when I was in training in the army. But this is much, much worse. I keep talking to myself about this, but why can't real life be like the movies? In the TV shows, the good guys always manage to run just far enough away and then dust themselves off after an explosion knocks them down.

I was wondering this as I lay in my hospital bed with tubes in me and monitors beeping. I just regained consciousness, and I wish I hadn't …

Robert Cho was still not a sight you wanted to see when you first woke up.

"Lev?" I croaked.

I could barely ask if she was OK. Everything hurt. Bad.

"Yes. Agent Levingston is alive but in critical condition. She is also in the ICU, but not ugly like you."

I smiled and grunted a laugh.

Ow! Laughing hurts. I could feel several broken ribs, and a lot more of me was messed up, too. I wish they had some high-tech, or magical, elixir to heal me like in those video games. No luck. This was going to be my new office for a while. The pain was unbearable.

"SWAT?" I mumbled.

Cho frowned and shook his head no.

I drifted back to sleep. I did not like the dreams that came.

———

I woke to a blinding light.

The sterile white walls and ceiling did nothing to calm me. My heart was beating rapidly, and I reached for my rifle in terror.

"Whha … Where?"

I couldn't think clearly, and the pain was horrible. A nurse had heard me and came in and rested her hand on my shoulder. I tried to brush it off reflexively, but my hand wouldn't move.

"You are still alive; try to relax, Mr. Grey."

The nurse appeared to be in her mid-forties and looked like someone who had been doing this ICU horrible shit for a long time.

I looked around—I was hooked up to an IV and monitors and was in four-point restraints.

"Wha … Why … am I …"

"Restrained?" she said.

I feebly nodded yes.

"Because you tried to remove the first nurse's head when you woke."

Then I felt terrible in a whole new way.

"I am … sorry," I croaked out, and my mouth felt like mush.

"It's OK, Mr. Grey; we know it is normal after waking up from combat."

She had done this before; she probably worked with veterans. She was busy checking my vitals and administering more clear liquid into my IV.

"You're at the UCHealth Memorial Hospital. You were brought here by Flight for Life."

I looked at the clear liquid that had been administered.

"Am I going night-night now?" I asked her.

She laughed; it was a pleasant laugh.

"No, well, maybe; I upped your painkiller a bit; it should hit soon."

"OK, thank you,"

She nodded and walked away.

Those painkillers do help; as the pain decreased, I started feeling woozy. Darkness fell again as I drifted away …

I snapped awake again and lunged up from the bed. Or tried to, but the pain stopped that *really* quick—

Well, at least the restraints are gone now, I thought.

Carefully and slowly, I sat up, then waited until the nurse returned to check on me. I needed to ask a question but was terrified of the answer—

I was going to ask her about Lev.

I'm not religious, but I silently prayed anyway that she was alive.

The nurse who walked in had a name tag that read "Jackie."

"Hello, Jackie, I need to know about Agent Levingston's condition," I asked.

"She is stable now and recovering," Nurse Jackie said.

I let out an audible sigh, and Nurse Jackie smiled. She was a different nurse than when I first awoke.

"She was in critical condition when she arrived. She had lost too much blood and was in hypovolemic shock; frankly, she should not be alive. Doctors are completely baffled …" She chuckled.

"God, it was fun to see their faces! Well, until I saw them take that stinger out—"

She visibly shuddered.

"It was like what you see from a bee, but gigantic. It was over three inches long! And it was jammed deep into the orbital bone—"

She looked up at me and realized it was probably hard for me to hear.

"I'm so sorry, Mr. Grey."

"It's OK, I needed to know," I replied.

"Well, she is conscious again, and the first thing she asked about was you …" She paused.

With a strange look on her face that I couldn't place, I watched her turn and leave the room.

The giant monster had done a number on Lev, but at least she was still alive.

SAC Cho had kept the press and senior management away from us. I could only imagine the PR nightmare he was facing. Not that I felt too bad for him—it turns out he has a better job.

I had some broken bones and internal injuries from the explosion, as did Lev. As the weeks passed, we took turns "racing" each other around the hallways with our IV bags on a rolling stand. We had to get up and move once every waking hour now that we were recovering.

She still looked amazing to me—even all swollen up with most of her head still in gauze.

As for me, they were still scheduling surgeries to take out shrapnel. Living through the explosion at the church, we ended up eating a lot of frag along with that concussive wave. At least we weren't in the fireball at the center. Not that you need to worry about the burning—if you are that close, the tiny pieces of you being on fire won't be of consequence …

We still had to fill out voluminous paperwork—CA-1s for traumatic injury, and CA-7 forms for everything the hospital was doing. We also couldn't make it to the SWAT officers' funerals because we were still invalid at that point, but several FAMs, OST, and CSPD officers had come to visit us.

The official story was frighteningly close to the truth.

All the newspapers reported that the New Era Revivalist Church members had barricaded themselves to avoid arrest for sponsoring the murders at Perry's truck stop. During the siege and subsequent battle against armed "cultists," the church members activated a bomb—killing everyone in the building. To include an entire SWAT team.

There was no mention of monsters, the snipers outside being killed, or of federal agents.

Not a bad cover-up, I thought.

Only one news agency got it right—*Crime Scene News*. Reporter Samantha Cox wrote an article about the attack. They added a video with close-ups of Lev and me going onto the Flight for Life helicopter and the giant piles of dead tentacles. Luckily, they were lambasted for making up a "fake" video, and the report went nowhere.

As for me not telling CSPD about it, F—that. As soon as Captain Gregory Hull visited me, he told me about the details they had of the SWAT operation, so I knew he knew. I gave him an "unofficial" SITREP to give to his officers at CSPD and help them fill in what had happened.

One that included every detail I could remember.

He appreciated it, and so did the other officers. Besides, it's not like they didn't already know about the monsters. They just wanted to know what happened.

So, Lev and I told them that SWAT had saved our lives and countless others if it had gotten out. Their bravery and dedication were beyond measure. They will never be forgotten. To say CSPD was pissed and wanted answers was the understatement of the century.

They were not the only ones wanting answers—

Samantha Cox kept trying to get in to see us—even after her article flopped—but we refused to talk to her. Her continued attempts were concerning—not just because she was the only reporter to visit our hospital continually, but because she was clearly on the right track and knew how to get evidence.

We had enough to worry about now; the press was management's problem.

Unfortunately, Lev and I were having horrific nightmares and PTSD. Seeing those impossible monsters was seriously messing with our heads. Something about the Big One was driving Lev to the brink of insanity, though.

Seeing it must have been truly horrible.

They were giving us narcotics and a bunch of other mental health medicines to help with the nightmares and constant pain. It helped, but she and I were not the same people we were before. We talked a lot and decided that we were going to see this through to the end. Especially now. Our bosses knew we would not be back for several months, but we would return to duty come hell or high water.

"Are the dreams of that Big One still coming every night?" I asked Lev.

"Yes, it's bad. The drugs help, but the vision of that ..." There was a long pause.

"That *thing*!"

I could see the fear on her face. It was a mirror of my own, I am sure. I have never been that terrified by anything. The incomprehensible creature she described kept creeping into my thoughts—even while I was awake. Both Lev and I were getting better physically. But mentally, we were in for a long struggle, and we both knew it. Somehow, she sensed that the Big One was still alive, out there somewhere.

There was a giant crater where the church basement used to be, and most of the church had collapsed. Luckily, the response by "F—ing Everyone," as the late Sergeant Donaldson had aptly said, happened quickly. The church did catch on fire from the explosion, but they were able to get Lev and me (both unconscious) to safety. The fact that it killed the monsters near us must be some miracle unless they died when the Big One did. I am hoping that is why.

"Do you think you'll ever get over seeing ..." I couldn't finish. I still couldn't fully see it; my mind wouldn't let me know what she had described, which she said didn't even honestly explain how enormous and grotesque it was.

"No," she finished for me.

For the next several months, we worked on our recovery. I don't know which costs the government more: the field office they remodeled or our hospital bills. Physically, we were steadily improving. Lev, inexplicably, was healing much faster than I was. I finally saw her without the gauze.

She looked at me plaintively.

I knew that even though she did not care about being a model, she did care that half her face had been ripped off. They had also removed that "stinger," which had a sac, presumably of poison, that was now empty. The fact that her right eye still worked, even though they did not expect it to recover, was nothing short of a miracle. It was still bloodshot and badly bruised around it.

"You are still hot, don't worry," I said.

"Yeah, right." She laughed.

I laughed, too.

She and I had grown close during our recovery.

We shared a bond of pain, recovery, loss, and never-ending fear that few others would understand. I often thought our shared time was better than any drug they had given me. And they had given me a lot.

We went for another walk and stopped to rest for a bit.

Then she hugged me for the first time.

I could feel her warmth and her shuddering. The fact she was holding it together, better than I was, is a testament to how strong-willed she was. We both held each other for a long time. I gently kissed her on the top of her head. She pulled her head away to look up and smile at me. The right part of her face barely moved. I smiled back. She was still pretty but looked fierce with the scarring on the right side of her face. And I would swear her right eye was a different shade of blue now. Just a little darker.

She turned her head to the right so I could only see the left side.

"I think this is my better side now for photo shoots. Whatcha think?"

Laughing, I replied I thought so, too.

We snuggled back into one another and into the aging couch in the central area of the hospital. She sighed as she put her head on my chest and fell asleep. Having a beautiful woman in my arms, softly sleeping, was a good feeling. She was fully relaxed, and I liked to think that I made her feel safe in my arms. I could feel myself dozing off.

———

Agent Lev

I can feel its slimy skin and the ripping of dozens of barbs, some with chunks of my face stuck to them. In an instant, I am walloped so hard that it strains my neck and throws me backward. But I can feel the stinger lodged just under my eye and see my blood on the tentacles. When I stood back up, I grabbed my M4. I can see the mouths are licking my blood off the tentacle. They smile at me after enjoying the taste of my flesh. I see the tentacles grabbing the other men and pulling them in, the gunfire and flash-bang grenades going off; I see Donaldson make it out alive, the others being dragged into it and absorbed. Limbs ripped away and swallowed, blood everywhere, and their horrible screaming that sounds like me—

I lunged out of bed and onto my feet. It was the middle of the night again, and I realized … *I was the one screaming.*

"Are you OK?" asked the duty nurse.

She must have come in at the end of my nightmare because she was already there when I awoke. It is the same every night; I wake up to my own screaming.

"Yeah, I'm OK."

It was a lie, and both of us knew it. She nodded and headed out of my room.

I let out a long sigh.

Since I was up, I went to the bathroom.

My injuries were healing fast, and that led to a problem. My recovery baffled the doctors. They said I was healing too fast. I didn't know what that meant …

Until now.

Looking in the mirror, I was horrified. Even though I am a severe tomboy—and must be to be able to compete in a male-dominated profession—I still care about my looks. I didn't waste a lot of time on beauty crap, but I took my good looks for granted.

Now, I don't.

There was a monster in the mirror staring back at me.

I now had one dark blue and green eye and one dazzling light blue eye. The blue/green eye was nestled on the right side of my face, all scar tissue. The speed at which I had healed made all my wounds scar terribly. I held back a sob but let the tears flow. Walking back, I sat down on the bed.

I had tapered off the psych meds, as had James. Thinking of him made me feel happy. I didn't want to admit that I was starting to have more loving feelings for him. I think he felt the same way—I sure hope he does, anyway. My heart skipped a beat at the thought he might not feel the same.

Could he love a monster?

We hadn't kissed, but we had held each other for dear life, which was an accurate assessment. Neither he nor I thought it wise to tell them how bad the nightmares were, especially now that the psych medicines were gone. But we agreed we had to get back out there and fight whatever the cause of these monsters was. And part of that pact was saying we were fine even if we weren't. I decided to lay back down and try to get back to sleep …

The morning sun was warming my face. I was glad I was able to fall back asleep. My stomach was grumbling, and I admit my appetite had not suffered. I can't believe how much I eat now! It must be the energy of all that healing.

I wanted to join James in the cafeteria for breakfast, so I got up and went to wait for him in the hall leading to it. James also gets up early, so I knew it would not be long.

I sat down and waited.

A few minutes later, I saw him coming down the hall. He gave me a huge, warm grin when he saw me. I stood and walked over to join him.

"Hi, James," I said.

"Hello, beautiful," he replied.

This is the first time he has said that to me!

Looking sharply at him, I could see he was not messing with me. There was caring in his eyes. He still thought I was beautiful! I could feel a surge of happiness going through me.

"You better mean it," I said, smiling.

James smiled also, and then he did something I never expected—

He reached forward, hugged me, and kissed me deeply. I shut my eyes and went with it—all those months of talking, cuddling, and walking together. Finally, I know he felt the same as I did. When we came up for air, we were both smiling. He had beautiful green eyes and a lovely smile. Mine was a half-smile, and I knew it. He saw the fear in my eyes.

"I love you, Lev … and I think you are beautiful inside and out, no matter what," he said.

I paused to think for only a moment.

"I love you too, James."

Then I added, "And I think you are beautiful, as well."

We both laughed. Then we held each other's hands and went to get breakfast …

After many more weeks of therapy at the hospital, I was better than new—literally.

James? Not so much.

But at least he was fit to return to duty—light duty anyway; he was still healing. James and I looked out at the snow. It was coming down steadily. Luckily, it's not like we had to drive anywhere.

"Do you want to go for our last walk at the hospital?" James asked with a smile.

He knew I did.

One of the highlights of our day was our walks. We were officially discharged from the hospital. He would still be doing therapy, but he could get around and learn things while we were in training. The FBI had set up two full months of training for us, the same training the rest of our team had already completed. We heard the new field office was now fully up and running—no new news of anything. Maybe we had stopped the only OI incident ever to occur.

I sighed; I doubted that very much.

"Is that a no?" James said, looking at me quizzically.

"No, no … I mean, yes … let's do the last walk. I was just thinking that more OIs are probably going to happen now. I can't imagine if it happened once … that it can't happen again," I said.

He nodded in agreement, took my hand, and we walked outside—our Uber to the airport was waiting.

I was cleared for full duty and flew as an armed LEO on a government-purchased ticket. James was flying as a civilian, with no weapons or gear, since he was not cleared for active duty.

We got in and held hands on the way to the airport. I put my head back and remembered with a smile …

———

A few weeks later, we had our last weekend together, and the sex with James had been incredible.

He had quickly looked past my scars and facial deformity. Plus, he had already told me that he thought I was a sexy, battle-tested warrior as far as he was concerned. As we lay in the bed naked, he ran his hands all over me and caressed me. Sighing, I leaned into him and put my leg over his. We snuggled into each other's arms as we had done a hundred times. I felt his strong hands as he massaged me, also for the hundredth time, and we could both feel the difficulty he had trying to push into my muscle.

The muscles had something running through them, and we both knew what those "somethings" were. We had already discovered that "poison" existed in that stinger, and it was turning me into something that was no longer fully human. I was terrified of what I might become, but he told me he was with me, no matter what.

God, did I love that man!

But we harbored a secret that didn't stay concealed for long. It happened while we were spending the weekend at the Broadmoor Hotel (we decided to celebrate being alive and splurge a bit.)

The revelation occurred when room service arrived for the first time, and I was taking a nap. There was a sudden, loud knocking at the door as the room service personnel arrived.

I can't recall how I found myself here.

I had been asleep and was now standing next to the bed. James was taken aback, and we both exchanged startled looks. It was precisely as

James had described with the SIM on the plane. I had transitioned from asleep to standing in a split second. He smiled, then turned, and headed to the door …

———

During the final months of our recovery, my healing baffled and puzzled the doctors. Medical staff wanted to run more tests, a lot more tests, but I said no. They had done X-rays, MRIs, and follow-up scans during my many procedures already, so they knew something unprecedented was occurring.

But, dammit, it was my body—not theirs!

So, I informed them of the Health Insurance Portability and Accountability Act (HIPAA), which protects patients' privacy, and that they were not to share my medical information.

They did not respect my HIPAA rights.

Even with my refusal, I am sure many damaging details about my new physiology had made their way to the FBI OST. The agency still cleared me for duty when it was apparent I was more than ready, but I knew they would keep a close eye on me.

I didn't blame them.

I turned to James and said, "Are you ready to be all you can be?"

He laughed at the army slogan reference and leaned his head slightly *up* to kiss me.

I chuckled, and so did he.

We both realized early on that I was infected with whatever that stinger had in it. At first, it was just my healing that was unusual. And I slept and ate *a lot*. Then I noticed James and others were looking at me eye to eye. I was now six feet, one inch tall. And I weighed in at an impossible 240 pounds—*although I don't think I look a pound over 220.*

I chuckled to myself as I thought about that.

For whatever reason, I was glad I wasn't as enlarged as the "full" SIMs. Otherwise, I would be *a lot* bigger.

Be thankful for the small miracles, I guess.

I thought about James's reaction when I started growing …

"I better be good to you, or you'll kick my ass!" James had said to me.

The scary part was it was true.

I was now much more potent and faster than any man. My bones were as strong as steel. And we all knew I had those horrible tentacles throughout my body. Somehow, though, I still had fully working organs and was alive.

No one knew why.

James and I had already seen what I could do. We even had to be careful during sex so I didn't hurt him. It was extraordinary but terrifying. Would the changes stop? Would I lose my humanity and become a "full" SIM?

Could I infect James?!

He said he would risk it.

James and I also discussed the possibility of my becoming a "full" SIM. I made him promise to do his duty and put me down if that time came. He was not happy to agree, but he did.

The medical staff asked what I was physically capable of, but I refused to show more than a slight increase in ability. I am sure they were more than just curious; they knew I was holding back.

It was obvious.

I am sure that someone in the government wanted to know, so it was a good thing we were in the secret OST program. Maybe it could stay under wraps for a while …

James and I had already tested what I could do.

We entered the gym late one night, and James ensured no one could get in. I looked up at the pull-up bar. My usual max was twelve clean pull-ups. I jumped up. My first pull-up was effortless. So was the tenth. When I got to thirty, I started doing one-handed pull-ups, then let go.

James was smiling.

"Why the shit-eating grin, baby?"

"Because I'm with the sexiest, strongest woman alive … And she loves me," he winked.

I smiled.

I was still "passable" as a human, but I did get strange looks everywhere I went—my days of "blending in" as a FAM were over. I could feel the looks of disgust and finally understood what it was like to be openly discriminated against—just because I looked different than what a "normal" woman should look like.

Not that I had any blame for them noticing. No one knew how to react to me now that I was a strong, powerful woman. Men, especially, are not used to seeing a woman as someone who is their physical equal —or more than their equal—and that scares them. The body deformation from the tentacles and the elongation of a few inches in my limbs and neck was not enough to be seen as inhuman, just as a deformed one with some kind of gigantism. And the fact that I looked like a pro bodybuilder on steroids didn't help any. I even had the super-low body fat of one. I cried when my all-natural breasts went from a 36C to a 52A. My perfect breasts were now a little saggy and a lot smaller as the fat had melted quickly away.

That made me all the happier that I have James.

We already let the agency know we were a couple and would be acting as one. And that if they had a problem with it, we would still be a couple, just as "former agents." It was civilian government service, not the military; we could quit whenever we bloody well felt like it.

They begrudgingly agreed.

We insisted that we stay assigned to the same field office and be treated as "permanent partners" from a work standpoint. Luckily, everything was so "not by the book" at this point that they agreed. Besides, they knew I was an asset *and* a liability. And we both told them that if I "turned," James would kill me. Or try—that scared me the most.

What if I killed him?

———

Agent James

Our flight home to Denver was much different than our normal ones.

Colorado Springs airport is not a large airport. Our block time was about an hour (the flight is only twenty minutes or so), and I am not sure why they sent us back this way. It seems like it would have been easier to come down to get us. Oh well, the government operates in unusual (and expensive) ways …

Getting to the sterile area and our gate did not take long.

With clothes on, Lev was still passable as a human, albeit a very unusual one. She sat just separate from me and was a little closer to the front of the plane. The looks of surprise and shock didn't bother me, but I could see the pain in her expression when she was looked at like a freak.

I can only imagine what she feels like right now.

The shocked looks didn't bother me that much. But the two men seated behind her were really starting to piss me off …

The two men behind her were college-aged and reasonably athletic. They were talking about her loudly—so they knew she could hear. I could hear comments like:

"F—king female bodybuilders. It's just so *GROSS*!"

"What the f—k? She looks like a dude!"

"Yeah. I bet she *is* a dude!"

They laughed.

I remembered my training. If she weren't going off on them, I wouldn't either. They were lucky I wasn't a civilian. Otherwise, I would be tempted to beat them senseless when the airplane door opened. The federal felony assault status, under maritime laws for an aircraft in flight, changes back to local laws when that door opens—and I knew it.

Their open hatred and bigotry of her, just for looking and being different from them, bothered me, and I knew it bothered her.

Even the flight attendants were ashen-faced but tried to be professional and friendly when they talked to her. They were surprised when she "half-smiled" and was friendly back. By the end of the flight, one of the female flight attendants was chatting with her in pleasant tones.

God bless her. I know how badly Lev needs that right now!

After getting bored at her lack of reaction, the two bigots behind

Lev finally switched to talking about sports. Who had what stats, who was getting traded, and for how much …

The flight landed without incident, but I noticed how on edge I was. I am glad I am not still a flying FAM, I am not sure I could do that anymore.

After getting off the plane, we walked together through Denver International Airport's B Concourse to the trains in the center. The train dropped us off on level five of the Jeppesen Terminal, and we walked over to baggage claim.

"Hey, I just had a thought—" before she had a chance to congratulate me, I continued, "I think we should call those NMC drivers FUD."

She just raised an eyebrow (her left one).

"Federal Uber Driver."

"Is that only for the ones with no personality?" she asked.

"Is there another version?"

We both chuckled at that.

Finally, our bags rolled around the carousel to us. I heaved my light bag up and onto the ground. Lev picked hers up like it was the weight of a purse.

After picking up our bags from the carousel, we went to level six. Like last time, we went where everyone else dropped off for departures. Then, we walked across the tarmac to where "official government-only" vehicles parked.

"I wonder which one is ours?" I joked.

Lev laughed. We both smiled, grabbed each other's hand, and walked over.

The black Chevy Suburban had illegally tinted windows. Well, it's illegal in Colorado except for government vehicles. The driver wore a black Battle Dress Uniform (BDU) and opaque black sunglasses. Some people wonder why the movies always show that stereotype. Well, I guess because it's true. Those *are* the vehicles we drive as "undercover" cars.

Hopefully, they weren't all blacked-out Chevy Suburbans …

I got the door for Lev. She gave me a half-smile, said, "Thank you, love," kissed me, and got in.

I got in the front passenger seat.

"Hey, guys, I'm Jim Phillips. It's an honor to finally meet you two. Thanks for everything you did in Colorado Springs."

We both nodded. It's hard to know what to say to compliments on surviving when a dozen of your colleagues are dead. I thought he could sense that.

"Sorry, guys, I know it was hell you went through."

"Thank you," Lev and I said at the same time.

"Jinx!" Phillips said, laughing.

We all chuckled.

Sure as hell, I had to eat my words. The driver was an NMC agent —buff and dangerous-looking like all of them—but super talkative and friendly. He even treated Lev like a fellow agent, not Frankenstein's monster. Jim was actually a nice dude.

CHAPTER 11
THE NEW OFFICE

OST DENFO
Agent James

THE SUBURBAN PULLED up to the garage door, and Jim radioed, "X-ray Four at sally port."

"Oscar One copies." The garage door opened, and we pulled inside. We learned later that Oscar was the code for "Office" and meant the person in charge of allowing entry to the sally port. And that "X-ray" was the call sign for the nuclear materials couriers, who were security for the facility and the vehicles.

Lev asked them why they chose X-ray.

"So that teams Alpha through Whiskey could be killed before we have to change our call sign," they told us.

Haha … Jerks—Gallows humor at its best.

This place had changed.

The destruction of the church, the death of an entire SWAT team, and the revelation of what we encountered had scared the living hell out of the very highest levels of government. Only the National Security Council, the FBI Director, SAC Cho, and our team officially knew what had happened.

But they did.

And they were freaking out.

Several high-powered people had way more questions than answers and were *very* unhappy with how the FBI handled it—it was almost as if no SOP existed to deal with unprecedented supernatural attacks.

Regardless, the President of the United States (POTUS) told our FBI director, and I quote: "You better not f—k this up."

So, no pressure at all …

Driving into a sealed room with cameras in the upper corners, I can see two NMCs (with SMGs and a K-9) coming out from a side door. Mounted in each corner, above the garage door leading inside, were some kind of remote-controlled machine guns. Looking up at them, I could also see several ominous holes above the garage door.

They were running scanners of some kind (probably just explosives sniffers), and used mirrors under the SUV. Since armored windows don't roll down, we opened all the doors and popped the trunk open. They also looked inside, checked each person's credentials, and ensured we were cleared to enter. Their K-9, a huge German shepherd, had stopped as soon as it entered the room.

His handler yanked on the leash, and the K-9 didn't budge.

"What the hell is wrong with you!" he growled at the dog.

He wasn't the only one growling.

The K-9s ears were back, and it let out a low growl. When he yanked again, hard, it whined and moved forward with trepidation. When it got to Lev, it backed away from her, with its head and tail down, and whimpered. Everyone had stopped and was looking at Lev. Pissing me off, I might add.

"Everyone getting a good look?!" I shouted.

"Sorry—" The dog handler said. "X-ray Six, vehicle is clear."

The inside door rolled up, and we drove in. Everywhere we looked in the bay were vehicles. Several Chevy Suburbans and one Tesla Model X were blacked out "cop style." A trained eye could see the undercover emergency lights on them. Every vehicle had a designated and marked space. No weird lingo. Just GOV One, Two, and Three.

MX One. POV One, Two, Three, etc. Three Model S Teslas were in the POV spaces, all different colors.

We parked in the empty "GOV One" spot, and everyone got out. We walked over to the door to leave the bay.

"Hey!" Jim shouted; Lev and I turned.

He had his hand out and a big grin.

"Where is my tip?" he said.

The other NMC guys were smiling, too. I guess they did have a sense of humor! They remembered our last time with them.

"Sorry, my bad!" I yelled back.

We all laughed.

This was a good start.

We walked through the door from the garage bay and into the main front room—where the pedestrian "sally port" and an NMC agent were. Another NMC agent waved at us, and we walked over and introduced ourselves.

"Agents Levingston and Grey. Good to meet you," I said.

He smiled and said, "I'm Terrance Jones. It's good to meet you both." He shook our hands and winced a little when he shook Lev's.

"Hell of a grip," he said, massaging his hand.

"Sorry, I do that sometimes," she said sheepishly.

"No worries. I'm just glad you are on our side," he replied.

Turning, he started walking and gave us the tour …

The office now looked like the specs and then some. Large signs in bold, capital letters labeled each area as you entered.

As promised, several 150-square-foot dorm-style rooms were in quarters. There was a small working kitchen and tables where you could eat in the mess. And there was a large, padded room labeled "TRAINING" for all "defensive measures" training.

We followed Jones into the Mission Control Room (MCC). Alan was there and smiled when he saw us. He came over and shook my hand vigorously, then turned to Lev. With a smile, he waved. She smiled knowingly and waved back.

Alan was smart.

He introduced us to the Intel/Ops team. Four people, who probably also had brains the size of Einstein, waved back at us. Several giant monitors showed all sorts of information in real time. Desks, computers, radios—everything that should be here was here.

Finally, we walked into the large conference room labeled BRIEFING.

We saw all our team members together again for the first time in months. They had all individually talked with us on the phone, visited us, and given their best wishes for our recovery. I am sure they also all knew about Lev's transformation. Even so, they could not hide their shock at seeing her now. Lev had learned, at this point, to wave.

"Hey, everyone," I said.

"Hi, you two," said Chayton. "We are glad you are back and in one piece. You both did a hell of a job!"

They all clapped. We nodded back with grim looks.

"OK, enough with the revelry, let's get to work," Chayton cut in.

I knew he was ready to get us up to speed. He took over from Terrance and showed us the many features of our office and the vehicles that no other field office would be allowed to have.

Well, maybe the NMC offices were like this; we wouldn't know. We didn't have "Q" Clearance as they did, plus we had no "need to know." Even though "Q" is just the Department of Energy's version of our top secret clearance, it was still a different clearance. So, we would never know.

Chayton guided us back to the garage bay, where we looked more closely at the vehicles. The Suburbans were labeled "GOV," the Model X as "MX," and the civilian-looking ones as "POV"—even though they technically were all "Government-Owned Vehicles." All the vehicles had armor and an HVAC "Bioweapon Defense Mode" that recirculated air while stopping outside contaminants. It sounds like science fiction, but it was just like what the Teslas had. It wouldn't surprise me if the Suburbans had Tesla HVAC systems, too. The vehicles' armor was impressive, and all the vehicles had souped-up and more powerful power plants.

Well, except the Teslas—they figured a thousand horsepower was enough.

The increased power wasn't for fun either; the armor added significantly to their weight. Performance can mean the difference between life and death in some circumstances. Compartments were built into each car/SUV to store everything from long arms to other gear securely. None of the "POVs" looked out of place. They were different colors, but all were Tesla Model S cars. All had police-style performance and durability-based modifications, so they could handle better and take some damage from what they encountered. All were picked to have some ground clearance.

There were no Porsche 911s or Corvettes. That was good. This wasn't *Miami Vice*, and I didn't see thousand-dollar trendy outfits in our future either. The Teslas were a surprise, though not too much, as US government agencies can only lease or buy "American" vehicles.

Our next stop was looking at the weapons built into the sally ports (vehicle and pedestrian) that would make short work of an intruder. All are controlled by the port operators—the "Oscars" I had mentioned. I could see how the Oscar was able to control the guns remotely, with a target reticle on the screen. Right now, it is aimed at the outer door.

Two sally ports were the only ways in or out; the other "doors" had been blacked out and made with bullet-resistant glass. Behind each fake door were the normal walls, and behind them were reinforced concrete walls that they had added to the inside of the entire building. There was no roof access from inside anymore. The whole building could be sealed with an independent HVAC system. The building had emergency landlines for comms, solar panels, and a battery system for power. I guess they had gotten a lot from Tesla. I learned it had its own satellite communications (SATCOM) relay as well. I wondered if they were using Starlink also—

"I know you saw the weapons on the way in, the two 7.62mm machine guns with armor-piercing rounds mixed in. The rounds will go through a vehicle, but the reinforced walls can stop them," Chayton said.

"What are those scary-looking holes over the garage door?" Lev asked.

"Those are for the gas—either CS or flammable gas that can be ignited. And no, it hasn't been tested yet."

"The pedestrian sally port has similar systems, but with 5.56mm rounds."

This was impressive. The G never gets to turn offices into a fortress like this one. Some serious strings had been pulled, and several regulations had been ignored. Last up was the armory. After extensive security procedures, we opened the door to the main armory.

"Wow!" Lev let out a whistle.

We all shuddered.

It came out as an angry, alien hissing sound.

"Sorry," she said again, looking embarrassed.

I was about to say something, but Chayton beat me to it.

"Don't be, Agent Levingston. We have intel about what's going on with you. Things are going to be different with you sometimes. We all understand that you're a critical part of our team. Understood?"

"Understood, sir," she replied.

Chayton nodded to her.

Neatly marked and separated into categories were sniper rifles, automatic rifles, SMGs, fully automatic shotguns, pistols, DM (hand-to-hand) weapons, and grenades. I did a double-take.

"Grenades?" I asked.

"Yes, the flash-bangs and smoke are standard issue. The CS gas grenades and concussion grenades are not here. Understood?"

"Yes, sir," Lev and I said in unison.

Now I *am* scared.

The fact that they were going to let us use offensive explosives, in any domestic circumstances, was unheard of.

There was another section for fully set up body armor outfits. Lev and I wandered over to it. A long row of exoskeleton-armored suits was stored, each standing upright like a person. A gas mask on each one, which could be attached to the helmets without taking them off, was in a side pouch. Other pouches with first aid kits, ammo pouches, and more were on tactical attachment points. I looked closer.

"Those are ExoM Exoskeleton suits," Chayton said, explaining our querying looks. "They can take three hits from an AK-47 from thirty-three feet, or so we are told. I hope we don't get to test that. They are passive, no power source. However, the suit redistributes 70 percent of the load weight to the ground so that you can carry more with less effort. There was a powered version called the 'Guardian XO,' but it was deemed impractical for combat use. It was more for just picking up and carrying around heavy stuff without concern for mobility. We have modified these ExoMs further—" He pointed and gesticulated as he talked. "You can see release tabs at the shoulders and the inseams. If you are hit in the limbs and have arterial bleed, you or your teammates pull one of these tabs …"

He reached out and pulled one of the suit shoulder tabs. There was a loud pop and hiss, and the shoulder pad moved up and back down. He pulled up on the pad, and we could see a Combat Application Tourniquet, or CAT, had been deployed with a simple CO_2 canister, just like the ones BB guns use. Those CO_2 canisters are easily replace-able in the field as well. Smart.

"Honestly, I don't know why this wasn't invented sooner. A lot more soldiers and officers would be alive today." Chayton shook his head in dismay.

"So … about those grenades that don't exist …" Lev said.

"They're not standard issue and are locked in another container. They are only for extreme circumstances. Determined by myself or SAC Cho. Clear?"

"Clear," we responded.

"Whatcha think?" Chayton said, smiling, now that the tour was over.

"Wow. Very impressive," I said.

"Glad they didn't think we made it all up," Lev joked.

"Yeah. The silence is killing us. Upstairs, the mega-brass wonders if we reinforced the barn door after the horses left." Chayton looked concerned.

Lev and I looked at each other—we knew what the other was thinking.

"God, I hope they are right," she said.

Chayton shrugged, and then he and I both nodded in agreement. He gave us a long look and said, "I need to talk to you both about something ..."

We both knew what was next.

"I know you are a couple now and have put in paperwork as domestic partners," he said. "But I need to know. Will your relationship cause you to take unnecessary risks to save the other when we get in combat again?"

We looked at each other.

Lev spoke first, "Absolutely."

I smiled; Chayton did not.

"Chayton, I'll take *any* risk to save *anyone* on our team, the same as I would for James. We are professionals," she said.

"I concur."

Wow, James, another great response. I mentally kicked myself.

Chayton smiled. "OK. I don't know why I thought it would be a problem. But as the TL, I had to ask it."

"We understand. It won't be a problem, boss," I said.

Next to me, Lev nodded. It was settled. We headed off to the mess to eat and to get a good night's sleep.

———

Lev and I stayed the night, as did the rest of the team. We were still assigned separate quarters because they were small and tailored for one person each. With our size, the bed was way too small for us to actually *sleep* together. So, we just "visited" each other a lot. There was no adolescent whispering; it was clear with our surreptitious hand-holding that we were a couple—but still professionals. They even assigned us side-by-side "dorm" rooms. We also made clear to the other team members, at Chayton's request, what we had said to him. No one was concerned. Besides, I think the priority for most battle plans was to revolve around Lev anyway. I think everyone was curious to see what she could do in battle.

Everyone but me.

They have rules about fraternizing in the government for a reason. I would do more for Lev's safety, and I knew she would for me, regardless of what we told Chayton. We knew they were not really OK with the situation, because we had to threaten to quit when they brought it up.

But they didn't want to lose Lev.

If it had only been me, I would have been back on flight duty with the FAMs by the end of the day. However, if Lev quit, they would lose one of their most powerful agents and have to assign a team to watch her 24/7, indefinitely. That would not be a practical decision.

Speaking of practical … the money, not to mention the strings they had to pull, to make this office were unprecedented. Nothing here was science fiction; we had no ray guns or magical, mystical artifacts to help us.

Anyway, these are the things I think of when I am up early. At times like this, though, my nightmares woke me up before dawn. Sometimes, I could get back to sleep. Other times, like now, I couldn't. So, I got ready and went to breakfast early.

It was nice to have the mess to myself, anyway. My black coffee let off a reassuring smell, and I liked seeing the steam come up. Plus, it gave me something to stare at as my mind wandered—

"Good morning, James." That was Morris, breaking me out of my daydreaming.

He also grabbed a cup of black coffee, but he added what looked like ten packets of sugar.

"Good God, man, how can you drink it with that much sugar?" I teased.

He smiled and replied, "How can you drink it without?"

I nodded and lifted my cup to the excellent comeback.

We sat quietly as the rest of the team made their way in over the next half hour.

Lev walked in.

Everyone had gotten used to seeing Lev, but they still had to fight the urge to look amazed when they saw her. That is not exactly the look she and I shared now. She half-smiled, got her coffee, and came to sit across from me.

"Morning, love." I kissed her.

F—them if anyone has a problem with it!

I looked around. There were a couple of "OK by me" looks and shrugs, but no one seemed concerned.

She had stopped wearing makeup.

There was just no way to do it without looking weird. After watching her try—and cry when it failed—she finally decided it was pointless. Besides, she always had a natural beauty that didn't need eyeshadow.

Because we had just gotten back, they wanted to test our team's readiness. So, we were put on Quick Reaction Force, or QRF, status for a month to train together and get used to the office and the new equipment. Even though they wanted to set up our training as soon as possible, there was a delay because they had to wait for us to be medically cleared before scheduling us for the training program. Also, they wanted us to gel as a team immediately in case another Occult Incident came calling.

This morning's first training block was DM. After breakfast, we were all gathered in the mat room. At 0700, Chayton walked in. We were already wearing our MMA fingerless gloves, mouth guards, and cups for groin protection.

"OK. We already know what we can do from our first sparring session many months ago," Chayton said. He shot a glance at Lev. "So, we're going to work some techniques, then do some … *light* … sparring."

It was clear that he had not done that before, and I could tell that by the quizzical look the rest of the team gave him—Lev had a knowing look—he was telling everyone to be very careful around her. We didn't need anyone going to the hospital because they decided to get competitive, not that I thought anyone was eager to spar with Lev anyway …

"Morris, you're with Lev," Chayton said.

Morris visibly gulped and then nodded yes.

"Alan with Larry. And James, you are with me until you have full medical clearance. One of you from each team get a knife from the wall."

Once we had gotten the blue knives, we formed a semicircle around our civilian instructor for that day. He was a man named "Bob," who was Vietnamese and had that scary look of someone who was a killer, and of someone who was not actually named "Bob."

"Bob's going to show us knife fighting," Chayton said.

I found it strange, considering knives would not take down the monsters we had fought—so I said something.

"Chayton, I have to ask—why are we learning knife fighting against monsters that we clearly can't kill with knives?" I asked.

"Just in case we fight people as well. Plus, we have no idea what else may be coming our way down the road. Plus, it's the government, and we already made a PowerPoint on it."

I laughed, and the others joined in.

Yeah, that actually sounds about right.

None of us were expecting to go straight into practicing techniques. The instructors used a process called Explain, Demonstrate, Imitate, and Practice or EDIP. First, he explained how to do it, then showed us the moves and counter moves slowly. Next, Chayton and "Bob" demonstrated it at near full speed. Then, we tried the techniques on each other slowly while the instructors (Chayton and Bob) walked around critiquing us. Last was full-speed practice. This is a honed method of teaching practical hands-on skills, and it works. Chayton and I took turns doing attacks, defenses, and counterattacks. Everything was going well …

———

Agent Lev

Greg Morris looked at me.

I was so happy!

Finally, someone was looking *down* at me again. It made me, briefly, feel like a woman again. He held the knife and came at me slowly. I deliberately stepped off at an angle, hit his weapon arm with both forearms and grabbed the arm. I made sure to do it lightly. The knife flew out of his hands when I hit his arm.

"Oof!" he grunted loudly.

Chayton turned to me. "Lightly, killer," he said.

Morris picked up the knife, and we tried again. I could tone it down, but I had to go *very* slowly.

I had the "Superman" problem.

Have you ever watched him pick up a car or catch one to save people?

Yup.

Have you ever watched him pet a dog?

Nope.

Not unless he wants to crush its head and flatten it on the sidewalk.

From Muay Thai, I learned that a strike always causes damage based on three factors: the mass and strength of the limb, the speed at which it is moving, and the precision of technique, which affects speed and accuracy. Now, I can add a fourth factor: bone density.

It was my turn to be the aggressor, so I took the knife and came at him very slowly.

It was still fast.

Morris stepped expertly out of its path and hit my forearm with both hands.

"Oof," he grunted again, although not as loud as the first time.

I saw him wince, but he continued moving in and wrapping my arm with both of his hands. He dropped his body weight onto my arm. Usually, the person goes down when a 260-pound man drops his entire body weight on an arm.

He hung in the air like a small child would.

I realized this and let myself go down to the ground. As I got ready to get up, he reflexively held out a hand to help me. It's not a sexist thing; we all help each other up. I shook my head no and shot to my feet.

He yelled out and jumped back.

Everyone turned in alarm; All was suddenly quiet.

"Well, I, for one, have seen that before," James said.

James pretended to yawn with his hand to his mouth, and there was some polite chuckling. *Thank you, my love!* Everyone resumed practicing techniques.

Curious about my new capabilities, I went to the heavy bag. Morris was still massaging his forearms, and he needed a break. So, while everyone else was practicing the technique repeatedly, I took a fighting stance and lightly hit the bag with a jab. It swayed away with the force of a hard kick. Next, I hit it at an average speed with an elbow strike. It dented and swung way up. I reflexively sidestepped and launched a hard round kick as it swung back down. It caught the bag and hurled it sidewise like I had done thousands of times. This time, though, it swung all the way up on its chain. There was stuffing sticking out from where I had hit it, and a large gash was visible.

"Well … crap," I said.

I reached out and steadied the bag. All was quiet behind me.

"You're all staring at me, aren't you?" I said without looking behind me.

"Just like I always do," said James in response as I turned to face everyone.

The rest nodded.

Alan said, "Yup!"

"Oh well. I think we needed a new bag anyway," Chayton said.

I turned back to look at the bag. My speed and strength were not human, but I was no superhero. The bag only tore because my bones were so hard. I looked closer. The elbow strike had cut it, but the kick had ripped it open.

As if hit with a metal bar.

We finished the DM session; I had bowed out of sparring.

No one seemed to mind.

It was time for lunch, and I was glad, as I was starving! They had brought in some chef to cook, and the food was nothing crazy, but wholesome. I noticed Morris and I ate nearly the same amount; I ate slightly more. Another thing about my new reality is that I stopped counting grams and calories. I just ate—a lot.

And I still had single-digit body fat levels.

I *never* thought I would say this, but I wished I could have a little more fat. I looked like I was about to do a professional bodybuilding show—complete with my A-cups. I frowned, returning my empty tray to the rack.

This afternoon, we were scheduled for academics and assembled in Briefing.

At least Chayton didn't step in with a stopwatch this time.

Our class was called "Anatomy of the SIM."

"OK, everyone, let's get started," said the instructor, Daniel Histon, addressing the class.

He was the same instructor we had at FLETC so many months ago. Judging by the group's bored expressions, I could tell this was for James's and my benefit. They had probably already taken the class. Looking at James and me, he said, "We know a lot more than we did last time you were briefed." He started the pictures with a new Power-Point on the projector.

"Physiologically, it seems the parasite works in symbiosis," he said.

I looked at him quizzically.

"I think I remember the proper word usage. Working together?" I asked.

"Yes. Two different organisms work together to the advantage of both. At least as far as capabilities go …"

He looked a little sheepish since we all knew I was somehow one of them.

"So, the creature that causes all this—we are just calling it a 'carrier'—gains access through the mouth and tears its way through the back of the throat to get to the brainstem, destroying the vocal cords in the process. We can see they healed rapidly, but the scar tissue probably affected how the voice would sound in a *big* way. Maybe that is why they didn't talk. It looks like they could have …"

The slide showed the damage to that area on one of the dead SIMs. It had already wholly healed before it was killed, but the scar tissue was clearly visible.

God knows I am aware of the scar tissue from rapid healing.

I am just glad that my "transformation" was from some kind of poison in that stinger, and not from having my throat ripped apart by a monster. I also can't imagine having a voice so terrible that I didn't dare speak. Mine was a bit deeper, and off from what it was before, but it still sounded like me—mostly.

There was a pause as he changed to another slide, and then continued, "It wreaks havoc on the brain, surging every kind of hormone and adrenaline. And it starts to convert muscle and bone. It also interweaves tentacles that run through every part of the body. It, somehow, hardens the bones and the tentacles, making them much more damage-resistant. And the alien 'muscle' in the tentacles is unlike anything we have seen. It doesn't match anything on Earth, in both how it is structured and how the labs come back ... *inconclusive*."

He took another long pause.

"This thing is completely alien; its labs and structure have our best people scratching their heads. We do know these tentacles can contract with incredible speed and force. And they are highly resistant to all forms of trauma. We've tried everything. Shooting it, burning it, freezing it, electrocuting it, you name it. Right now, the best defense is still high explosives or hitting the creature attached to the brain stem. We have learned a lot since you and SWAT went up against them."

I looked at James, who looked pale. I knew it was worry for me and how we both felt when he said, "SWAT."

James and I knew those men—they had laid down their lives against these monsters and saved us.

"Sorry," Daniel said.

He had seen the sudden change in our demeanor.

"It's OK. Carry on, sir," I said.

I knew this was hard for him to teach, especially since he was looking out at me.

At one of "*them*."

"So, the best bet is to shoot the brainstem area where the carrier is. That will kill the SIM. As for fire and freezing? It does a number on the 'person' part of it. But it looks like that is redundant. In other words, the tentacles can operate without needing the host human's muscles, organs, or bones. As far as the creature part of it, it seems immune to temperature changes. It reminds us of the Tardigrade micro-animal. Except it doesn't hibernate, it is just … unaffected."

I already knew that part. When I got cold or hot, I could feel—or not feel, I should say—the parts of me that were "it." I didn't sweat or blink anymore either, and I had a very high body temperature. Not that that freaked me out or anything …

"Does it make any difference what round hits the carrier?' James asked.

"No, we now know that rifle or pistol rounds can kill the carrier and thus the SIM. The good news is, we know how to kill it. Just nail this guy," he pointed to the picture on the screen, with all the skin removed from the head of one of the dead SIMs. The red dot from his laser pointer was on the grayish/purple beastie, and a chunk from James's bullet was missing.

"The other SIM's carrier had most of the creature gone. Rifle rounds do an even better job of destroying it. Do you have any other questions?"

"CCTV footage. Were you able to glean anything from that? How it moves, how fast is it, etcetera?" Lev asked.

"What little we got from cameras at the truck stop incident, we turned upside down. Our computer techs looked at everything: how it vectors, the top speed and acceleration, and even how it responds to bullet hits," Daniel responded.

With that, he handed James and me pamphlets on the creatures.

"Everyone else already got this and memorized the pertinent facts. It'll make some nice evening reading with a cup of tea," he said.

He gave us a moment to skim it.

On average, the SIM-hybrid saw a 10 percent increase in height and limb reach and a 50 percent increase in body weight. Those are the SIMs created by the poison from the stingers.

Jesus, that is me.

The "full" SIMS, the ones created by the carriers, had a 20 percent increase in height and a doubling of body weight. All "versions" had low single-digit body fat levels. Acceleration was amazing. The SIMs we fought topped out at over thirty miles per hour and accelerated to that speed in just over a second. The smaller SIM hit thirty-four miles per hour in 1.13 seconds, estimated. With a longer run, it might top out at around forty miles per hour. It slightly out-accelerates a cheetah, even if it doesn't go as fast as one.

The stats for the cheetah were from zero, to its top speed of sixty miles per hour in about three seconds. The fastest human sprinter hit a top speed of 27.33 miles per hour, 67 meters into a 9.3-second 100-meter dash. And these were all faster than that. Ugh. No one is getting away from one—unless they are a cheetah.

We looked up from our pamphlets.

"That's all we have right now. None of the non-human lab results matched anything on Earth … None."

"Thanks," James said.

With that, the briefing was over.

CHAPTER 12
NEW BEGINNINGS

The Reverend

I KNOW the Feds might still be looking for me, but at least they did not know of the tome.

The "cover story" about the NER Church was all over the news.

They said we had barricaded ourselves and fought to the end, blowing up a bomb and killing everyone. The news agencies had no idea how right they were, except I am sure it wasn't us that triggered a bomb—I was the only survivor before they even got there. Either they brought explosives, or they used the demolition charges that were left in the church.

I have no idea why they would blow themselves up, though.

Additionally, there was no mention of monsters, Feds, or wanted persons. Hopefully, they thought I died in the explosion.

However, I was distraught that I had somehow failed. There was no Messenger to guide me now. After it had directed me away from the NER church and told me to take the tome, it stopped communicating with me.

I know I cannot ever get the insurance money for the church, but luckily, there was an account for it that no one knew about.

My account.

Embezzling was probably the least of my crimes at this point. I only kept paper records of those actions and mine were destroyed in the fire. The Colorado Springs **PD** Officer, Vincent O'Donnell, had helped me create a fake ID just in case.

He also taught me not to leave a trail for the police to follow.

I did my best to leave no evidence that I existed; I only used cash and the fake ID, and only when absolutely necessary. I no longer had any connection to the late Reverend Doctor Gregory Turner, the Third.

Once I made it out of the police dragnet (I had taken a ride in a trailer full of manure on the way to a farm), I rented a cheap hotel and cleaned up. The following day, I bought an affordable—under $10,000 —used car, all in cash, at the sleaziest car dealership I could find. Then, I made my way to California. I had no guidance; I just wanted to escape Colorado.

A new division of the ultra-devout needed to be formed, and another identical altar and platform had to be made for the precious tome I was carrying.

These things took time.

Luckily, after weeks of searching for the right fit, I finally found my church. The long process of winning over my flock, building the altar, and summoning the Deathwalkers could start again. Soon, my Lord would return; I had faith.

———

My new church was a blessing.

A church in Long Beach, California, had just lost its pastor to a heart attack.

It was time for an introduction.

"Hello, you must be Reverend Clark," the Hope Church of Salvation woman said to me. She reached out and shook my hand.

My fake ID did not quite match my actual appearance, so I would have to be careful not to run afoul of the law and to avoid any official contact with the police. I was now one Jeremy Clark from Grand Junction, Colorado.

"I am. A pleasure to meet you, Miss …" I trailed off.

"Miss Bernal. You can call me Sue," she said with a smile.

Unless my eyes deceived me, I could sense she was attracted to me.

"Miss Bernal—Sue—the pleasure is mine."

We held each other's hands much longer than was customary.

"Let me show you around …" She gestured, and I followed her inside the church.

It was a magnificent church—not massive or flashy, but very ornate—especially inside. Sitting on extremely valuable real estate on Naples Island, it was in a developed area, not remote like the New Era Revivalist church.

"This is Paul and Deacon," she said by way of introduction.

I reached out and shook hands.

"Deacon …?" I said.

He laughed.

"Yeah, Deacon. With a name like that, it is no wonder I wound up in the Seminary!"

After some polite chuckling, he continued.

"Mr. Clark, I hate to get straight to the point, but after the unfortunate passing of Reverend Silverman, we are desperately in need of a new pastor …" He looked at me expectantly.

I noticed Paul and Sue were also looking expectantly at me. Sue's look, in particular, was one of wanting …

"I would be honored to lead your flock to eternal salvation," I said.

"Thank the Heavens!" Deacon said.

I shook their hands and got down to the brass tacks of working at my new church …

The next Sunday service came quickly, and I came out and went to the lectern.

A warm welcome of clapping ensued.

My new church seemed overjoyed to have me.

The Hope Church of Salvation parishioners were ecstatic to learn that a seasoned and devout "Fire and Brimstone" Reverend would lead them—they did not know just how blessed they were …

"Welcome, everyone. I wanted to express my gratitude for this opportunity. The opportunity to lead you to salvation in His holy name. God be praised."

"God be praised!" from the congregation.

"I'll start with Genesis, as we are quickly nearing the End Times —" I began.

The rest of the sermon went well, and by the end, I was well on my way to establishing my more hard-core religious philosophy.

———

I now only shower before services and am otherwise a recluse.

I had spent the winter and spring months preaching, and the new congregation loved me now. I also painstakingly created a new altar and platform in the cloakroom of the new church. Finally, after finishing the altar and platform, I placed the tome on top. After such a long silence, the Messenger finally spoke to me again.

"*Well done. You know what you must do.*"

That is all the Messenger said, but I did know what to do.

My new congregation was just as hard-core as the last one. We would have no trouble creating a new "action arm" for our divine purpose. I had started thinking of the Angel and me as a "we" since it guided me daily now. I learned so much from the tome thanks to the Angel's guidance. It showed me how to tap the energy of the other plane to stay awake longer and learn even more.

It was glorious!

The knowledge of this other plane and the impossible creatures in it was magical. It also told me the name of our Savior to make its transition to our world easier: Ashta'goth, the Devourer.

My Lord was eager to return to our world, just as I was eager for it to start the Ascension.

Today is Sunday, and I knew it was the right time to create my new "Wrath of God" army. The church was packed, as I had asked everyone in the Hope Church of Salvation to attend today's sermon. There was some light talking as I walked in and took the podium. I raised my hands, and everyone quieted down.

"The Ascension is upon us," I said.

As before, many platitudes to the Lord sprang, unbidden, from many happy mouths.

"Settle, … settle. Yes, *yes*, this is excellent news! It has been foretold that the living unbelievers and the wicked dead, now raised to life, will be judged. They will then be cast into the lake of fire. The saved will live forever in a new Heaven and Earth. So, be thankful and blessed. For we have been shown the way to salvation!"

I paused for effect.

"What does this mean, you ask? It means a great Messenger has been sent to put God's judgment and wrath upon the nonbelievers and the impure! And that all will be judged, and many shall be found wanting. He will come for believers, both living and dead, and they shall rise into the sky to meet Him."

I walked around the podium to be closer to them, lowering my voice so they had to concentrate on my words.

"This will be a hard period for all. But the reward of Heaven awaits all who believe in and aid in the Ascension's imminent arrival," I said.

I paused before continuing.

"We are truly blessed here today. The Angel, perhaps *the* Archangel, has spoken. A new era will begin in Heaven and Earth."

The thought of more than one Earth was on my mind.

"This will happen immediately after God's Messenger of the End Times arrives and destroys the wicked. All, both the living and the risen dead, shall go to Him to be judged! Those unworthy of his love and everlasting peace shall be thrown into the lake of fire!" I looked around.

I knew I had repeated myself, but that drove the message home. Everyone was staring at me with big eyes.

"Can you imagine the glory of the new Earth? Heaven's own Guardian has been sent to us! That Guardian is coming …" There was another long pause, and I continued, "How, Reverend Clark, you ask? How do you know of its arrival?"

I paused again for effect and walked to the cloakroom door as I spoke.

"Because it has been foretold to me by the Angel … And …By its command …The altar it arrives on is now here."

With that, I opened the door to the large cloakroom. The intricately carved white altar and the large, inscribed platform were visible. Sitting atop the altar was the invaluable tome.

"The reign of Heaven on Earth begins … Very soon."

Everyone got up and trepidatiously entered to stand before the altar.

None dared to touch.

"I know you all believe," I said as I approached it. "For those of you who are willing and able, I'm afraid I may need your help to defend this altar until the Ascension is complete. Those who are unable —the old, the infirm, the children—what of you? Fear not; you're still saved but will tend to the others while the *Protectors* (said with a Capital 'P') ensure time to complete the Angel's calling. I'll need the Protectorate to stay after service for a special calling."

"Thank you all for joining in today's sermon. Go forth on glad tidings!"

"Thank you, Reverend."

"Have a blessed day."

"Bless you, Reverend."

These and many more platitudes came my way.

I engaged in small talk with them until only the Protectorate remained. Two dozen men and women stood before me.

"Welcome, fellow faithful servants. We have a unique opportunity before us."

I waited a long moment, not just for effect but to assure myself of the following crucial words I would speak.

"I have had a recent visitation by the Angel. And the process begins now, today."

Gasps.

Julia, one of the most fervent of the flock, covered her mouth in surprise.

"When?" she asked. "What did it say?" asked another. "Is the time upon us now?" came from a third voice. Many more questions erupted at once, but there were no looks of scorn or disbelief. That was a good sign.

"The Angel has been speaking to me daily for almost a month now," I lied.

There would be no need to scare them with the tale of the first attempt, so many months ago.

"The Angel has also told me it is time, and I'll need you all to meet with me at nine a.m. next Saturday while the church is not in session. Cancel any plans you must. The Angel has commanded it."

Nods all around.

"Welcome to the 'Protectorate' movement," I said.

From my prior hubris, I learned to change the elite group's name in our movement in case the WOG name had gotten out.

"It is a secret. You're to tell no one. Is that understood?" I asked.

Nods again.

"Say it out loud: 'I will tell no one.'"

Each of them, in turn, said it.

"Thank you for your service to the Lord. The Heavens will surely welcome you for your service." With that, and a nod, they were dismissed …

Saturday morning came, and they assembled—as I had asked them to—this time in the back cloakroom. This church had no basement rectory, so this would have to do.

"Good morning, Protectorate," I said.

"Good morning, Reverend," they all replied.

I could hear appreciative sounds as they approached the white altar and platform again. It was identical, in every detail, to the one that was before. Only there was no faint silver aura on the tome. Sweet Margret had been lost in the last battle, along with those blaspheming heretics that had ruined it. I still did not know the plan for "activating" the altar. I tried to have others touch the book, but nothing happened. Disconcerting, but I put my faith in our holy Father—He will guide us. I have no doubt now that I was spared for this reason. That was why I was guided away from the NER Church by the hand of God. There was no other rational explanation …

After they looked at and finally touched almost everything, I interjected.

"This was built precisely as directed from above."

Roy was the first to speak. He was a mild-mannered man in his mid-fifties.

"What is its purpose, Reverend?"

"Glad you asked, Roy," I smiled. "It is to call forth messengers of God's will, His servants, prophets or Messengers, we could call them."

The looks on their faces were angelic. This is what every true believer, deep in their heart, hopes for. That one day, Ascension would come. The faithful, the pure of heart and action, would earn their rightful place in Heaven forever—and the unfaithful would be cast into the lake of fire.

"After the Messengers come, there'll be wrath upon the unfaithful. This will be followed by the great Devourer, who will start—and finish —the Ascension, in God's name. So it has been foretold to me by the Angel just as the Ascension has been foretold to us our whole lives," I said.

It's time to get to work … again.

Getting "volunteers" this time was easy—I just didn't tell them about the change process.

I quickly got my two eager volunteers: Nathan Lynch and Gustav "Gust" Tanner.

Again, both had pasts that made them seek redemption and were keen to leave the world that had oppressed them. Both had struggled with addiction and the legal and social ramifications that came with those uncontrolled addictions: each had DUIs and had been divorced by their wives.

We chanted and waited. All was as before, but there was no change. We waited … and we waited.

Finally, Tanner said, "I'm sorry, but I need to pee."

I was livid.

This was embarrassing, but worse, it had been ineffectual.

"It's I who is sorry," I replied.

It should have worked!

I hoped the Angel could tell me what I did wrong. They all left, and I didn't like the looks some of them gave me—the "you are a fraud" kind of looks.

After they left, I closed the church for the night. I really hoped the Angel would visit soon.

Had I lacked faith? Was I too proud? Had I acted with hubris? Did I sin or miss something in the summoning chant?

I guess the summoning would have to wait. I walked back into the cloakroom and sat on the platform. Hopefully, it was not blasphemy to do so, but I was trying to think. What did it want? How can I make it happen without the conduit?! Margret had been killed at the church. If there had been survivors from my flock, they would be in jail, and I would have seen something about it on the news. At least the police did not seem to be looking for me yet.

There must be another way to bring forth the *Others* again.

The next church service was muted. I received several pitying and skeptical looks, which was not a good feeling. It was clear that I needed to win them back, and soon.

After several days, I knew I was on the cusp of a great revelation. Something I had read was pulling at the corners of my mind—

"A conduit was the first person to find the tome and must be a devout believer ..."

Could it be that simple?

I had a thought—I would try it tomorrow. I called Winston, a member of our church ...

The following day arrived, and Winston Holmstock, also a member of the Protectorate, had come as I asked.

"Good morning, Reverend. You wanted to see me?" he said.

"Yes, Winston. I need you to do me a favor," I said.

"Anything," he replied in earnest.

"I want you to take that tome—" I pointed at the altar and tome "—and hide it somewhere in the church."

He looked at me like I was insane.

"It must not be in the open, but hidden. But not so much that I cannot find it in more than a day or two of searching," I instructed him.

He was nodding and resisting the urge to ask me questions. He went and retrieved the book.

"Do it now and come back to me when you are done. Do you understand?"

"Yes, Reverend," he replied.

He walked out with the heavy tome.

I smiled.

I will be amazed if this works. Soon, the scavenger hunt would begin. I still had two full days before my next sermon.

———

I did not find it that day.

I hoped he had done as instructed—including not telling anyone about our encounter and my strange request.

The following day, after searching everywhere, I still had not found it. Suddenly, I felt an urge to look one more time. I walked into the church's administrative office. I had already looked everywhere it could fit in.

Nothing.

I sat down and let out a long sigh. My neck was tense from stress and from looking, literally, high and low. I just needed to relax and think! Where could it be? I looked up for guidance.

That is when I saw it.

The ceiling in this room had that office drop-down tile ceiling, where individual panels can be pushed up and taken down to access lights and HVAC stuff. One was just slightly ajar. I climbed up onto the desk and pushed the tile in and over. It bumped something. I reached up inside and felt around.

It was next to the edge of the tile I had opened—

The tome, finally!

I felt a strange sensation when I touched it.

I quickly got it down, not even bothering to replace the panel. Taking it to my office, I sat in my comfortable leather chair behind an enormous mahogany desk.

Carefully, I opened it.

The sensation I had when I touched it was instantly magnified a hundredfold. Everything had taken on that silver hue the exploration team had described. I could feel the power flowing through me.

It was glorious!

But then, I sensed motion all around me. Something … *some things* were starting to take form.

Suddenly, without warning, the world opened—

But not my world.

The silver hue had engulfed my body, and dozens, maybe hundreds, of creatures were everywhere I looked. One, about the size of a shark, with a giant maw and covered in eyes, pincers, and other orifices spewing a toxic-looking sludge, came straight at me with its mouth open wide. It sensed me, and I it. It rushed forward, and I could see its flagellating tails, with stingers on each end. It made this horrible sucking, screeching noise and bit down over my entire head.

"AAHH!"

I let out a shrill scream.

And then uncontrollable laughing.

It had passed right through me. The silver aura emanating from me became blinding, and I screamed and fell out of the chair and onto the floor. Curled in a fetal ball, I laughed uncontrollably until I passed out from fear—

I don't know when, but many hours must have passed. I could see the last rays of sunlight coming through the window.

The monsters were all around me!

They were going through everything, even me, as if nothing existed. Some were curious or maybe hungry. I had stopped trying to shoo them away. They did not see my motions. Occasionally, one sensed me in some way—it would charge at me, horrible mouths open wide with sharp teeth, only to go through me and continue. This must be what poor Margret saw. It was marvelous and terrifying at the same time.

I knew what I needed to do. I ate quickly and tried to get to sleep. Sunday service was the next day, and it was going to be busy …

The dawn broke, and I awoke to the sounds of nature outside. After getting ready, I put on my finest raiment once again. I watched and listened from my office as the parishioners started to come in to be seated for the day's service. I could see some of them from my office and could hear them as well. Many were laughing, probably at me. Since last week's Protectorate meeting, they had clearly broken their promises, as I saw several people gesticulating some of my movements from the previous week. I heard "Charlatan," "Quack," and "Fraud" being uttered …

It was time for them to change their tune.

I entered the room, and all fell silent. No one could miss the subtle aura that surrounded me.

"As you can see, I have solved the problem of finding the conduit. That conduit is now me."

The about-face was comical. One moment, they were getting ready to ridicule me; the next, they were back to being true believers.

"This aura … you see it … do you not?" I asked.

Many affirming, nodding heads.

"As the members of the Protectorate clearly can't obey a simple instruction, you're all aware of what happened. Or, to be precise, what did not happen last Saturday? I am here to tell you that the Ascension begins today … NOW!"

They all jumped.

I had not meant to be so forceful, but it came out suddenly from my rage! They recoiled at my booming voice—I could hear its echo in the large room.

"Two of you will volunteer to be the new blessed ones, the heralds of the good tidings of the Ascension. Your place in Heaven is forever assured."

I looked out among them. Most averted their gaze, but some stared with rapture at me. None, however, volunteered. So, I did my signature move and walked around the podium to stand near the first row of pews.

"*No one …?*" I asked incredulously.

There was a long pause.

"I would be honored, Reverend."

That was Paul Jones—a dishwasher from Huntington Beach. He was single, having suffered the shame of a divorce he did not want. His unfaithful ex-wife wanted someone "more successful."

I nodded.

"Welcome. Your sins are forever absolved, and you'll be remembered as a hero of salvation—a true warrior of God!"

Some started clapping, and others joined in. I did not move to stop it.

I clapped and said, "Hallelujah!"

Others joined in, and several more volunteered, so I picked Cathrine McKinkel because of her lack of familial ties. She was also a divorcee; her husband had left her after their only daughter was diagnosed with terminal brain cancer. Her daughter died three days after the divorce was final.

"Today will be a different service. As you can see from my holiday attire, today is a special day—a new holy day—the day of atonement. I was told that all of you shall confess your sins to God now, and then we'll wash them away. In Saturday's evening service, out in the ocean, you'll thoroughly cleanse your soul in holy waters," I said.

Many questioning looks came my way, but I didn't indulge them. They would know soon enough.

"In the name of our Lord and Savior, I ask you to bow your heads in prayer and ask forgiveness for all your sins. Committing yourselves to the Ascension will forgive all you have sinned. Pray now, quietly. It's your time to speak with the Lord and be forgiven."

With that, I clasped my hands and joined them. All was quiet except for some light muttering of prayers from some of them. Unlike them, I was not praying. I was thinking.

"Amen," I said.

Enough time had passed for them to have finished.

"I'll take the two of you after service, along with … my disobedient Protectorate." I looked them all in the eye with stern disdain.

They were suitably cowed.

"The rest of you shall join me at the Long Beach Shoreline Marina, Rainbow Harbor, next Saturday at six p.m. I have procured a boat for us all. We'll wash away our sins in the ocean as we receive the final blessing before the Ascension begins. The Angel has decreed it so. Go forth and enjoy your final mortal days before we rise together!" I said.

They looked scared but happy. Ascension is what we all dream of. The world, and especially America, had given in to sin. Things that once were an abomination, things that would have a sinner put to death on the spot, were now being "defended" as though spitting in the face of God was some new "right."

Blasphemers all!

I broke my daze and said, "See you all this Saturday."

I ended the service and insisted that only the Protectorate and the two volunteers could stay. Once again, I admonished everyone to remain silent about our endeavor.

We assembled in the cloakroom for a second attempt. The time had arrived, and I had Paul and Cathrine get naked. I noticed a few men stealing glances at her comely naked body.

"Do not give in to the temptations of the flesh!" I scolded them.

The guilty men were suitably chastised.

"Sorry, Reverend," they said.

They turned to a very naked and pretty Cathrine and muttered, "Sorry, Cathrine."

She sheepishly said, "It's OK."

The two of them lay on the platform next to the altar. We all began to chant. Ultimately, I started seeing everything get brighter with that silver hue.

It is working as it did the first time so many months ago!

The light and the pain it brought were too much. With a frantic yell, I could hear the others crying out in pain as well, the blinding light became too much. I fell to the floor, as did the others, unconscious.

Once again, I woke to the setting sun. Paul and Cathrine were already gone. I tried to comfort myself and reign in my fear. The inhuman creatures all around me were not helping. Others, who had just awoken, saw my fear but assumed it was from the ordeal we had just experienced. In reality, I was just worried that the Deathwalkers were gone when I awoke. I am sure that we have succeeded, however.

"You have all done well." I smiled. "Go now. I'll tell you more at Saturday's sermon. Be there at six; do not be late. The Ascension will be soon, and we shall all rise to Heaven together!"

I wondered darkly, where *had* the two Deathwalkers gone?

CHAPTER 13
BOLSA CHICA

The Alternate Plane of Existence
Ashta'goth

THE SHOCK of violently shifting back to its home plane was excruciating. Not from pain—it did not feel—but from rage. Now, it had to reach out to the priest again and start all over. Not that this was a problem. It had lived for thousands of years, so months—and even years—were the blink of an eye to it.

Last time, it had underestimated the speed and efficiency of these humans. They had destroyed the altar before it could be freed from it. This time, it would be released from the altar before starting its rampage of the entire world.

This time, it would be freed!

The priest would join the final *other* and use their combined power to bring Ashta'goth back to this world. He would go with Ashta'goth until he stopped being useful, at which point he would also be absorbed.

Ashta'goth has not yet fully understood humans. They were still new to it, so it did not anticipate the quick response from the first

Deathwalker attacks. It had sent out each of them just to cause mayhem. Each had figured out their own "best way" to do that. It did not think these *police* could backtrack their movements to the church. Their ability to find it using the Deathwalker corpses was impressive—so it needed to be much bigger this time before they eventually found it again. In its world, eating hundreds—or even thousands—of creatures in a day was normal. There was no "alarm" to deaths in its existence. It is strange how attached humans were to just a few measly deaths—it made no sense to it. But it had not grown to its size by being stupid; it learned. Quickly.

This time, it would grow in secret.

As it grew, it would shed the Uth'raliegh. What the humans had called "tentacle things." They were not highly intelligent but seemed more brutal than the humans they killed. In its plane of existence, they were primarily bottom-of-the-food-chain prey. They could follow basic commands:

Go to sounds and movement.

Kill living things.

That was about all they were suitable for—besides being eaten. They offered no sustenance, though. They were more like offal. Nourishing to lesser creatures, but a waste product to it. It would never have guessed they would be useful if not for how weak these humans were. It had decided that the humans who now followed the priest would no longer be needed.

He would have them brought together to be devoured by it.

Then, the priest and it would find a place to go afterward.

Somewhere isolated and away from other people, where it could eat the things it needed to get bigger and bigger in secret. But first, the priest had to do one final chant to release it. It would still be tied to the altar that the new conduit—the priest—had used to summon the *Others*. Once freed, though, it could move and grow.

It could already get the priest to open the floodgates to its plane of existence if it wanted to. But the trick was only to open it far enough and long enough for it to get through. It wanted this plane to itself.

No predators, only prey.

Time to talk to the priest again.

———

Monday—the Hope Church of Salvation
The Reverend

The release of the third *Other* was more accessible this time. It was Monday, the day after the sermon. Everything went smoothly, and the *Other* appeared on the pedestal—just like last time. The creatures from beyond were swirling around me. But now they were a comfort. I laughed and laughed. My hands had started to tremble and would not stop. I was weary of this earthly existence and longed to be one with my new master. To witness His weapon of Armageddon and the great destruction it would cause before rising into the sky. All I had to do was one last chant, and it would be free! Free to bring forth the End Times. It was glorious! I smiled nonstop. Well, when I wasn't laughing anyway.

The last *Other* called me to it.

From the Angel and the scripture of the tome, I knew that I must join it to have the power needed to call forth my Lord and free it from the altar.

I put out my hand.

It stretched out its amorphous body and grabbed my outstretched hand. I could feel the creature's heat as a thousand little cilia and a hundred tentacles pulled it up my arm. It left a horrible-smelling purplish slime as it touched my shoulder. Sensing where I was most vulnerable, it encircled my neck. But it did not harm me.

It was like a writhing scarf protecting me! It was so comforting ...

I felt hundreds of little stings as it latched on to me. I would be carrying it, but it was there to protect me. Somehow, I just knew.

Suddenly, I could feel the change within me.

The suffering of others was part of God's plan all along! Even the most pious among us must suffer for our sins at the hands of Ashta'-goth and his servitors. I no longer felt any remorse, only joy in their suffering—in my suffering. Our physical bodies were not our immortal ones.

With my task of summoning Ashta'goth completed again, it was time to free him from the altar …

The final incantation took several days. I did not sleep, eat, or bathe. Finally, it was done.

Like a little purple/grey clay ball, the tiny creature that sat patiently waiting on the pedestal would become the great Devourer.

The salvation of our souls.

It looked so small and helpless. I felt a sudden urge—I was hungry to eat it—but I resisted. As I finished the final words, I could see the lump of clay pulsating. This incantation was much more potent, as I was a Deathwalker now. It could bring more of itself into our plane this time.

Suddenly, it was everywhere.

The little ball grew. I started to see mouths open and shut, horrible sharp teeth inside each one. That same purplish goo was oozing out of a hundred orifices. Tentacles and cilia sprouted everywhere. Then, the tentacles started sprouting barbs, suckers, and stingers. Everywhere was swirling. Things appearing and being reabsorbed. I watched mouths hungrily eating any tentacle that came near them. There was a din of squelching, screeching, babbling mouths, and smacking sounds. It was impossible to stop looking …

Something in me was different now.

Deep in my heart, I knew this was God's true Messenger, and I would do anything for my new Lord! Knowing that others would die horrible deaths by joining it did not concern me—it excited me! This was the most beautiful thing I had ever seen, and I yearned to be one with it—for all of time. That would be a gift on my way to Heaven. I reached out to touch my Lord without thought, and a mouth snapped at me—

SNAP!

The stump of my arm, where my hand once was, started spurting blood. Laughing maniacally, I sprayed it all over my new God. Mouths hungrily formed, and grotesque, alien tongues licked up every drop. Suddenly, I felt woozy, and my eyelids slowly dropped …

I awoke to a new sensation; I had enjoyed feeding myself to it! My greatest desire now is to serve and please Ashta'goth, the Devourer!

Looking down at my arm, I could see that everything, from my wrist down, was now a writhing mass of tentacles.

It is beautiful! Thank you, my Lord, thank you!

The Numil'e, as my Lord told me the *Others* are called, had moved to my arm and made this beautiful appendage! I was eternally thankful.

However, I kept my distance from my Lord this time as I prayed to it.

My Lord was entirely here now—It filled the room. There were flying monstrosities everywhere that would pop out of it and fly around the room, only for most to be eaten again by mouths—or seized and pulled into it by tentacles. I kept away from it this time, for I knew it would absorb me. Even though I longed for that, my master said there were things I must do first—

My first command now was guiding it. We would head into the one place the humans could not go—where food is plentiful and would not be missed. My flock would also go there to join with it forever …

I struggled to walk back to my bed; I was exhausted like I had never been before. I fell asleep almost immediately.

When I awoke late the next morning, the sun shone brightly in the room. Everything was so vividly colored. I reached for my nightstand and felt for my glasses. Finding them, I put them on reflexively. Everything around me was blurry, giving me a headache, so I took them off.

Good Lord!

My vision was perfect.

I was no longer nearsighted. I looked down and saw my feet hanging over the edge of the bed. The bed groaned as I got up. Something had happened—something marvelous. I went to the bathroom and looked in the mirror in astonishment!

While I was sleeping, the *Other* had changed me into a Deathwalker.

I was now a very tall man, highly muscular with very little body fat. My hair had grown out and was jet black. Plus, my eyes had miraculously changed color! They were now deep black, the color of the abyss. I was now a very imposing figure!

Perfect for my sermons.

The other good news is that I looked so different that if a BOLO was put out for me, the average cop could not recognize me now. They would be looking for a 5-foot, 8-inch, 160-pound man. One that was ordinary looking, with slight muscle and average body fat.

That man was gone—only the Deathwalker version of me remained.

How things change …

———

Saturday—6 p.m.—Long Beach Shoreline Marina, Rainbow Harbor

I spoke amiably with my flock as they boarded the boat. Their astonishment at my transformation only increased my authority.

"The time has come. The time to be cleansed and freed from your sins before the Ascension begins—" I began.

"Reverend, what miracle has occurred to change you so?" Sue Bernal interrupted.

If she had some feelings for me before, they were downright covetous now. No worries, all her sins would be washed away …

"Hello, Sue—" I smiled warmly, and the attention was still welcomed. "As you all can see, I am now a Deathwalker."

There were several gasps from some, but all listened with rapt attention.

"Today—the day of cleansing—has arrived. We will be on the water shortly. Captain Orin Kloss will give you a briefing before we start; please give him your complete attention …"

I stepped aside as everyone boarded, and Captain Kloss came down from the flybridge to give a matter-of-fact safety briefing. He had clearly given it many times before, as he did it all from rote. As he spoke, the boat was heading out to sea. After ensuring everyone was comfortable and knew all the safety rules, he left to man the helm.

It felt surreal. Here we were, all enjoying the ride out deep into the Pacific Ocean as I led them to their gruesome deaths …

It *was* a lovely evening, though. The sun was low on the horizon, and the boat stopped and bobbed gently in the water. Looking toward the stern, I could see no sign of land.

Good. We are far enough out now.

"Alright, everyone!" I shouted so that all could hear me. "One at a time, women and children first. Help each other into the water, please!"

I watched and waited as everyone else from the church got into the water on the boat's port side. Once they were all in, I addressed them from the side of the ship.

"Today is a blessed day!" I yelled. "For the End Times have already started, and your day of ascension has come!"

Their eyes were big as they bobbed in the swells of the ocean, and they all wore life vests—safety first, of course. I heard cries of joy. Some were clearly crying in happiness as well.

"Do not be afraid. The Harbinger is here. You may call it—Ashta'goth, the Devourer!"

The crew looked at me with big grins. They looked at each other and rolled their eyes, and some even laughed.

Nonbelievers, I thought.

They would be having a much harder time than us. While my flock will rise to their salvation, the heretics will be left behind. Ashta'goth, the Devourer, would destroy all. But a lake of fire was in the crew's eternal future …

The first person went under without any warning—it had begun.

"What the hell?!" The ship's captain yelled.

The crew saw and was already getting the gear to save whoever went under.

They stopped cold at what they saw next.

Tentacles emerged from the water everywhere around the boat.

They were an unnatural shade of purple and grey and covered with barbs, suckers, and stingers.

AAHH! HELP! AAHH! SQUISH!—

Some of the people were immediately pulled under, only to see a big bubble of blood and gore surface where they once were. Others were picked up out of the water for all to see. It then scrunched them in its tentacles, like they were ripe bananas—squishing out their guts—before pulling their corpses under the waves.

Everyone was screaming and trying to swim to the boat, and the sea was red with blood …

It should bother me more; why does it not bother me?

Seeing the children being tortured, especially, should bother me—at least a little. Some of me still had empathy—but it was small and fading fast. God must have wanted his pound of flesh. That is why the horror they are enduring must be happening: It punishes them for their earthly sins before letting them ascend.

Yes, that must be it!

One last corporal punishment for their atonement.

I smiled.

Indeed, they were fortunate to receive His blessing, regardless of their pain and fear. In the end, all would be as foretold.

They were free and blessed now.

I could feel the boat tilt as the captain turned the helm toward shore and started to apply throttle.

We can't have that, can we?

Drawing my pistol, I walked up to the flybridge. The captain turned and opened his mouth to ask something angrily—but no one will ever know his question.

BANG!

My pistol spit fire and put a round into his open mouth.

Saturday—9 p.m.—Bolsa Chica Beach
Christy

"Goddammit, Kevin!" I yelled.

He laughed as he ran off. He had dropped an ice cube in my bra.

Kevin was a good-looking man. He had the tan everyone in Southern California seemed to have, but his was darker from the weekends he spent surfing. He wasn't a bodybuilder but was tall with taut muscles and the palest blue eyes I had ever seen. I could feel myself getting aroused; it felt good.

My large breasts were visible in my bikini top in the firelight, and he was obviously into me.

We all decided that a beachfront party with a fire and some music would be the way to end a semester of study at Cal State Long Beach. We chose Bolsa Chica Beach and had a nice fire in one of the rings. Even though alcohol was not allowed, our colas were heavily "fortified," and we had all eaten marijuana gummies like candy.

So, we were all having a lot of fun.

Chris was playing the guitar, and he was pretty good at it. Sherry and her boyfriend Craig were chatting in the shallow surf. Everyone was mellow and having a good time. I looked over at Kevin, who was smiling at me while talking with his buddy, Chip.

I thought about Kevin fondly—*F— it, why not?* I thought.

"Hey, Kevin."

He turned and looked at me.

"Are you just going to leave this ice cube, or will you come get it out?" I asked.

I resisted laughing as his eyes almost bulged out of his head. The others did laugh, and I could see the other men discreetly ogling me, knowing what was next.

He came right over and sat down next to me. He reached out slowly and ran his hand down my left breast. The others were watching and smirking. He reached lower into my bikini top. My nipples hardened as he caressed my breast.

"Keep looking," I said in a husky voice.

His hand felt *so* good … He put his other hand around my waist. My excitement grew as he ran his hand over to my other breast next.

The ice cube had melted, and he slid his hand nicely inside my bikini top. His other hand reached up to unfasten my top.

"No," I said. "Public beach, remember?"

I leaned over his ear and whispered, "You can have it all; if you have a place, we can go …" I could see him react immediately. From the sudden bulge, it looked like he was well-endowed, too—

"Help!" Sherry suddenly screamed in terror from the water.

She was only wading in the gentle surf.

"He went under!" She screamed.

How? They were only waist deep, and the tide was mellow; there was no significant undertow.

We all jumped up.

My libido was now at zero as I watched Sherry frantically trying to locate where Craig had gone under.

We all ran into the water to help look for him …

———

Ashta'goth

Floating just offshore, Ashta'goth waited.

It thought about what had happened. One of the crew had made it to the radio to put out a mayday. Too bad its tentacle reached in and took him before he could. They all screamed in terror as it took them down one by one. Sometimes, it even raised a part of itself to torture them more so that others could see. In the sun's dying rays, the last of them were pulled under and into it. Several had tried to swim away, only to be grabbed and pulled into it. Some of the cultists were excellent swimmers; Those it pulled in, over and over, until they tired. Then it would nibble little bites out of them.

It fed on their terror as much as it did on their flesh.

"The police" had ruined its fun last time. The cultists were enjoyable, but the police had to be killed too quickly for its taste. It looked forward to more of them coming again. Perhaps it could stretch out their deaths more for its enjoyment …

After killing all except the priest, it grabbed the boat's keel and pulled it close to shore. As it cruised in toward shore, Reverend Turner dumped the captain's body overboard. As it hit the water, Ashta'goth grabbed him and added him to its preponderance.

Once close to the beach, the priest dived in and swam to shore. After seeing that he was safely ashore, it pulled the boat back, far out to sea, and then sunk it to the bottom.

There, Ashta'goth stayed.

Floating underwater and sensing the ocean around it, all the way to the shore, it could "see," in its alien way, both short and long distances simultaneously in all directions. Night had fallen, but that did not affect its senses; bright light and complete darkness did not affect its abilities.

It was glad it had decided to use the priest as a guide. He had recommended the ocean, which was safe because humans couldn't see well in it. The ocean's fish and creatures had helped it grow but didn't nurture its need for an adversary.

In its existence, it had to fight or run from creatures that were bigger or more brutal than it. The need for a challenge was growing.

It sensed prey nearby—a shark was moving toward it. The smell of blood drew it in like a siren song. It came in fast and bit out a massive chunk of it. The tentacles quickly seized it, and it suffered hundreds of bites as it was pulled in and eaten.

Ashta'goth moved on.

The water was much easier to move in as it glided along, instead of the plumping and bumping movement on land.

Next, it saw a pod of dolphins. Unlike the sharks it had eaten, they took one look at it and swam away as fast as they could. Luckily for them, it was faster than Ashta'goth could glide after them. It watched as the dolphins receded into the distance and disappeared.

Time passed, and it waited in the darkness of depth and nighttime

...

Now, it sensed more life in the ocean nearby. Two humans were walking in the shallow water near the shore.

How insane these humans must be!

To walk into something where predators lurked, especially at night when they could not see. Predators that they could not hope to see or sense in time.

Why would they do something so stupid?

No matter. It knew it would bring those "other humans" the priest spoke of, but it desired to fight and absorb them anyway. It was already far too big to move into the shallows, so it let itself stretch and thin out.

It encircled all around them.

The first one was yanked down so fast that the other let out a terrified scream; oh, how it enjoyed their terror! It could feel the one it grabbed panicking as it slowly absorbed him. Hundreds of mouths had formed to chew him to bits and pull him inside. The tentacles that had grabbed him helped feed him—and the remaining floating parts of him —to the mouths. Soon, more people waded in.

Amazed, it was.

Were they committing suicide? Did they want to die?

It knew these deaths would bring the police, but they would be coming soon anyway. For this reason, the priest advised it against eating his entire congregation, but it thrived on adversarial confrontation. With no predators to run from, it was bored with easy prey.

It wanted a challenge!

Wandering the sea near the shore, it absorbed anything alive that was unfortunate enough to cross its path.

It was already bigger than any creature on Earth.

———

Saturday—10 p.m.—Bolsa Chica Beach
Officer Janet

Officer Janet Greggs had gotten the swing shift. She would be off work in one more hour. Even though Saturday was the last day of her work week.

She wondered to herself if this was what she wanted.

LAPD had been courting her to apply with them. It would be good to work on actual serious crimes instead of policing a bunch of college kids to make sure they were following the mundane laws on drinking, drugs, and public indecency.

Walking along, she could see the fire on the beach. Fires were supposed to be out by ten p.m. Sighing, she walked over. As she got closer, she could see no one nearby.

An unattended fire? God, these college kids were something. Was it so hard to put out a fire before you left …

This did not put her in a good mood. When she found them, these kids would get a talking-to, maybe even a ticket or two.

Huh, that's weird, she thought.

As she got closer, she could see the fire had been tended to recently, and that's not all. There were clothes, blankets, food and drinks, and even a guitar. All were just left there like everyone had gotten up suddenly.

What? They just left? Who leaves behind a guitar?

Cop-sense tingling, she keyed her radio.

"Adam Six to dispatch—"

A very short delay. "Dispatch, go Adam Six."

"I have an unattended fire at the beach, but maybe a half dozen people left all of their stuff, including a guitar and clothes—" She broke comms for a moment. "There is no sign of foul play, but no one leaves everything like this. Something is up. I need backup to my location."

I slowly turned in place. Everyone else on the beach had left, and there were no sounds of talking or laughing. I was alone on the beach, with only the sound of the waves gently lapping on shore, not even an annoying gull. This was eerily peculiar; something felt very off.

"Emergent?" Dispatch asked me.

"No. But don't waste time, either. Expedite, not urgent."

"Copy. Units in route."

"Copy. Out."

While I waited for backup, I felt uneasy. It looked like I might be getting some overtime tonight.

I put on nitrile gloves and went through the missing people's belongings: cell phones, wallets—with IDs, credit cards, and money—and car keys. No, they had not left. They had been taken.

What the hell?

The other two squad cars arrived in under five minutes.

"Hey, Greggs, what-we-got?" That was Donald Paulson.

He was a good guy, but he sometimes mushed his words together.

"Well, it looks like we have seven missing college-aged kids. Their IDs all show them in their early to late twenties. They left wallets, car keys, clothes, you name it, along with a lit fire," I told him.

"Damn, no one does that," he said.

"Yup," I agreed.

He looked at the other officer who had shown up. "Guess we need to call in Search and Rescue," he said.

He reached up and keyed his mic, "Sam Two, this is Adam Three. Over."

Our police radios made a little "bleep" at the end of transmissions, so saying "over" was redundant. However, at least for the prior military, it is a tough habit to break.

"Sam Two, go ahead."

"We need S&R and divers to our location. We have seven missing persons under unusual circumstances. Over."

"Will do. I'm en route to you. Fill me in when I get there."

"Copy that, see you soon. Out."

Sergeant Williams, Sam Two, showed up about ten minutes later. Several other officers arrived to tape the area as a crime scene while waiting for CSI.

This would be a tough one for them.

Beaches aren't known for their ability to preserve forensic evidence, so they knew they had to hurry up.

They made it out admirably fast, but it was still well past midnight by the time the scene was secure, and they were well into evidence collection.

A couple of divers had shown up, along with a police boat, to try to light up the water. Luckily, it was late enough that there were no looky-loos. In today's modern world, that meant live feed videos that invariably caught the media's attention—the last thing we wanted.

Also, the lieutenant had been woken up, and, probably out of spite as much as duty, he woke up the captain.

Swell.

If there weren't any foul play, I would be the butt of jokes for the next month.

I looked out over the water at the boat circling. Shining its spotlight down into the depths, there was no hope they would see something. But it gave the divers some light. They had finished suiting up and flipped over backward into the dark water. There was nothing more for me to do tonight.

"Hey, Sarge, do you still need me, or can I go in, give that report, and go home?"

"No. You're done. Go ahead and do the report and call it a night," Sergeant Williams said as I turned to go.

"Hey," he said.

I turned back to him.

"Good job. There is definitely something very wrong here. Have a good night, Greggs."

"Night, Sergeant," I replied.

I headed back to the station to finish my report and then go home, glad to know I was done with my part.

It turns out that was far from the case.

———

Ashta'goth

Ashta'goth, now far out at sea, could sense the ship near the shore. A few well-adapted humans with fish-like fin feet had dived into the water at night. Ashta'goth couldn't help but admire their bravery, though not their stupidity. It would typically have come closer and devoured these fish people, perhaps even giving their boat a few "taps" to scare them. However, the priest had warned Ashta'goth of something they called "Sonar"—a tool that could "see" any significant thing's size, shape, and movement. Ashta'goth had no fear of them; the decision to spare them was methodical. It wanted the ones that came before—these *police* and *SWAT* creatures. Besides, the priest had said the *federal* ones would also come and probably be ready for it this time.

If it could laugh, it would. They would not be prepared, but they would be much more fun for it.

It floated in place and watched. It would not be long …

CHAPTER 14

MISSING PERSONS

Saturday—8 p.m.—OST DENFO
Agent James

WE WERE all in the Morale, Welfare, and Recreation room. I could see vending machines, an arcade machine with several thousand built-in games, foosball, a pool table, a card table, and many books and board games. Plus, there were a bunch of comfy chairs and a section in the corner to watch a big-screen TV. There was also a dart board. It was not precisely home, but it was a lot better than nothing when we were on QRF status and done training for the day.

I went over to the "library," which was an entire wall of books. I was looking forward to a light-hearted comedy or maybe even a comic book. I started perusing the titles and authors:

H. P. Lovecraft, Anne Rice, Mark Everett Stone, Steven King.

Compendium of Monsters, Lore and Legend, The Deep Ones.

Hmm. I guess only books about learning our enemy.

I finally found "On Combat"—a book about, you guessed it, surviving combat.

It would have been nice to read this *before* I joined OST …

Most of us had already been reading horror books, not for fun, but to learn about future enemies. That was Chayton's idea. I sat in one of the comfortable chairs across from Lev. We shared a warm smile. It didn't take long before we all headed to our rooms for an evening of shut-eye.

Lev winked at me as she left the room. It was strange to see she had to consciously blink. I had gotten used to her not blinking or sweating—even though she was uncomfortably warm to the touch.

Looks like I may get to sleep a little later than the others.

———

We were all dead asleep when the overhead page came—

BEEP! "All QRF, report to BRIEFING room. I say again, all QRF, report to BRIEFING."

That was Chayton's voice.

Oh, crud, this can't be good.

I threw on my clothes and shoes. We had been told we had ten minutes to get there unless he said STAT, which meant skip your clothes and get your ass there on the double. I arrived in six minutes and was the second-to-last person to arrive. Skag was last and looked particularly bedraggled. Eight minutes past the page, he turned off the clock on the wall. It had big red LED numbers that had counted down to 1:53.

"That was a good response. Now, grab a coffee from the mess, and be back in 5," Chayton said.

We did so. It was now 0352 in the morning. Once we were all reassembled, he got started. The projector already had a police report up on the screen. A Long Beach Police Department officer named Janet Greggs had submitted the report at 0155. Alan's team found it at 0325, and he woke Chayton to report it. Then Chayton sent out the overhead page at 0338; it was also surprisingly loud.

"OK, I know you're all eager to start," Chayton said without any hint of sarcasm.

Chayton looked like he had a whole night's rest, even though he was also in clothes he had thrown on in a hurry. I hated how he could always look like that, even without sleep. It's almost like he was a former marine or something.

"As you can see, we got a suspicious report. I know you've all read it by now," he said.

"Seven people disappeared from a beach in Southern California. They left everything behind and were gone without a trace. I hate to say this, but we might have another OI."

"Good. I want payback." That was Morris.

We all nodded our agreement.

"I'm glad to hear that. Just make sure to keep it professional, not emotional. Check?"

A chorus of "Checks."

"Alright, this happened on Bolsa Chica Beach in Long Beach, California. Harbor Police and divers are looking for any signs of them as we speak. Nothing yet," Chayton said.

Alan came into the briefing room and talked quickly with Chayton alone. He then left, probably back to the MCC. He looked haggard. We got up early, but he had been up. Chayton turned to us; it was time to get the show on the road.

"Time to go snooping around. Team Bravo will be Morris and James, and Levingston and Skaggs will be Charlie. Alan is staying. I want his help in MCC this time, plus he needs to crash; he has been up for a while … We'll take the POVs to Centennial Airport, so load them up with your stuff. I am Team Alpha, and my call sign is Frank One if you need me. We'll meet in the armory for an equipment issue—"

Chayton stopped and looked at his watch.

"At 0515. Get cleaned up, eat something, and pack your bags in your POVs. See you at armory."

I returned to my little "dorm" room, showered, and grabbed my already-packed bags. As I bent to pick them up, I could feel my pistol dig into my waist. I had developed callouses, in a non-sexy way, from carrying the gun in my front, center waistband area. Fast on the draw from concealment, but not great for comfort.

I went to the garage bay and threw my stuff into the car. It was a silver, new-generation Tesla Model S long-range—or at least it looked like one. The car was actually a new Model S Plaid; they just removed the "Plaid" badge and repainted the brake calipers. Now, it was "just" a Long-Range model to anyone looking.

They must have an agreement with Tesla or something. The car drew some attention, but they wanted that HVAC system with the "Bioweapon Defense Mode." No joke: they call it that at Tesla.

Let's hope we don't have to test the accuracy of the term.

I found out they originally wanted to put an old Model S body on it, but it was impractical. And they needed the new one's power, range, and weight capacity. It also allowed it to have excellent handling, an adjustable suspension, and enough horsepower to handle all the extra weight, which was substantial. It had the new battery system that Tesla had developed, so it had about 300 miles of range, even with over a thousand horsepower.

It also had the "track pack" to reach a 206-mph top speed. Nobody in their right mind would go that fast in a car that weighs over 4,800 pounds stock. Ours weighed in several hundred pounds heavier. They mainly wanted it to have the adjustability of the optional track package. Ours would not quite have the range and acceleration of the original because of all the extra weight.

They also had the new "Smart Tint" window films. These were dimmable from transparent to opaque. When parked, it turned opaque black. It's important to conceal our gear and weapons. Having someone look in and see them would quickly become a problem.

We were also guinea pigs for a new heavy-duty run-flat tire that Pirelli had made. They were developing new tires for a military contract and agreed to make a test run with the tires for our cars. They looked like the Pirelli Zeros that came with it but were heavily reinforced to reduce the chance of failure. Why didn't they have these on the new cars? As you can guess, it made for a much louder and bumpier ride.

I noticed Greg Morris's stuff was already in the back, so I added mine. I hit the button, and the tailgate automatically came down, and I went off to mess to grab breakfast and a coffee.

At 0515, we all met in armory. Chayton had already set up our

ExoM suits with all the mandatory gear and loaded magazines in pouches attached.

We just had to add weapons.

He gave us each a bandolier of flash-bang grenades since we knew they at least stunned the last ones. That was in addition to the six already on the armor. We picked out our choice of pistol, as long as it was a Glock 19, and were also issued an MP5 SMG, an M700PSS sniper rifle with a starlight scope, and a lethal-looking assault rifle—

It was an FN SCAR H-Mk2 with the 40GL grenade launcher attached below it on one of the Picatinny rails. It had the RFID tag for tracking it, at least at close range, the "Smartcore" shot counter, to see exactly how many shots remained, and the FCU Mk3. The Mk3 measured and calculated range, temperature, and slope angle to adjust the aiming point for a first-round hit. It used visible and IR lasers to determine the range and to "Laz," or laser, the target before firing. It's too bad that our grenades were only flash-bangs and smoke.

We had already been to Buckley Space Force Base several times to practice with all of them on their ranges, and we had become quite proficient. The Bureau had "borrowed" a FAM instructor and a military instructor to teach us the weapon systems. They all sounded sci-fi but were commercially available weapon systems—not some ultra-secret new ones.

We even looked them up on the Internet.

They were not available to standard citizens but only to the military and police. I appreciated that all our weapons used the same 9mm and 7.62mm bullets for interchangeability.

With all the full magazines on the armor, we just had to grab the rifles and SMG and holster the pistol onto it. We found it was easier to get into the armor, carry everything to the car, and then take the armor off and throw it in. Plus, we had done exactly that dozens of times already. It was a drill Chayton made us practice regularly until we were very fast at it.

The car's rear was already set up with spots for storing everything. Although the original vehicle had room for four, or five in a pinch, the back was now designed around three "operators." There was only one rear seat now to allow space for all three complete gear sets. Casual inspection from the outside would reveal nothing unusual, but inside, it had been gutted and rebuilt for mission purposes. The third person was there solely to guard the car. The NMC guys always did that. They assigned one to each vehicle, and they always sat in the back right seat. Each of our battle-buddy teams got one car.

They had assigned me as Bravo team leader, with Morris as my new BB. Lev was given Skaggs. Chayton was solo, except for his NMC agent, since Alan was sitting this one out from going to the field. We hit the sally port individually and headed to Centennial Airport.

Our three cars arrived at Centennial Airport with no problems. Traffic was light this early in the morning, and we were there quickly.

Once we made it to our hangar, we pulled in, and they shut the door behind us. Sure enough, a man in Air Force fatigues was there to help load our vehicles properly onto the plane. It was a military C-130 cargo plane. Each BB team had one car, so we had three in total.

Plus, the not-so-subtle Model X was already locked in place. That was one of the NMC vehicles. They declined to elaborate but said it was for "heavy-fire backup."

Not ominous at all ...

I would have preferred the NMC guys to join us instead of babysitting cars, but they had their orders. The government didn't want to risk losing automatic weapons, grenades, and modified cars to a tow truck or thief. Besides, guarding valuable vehicles and what was in them was kinda their thing ...

Each ExoM suit alone was valued at over $100,000.

OK, we are officially *way* better prepared than we were the first time! No crazy spy stuff or space-age military hardware, but all the stuff an agent could want. Although damn suspicious that we had all of it.

Now that we were prepared, the airman gave us a final in-flight emergency brief in case of a crash or other emergency during the flight. We completed our final preparations, and once we received clearance, we took off into the sky.

It was that time of year in Denver when we rarely had snow, and when we did, the sun had melted it all away the next day. At least there was no snow where we were going in California.

We landed later that morning and went to the exit through Edwards Air Force Base, i.e., AFB. There was a line of cars this morning, but it was a short wait. We drove down the I-15 and I-405 freeways until we reached Long Beach. Morris and I went to see Long Beach PD while Chayton, Lev, and Skaggs started looking into local leads.

Sadly, in civilian clothes, I could only hide the handgun and a switchblade knife. The rest was just too bulky.

They had issued us "bulletproof clothing," however. Fancy new bullet-resistant T-shirts that cost a pretty penny, I am sure. They were warmer but looked like regular clothes.

Crazy, the new stuff that is available on the market today.

Our "T-shirts" combined limited aspects of both bullet and knife resistance. Not that the impact wouldn't suck royally. But a bullet or blade *inside me* would be worse. I had never been stabbed or shot … yet.

Jesus, this new job was as dangerous as all get-out.

I am glad the G had our back on this one. They had seriously raided the piggy bank for this group.

———

Morris and I pulled into the Long Beach PD, or LBPD, visitor lot and got out. Edward "Ed" Baker, the one Lev and I had teased months ago, stayed with the car. He was still quiet but now talked some with us on the drive.

There was a news van out front; That was not great news for us.

Luckily, we weren't in the blacked-out Suburban, or they would have been all over us. Not that I have a problem with the press, mind you. It's just that I don't want to have to skirt questions and have my face on the news while doing undercover work.

I wonder what story they were here for?

We walked up to the receptionist, who sat behind a thick "glass" window—probably bullet-resistant.

"Agents Grey and Morris, here to see Sergeant Williams," I said.

The woman smiled; her name tag said "Vicky."

She buzzed us in.

Once inside, we saw an officer of average height, probably 5 feet, 10 inches, a fit Black male with Sergeant stripes and "WILLIAMS" on his name tag.

"Sergeant Williams, it's good to meet you. My name is Greg Morris; this is James Grey," Morris said.

He looked at both of us and said, "It's great to have you both here. I assume you're helping with the case of missing persons."

We both nodded affirmatively.

"Which one?" he asked.

Morris and I looked at each other; It wasn't lost on Sergeant Williams. He chuckled.

"Guess you didn't know of our most recent development," he said.

"Turns out an entire group of people, including entire families, have just disappeared on the same night as our seven college kids. They took out a boat and never returned."

I felt sick—and it showed.

Morris saw my look, and his wasn't much better.

Sergeant Williams, being a police officer, did not miss our visceral reactions to what he said.

"Uh-oh." That was all he said before adding, "What is going on? And don't BS me."

"Is there somewhere we can talk privately?" I motioned as we were still in the entry lobby.

He nodded, and we headed to the back of the station and entered a small briefing room.

"OK," I started. "Yes, we knew of the seven. No, we did not know about the other group."

I handed him a nondisclosure agreement/sensitive documents release form.

He took it and skimmed it. After the Colorado Springs incident, the government needed to keep things under wraps.

"That bad, huh," he said when he looked up.

"Worse," said Morris.

"OK. I need to verify with Captain Billings first, but I'm sure he'll be down with it—whatever *it* is. Although, I may as well bring him one of these too." He lifted the document.

I handed him another.

"We are trying to limit the number of people in the know. Can we trust it to be just you and him for now?"

He shot me a stern look.

"Look, we're going to share everything necessary to protect you and your officers, and you have every right to do the same," I said and handed him a few more of the release forms. "But once we brief you, you'll understand why this must be kept hush-hush. There won't be anything officially written down from the briefing. Agreed?"

He nodded his head and left. A few minutes later, he came back with the captain beside him.

"I'm Captain Ron Billings. Nice to meet you." He shook our hands as we introduced ourselves. He motioned to the seats, and everyone except me sat down—time to start.

"OK, the reason I looked like I ate a turnip when you told me about the boat is because that happened before … with an entire church," I said.

The sergeant and captain both sat up straighter in their seats. I had their undivided attention.

"We are fighting an enemy that killed everyone in the New Era Revivalist Church in Colorado Springs."

Their eyes were bulging now.

"And killed an entire twelve-man SWAT team from CSPD. I was there."

"Oh … My God—" That was the captain.

"What in the hell did you bring us?" He was starting to get angry.

I laughed, and they looked at me like I was insane.

"I can promise you one thing, captain. I did not 'bring' these monsters. That was someone else; someone bad."

There was utter silence.

"Please explain yourself," the captain said *way* too calmly.

I could tell he was getting ready to go off.

The fact that I was telling him about a massive cover-up of what actually happened in Colorado Springs was not the best way to ingratiate yourself with an officer of the law …

"The explosion in Colorado Springs *was* an explosion. But it was commercially available demolition blasting charges that the cult was using to booby trap the entrances. They were ready for a siege. They had extra charges in the rectory because it was a much bigger boom than we expected. They were pulling shrapnel out of me for weeks."

Sergeant Williams blanched a little at that. Many scars on my face and arms from the surgeries were still clearly visible.

The captain then asked, "Are you telling me that an entire SWAT team was killed by a church full of cultists, *and* you killed them all and blew up the church? Or the monsters did? Or, what?"

I smiled and said, "No. The cultists had barricaded themselves inside the church. That was their plan: to stay and fight. However, it turns out that barricading themselves in *with* the monsters was a bad idea. We found the cultists—or I should say pieces of cultists—everywhere.

"When we breached, it blew some of their booby traps. Once inside, we contacted multiple tentacle things. We are abbreviating them as TTs now. My math is fuzzy; I was a bit busy then, but we figured out it was at least twenty of them in total. Probably more."

"Don't forget the Big One," Morris added.

They saw the sick look on my face.

"The Big One is not something you ever want to face, and I mean that literally. Lev—she is another one of our agents—has seen it, and she tried to describe it to me. I never saw it, but the sounds it made were beyond horrible. I still have nightmares every night about it. And so does Lev, as you can imagine. I can promise you that you'll never be the same if you see it."

They could see the bags under my eyes and the tortured look on my face.

I continued, "The Big One is almost un-killable. I don't think every bullet we had could have killed it. Sergeant Donaldson and his team sacrificed their lives to set up the demo charges. The ones I detonated."

I took a minute. Talking about it again really sucked.

Morris gave me a questioning look. The one that said, *do you need me to take over?* I subtly shook my head no.

"Please dim the lights and turn on the projector," I said.

Morris booted up the laptop and turned on the projector. He then used my encrypted flash drive to access the PowerPoint presentation for the OI briefing. A picture of a vivisected SIM popped up on the screen.

"Woah," said Williams.

The captain covered his mouth. I think he may have almost barfed.

"W-T-F is that?" I started. "*That* is a SIM. Short for a Simulant. It's a bigger, stronger, and much faster version of the person it was created from. And, before you say it, we have fought them already, and no, they are not f—ing human. They are aliens, or whatever; all we know is the lab tests come back inconclusive and that the parasite forms a symbiotic fusion of man and it. This means that the alien parts don't match anything on record. I'll wait while this all sinks in." I sat down and crossed my arms.

I will give them credit. They took it well.

"Wow, you aren't joking, are you?" the captain said.

"No, these things are lethal," I responded. "It takes a shot to the brain stem to kill one of the SIMs. Everywhere else just pisses them off. Your packets—which you'll not keep—tell you everything about them and what we know. I hope you can understand why we don't want this to be a department-wide memo."

I pulled out a stack of the nondisclosure agreement forms.

"It is your call, captain, but I recommend reading in everyone on SWAT and any officers you assign to a task force to deal with this. And only use them. Everyone you tell will think you are f—ing with them until you have them come in for another briefing with me. But if we don't tell them, we risk them more. They need to know everything we know about these things. What works and what doesn't, and what they are capable of."

Both nodded, and they started to read, eyes getting wider. I waited until they had finished.

"The fact that another entire group of people is unaccounted for cannot be a coincidence. I guess whoever summoned the Big One somehow survived the last attacks. Or worse, there is more than one sect of cultists," I said. "Let's hope it's the first."

"So, you are saying there are many of them ..." The captain's finger scrolled down the document.

"TTs, SIMs, and the Big One?" he asked as he looked back up.

He looked like he had eaten the same turnip I did.

"Yup," I replied.

"The 'good news'—" I did the finger air-quotes motion "is when we killed the big one, the others seemed to die along with it. So, they are connected somehow."

"Yeah, and the bad news is it's somehow back, right?" Williams said.

I let out a deep sigh.

"It looks that way, yes."

"Alright, if you are for real, what do you need? If not, and you are playing some stupid joke, I'll put you in jail for false reporting, Fed or no Fed," the captain said.

"Fair enough ... I need you to get me whatever officers you decide to put on the task force and have them get that briefing with me ASAP," I replied.

Captain Billings nodded.

"You guys are pros at what you do. Share what you find out about the missing persons in both groups. We'll share what we find out. Our agencies will work together—for real—because our lives depend on it. I'll never stop feeling sick about that SWAT team ... and what they did to protect everyone, including me. Your officers will be in harm's way, so we need to know who to read in on the task force. I would recommend having SWAT on standby. Higher caliber rounds hurt them more, and flash-bang grenades stun the tentacle ones for at least a few seconds. It takes a clean shot to the brain-stem area to kill a SIM and a ton of bullets to kill the tentacle things."

"How much is a ton?" Williams asked.

"Around a hundred unless you get lucky. There is nothing to aim at; they are just a seven-foot ball of lethal tentacles. They kill by tearing off all your limbs at once—including this one," I pointed at my head.

Williams gulped. "Wow. This is not how I expected my day to go."

I laughed.

"Yeah, I never expected to be here either. I was an air marshal, not some 'X-Files' agent, until I ran into that SIM on my plane … Alright, now that you have finished the packets, we'll get started on this," I said. "Morris and I are not on vacation here. The other members of my team are out looking now as well. We want these creatures and any people involved found and neutralized as badly as you."

They gave me a stern look when I said: "neutralized."

"Look, you can arrest law-breaking people if they surrender. But make no mistake, the creatures are death incarnate. Please don't do anything but run or kill them. There is no 'arrest' with them. Trust me on this."

They both nodded, mollified.

"My turn, I guess," said the captain.

"The seven missing college kids and the 'boat group,'—what we call them for now—all left their vehicles in the parking lot. It looked like a damn car dealership. The boat group just left their cars. We got into all of them and got registrations, then impounded them. The boat group had left overgarments, leading us to believe they went onto the water. The "Siren's Song" tourist ship was chartered, with six crew, to take about thirty people onto the water yesterday at six p.m. It never returned. It had been registered as paid in full by one Paul Jones, who worked as a dishwasher in Huntington Beach. He is divorced, has no kids, and no living parents or siblings. I alerted the Long Beach Harbor Patrol, and they are looking for it. So far, no sign of it on or below the water. Some vehicles had car keys hidden in magnetic key holders or on their tires, but most were missing. Probably with the vics …"

He paused to think, then continued—

"I won't lie; even our detectives are at a loss. How do over thirty people disappear without a trace?"

"They must have gone out on the water voluntarily or been killed elsewhere. If our alien buddies got them, there would be a lot of blood on the beach," Morris said.

I nodded in agreement.

"We ran 27,28,29s on them to get vehicle, personal, and warrant info. A couple had open arrest warrants but for minor nonviolent offenses. Also, as guessed, all seven college kids are enrolled at Cal State Long Beach. We need to check further into the boat group and are doing that now," the captain said, indicating that he was finished by leaning back in his chair.

"Hold on," I said, pulling out my government cell phone. I texted Chayton the information we had gotten so his team could check up on leads.

"OK, my guys are on it, too," I said.

"Your guys?" Morris said with a smirk.

"Whatever, wise-ass, you know what I mean," I smiled.

"Will you tell me who is on your strike team, their call signs, and that they have gotten the full brief?" I asked the captain.

"Will do; you do the same with your call signs," he replied.

"Check," I responded.

The meeting was over.

I didn't want our actual names on any reports and told him so. I had wanted to give the captain call signs like Jolly One for Chayton and Merry One for Morris. However, he said we all had to be "Frank" designations to make it easy for his strike team to know we were the *federal* part of the ad hoc task force. Makes sense. Oh well, I liked mine better. Probably for the best, though.

———

Morris and I walked out of the building. There was a nice breeze, and the sun was shining. I sure do like California's weather better than Denver's.

We got in our car.

Tall, dark, and scary had been guarding it.

"Ideas?" I asked Morris. He just shook his head no.

"Alrighty then. Hungry?" I asked.

"Starving," he responded.

"OK, let's get some chow and brainstorm some ideas." He nodded in agreement.

Traffic was steady as we went down Pacific Coast Highway, or PCH as we call it. When we got to Second Street, we pulled into the In-N-Out Burger.

"Guard," I said to Baker—as Morris and I exited.

He showed me that I was number one with his middle finger.

Morris laughed, and we went inside. The place is always hopping, but they quickly got the orders out. Morris grabbed a table while I waited for our food. I ordered three Double-Doubles, each with fries and a Coke.

We were just finishing lunch when my phone rang; it was Chayton.

"Hey, Chayton. What have you got, boss?" I asked.

"The church angle seems to be panning out. So far, at least three vics worked at the Hope Church of Salvation in Naples. So that gives us a starting point for the rest. My guess is they are all affiliated with the church somehow. We are checking on the next of kin on the vehicles' registered owners now. I'm not sure if I'm hoping they are all church-affiliated," Chayton said.

"Deja vu, if so. And not in a good way," I replied.

"Yeah. Sorry, man. I think the Big One is back. And off its leash to boot," Chayton said.

I thought about what he said for a long minute.

"I think we should bring in X-ray heavy for QRF, just in case," I said.

X-ray Heavy was the call sign for the Model X, which had NMC guys in it. We were told it had serious firepower to help us against the alien creatures. Chayton, the team leader, would make the decision.

He didn't hesitate.

"Agreed. I'll also see if we can get the Coast Guard or Navy, but it'll be tough. Whether we fill them in or not, I doubt we can convince them of the threat. Hopefully, the NSC can help," Chayton said.

"I have to agree. It's a small miracle we convinced the LBPD. The pictures helped, but I doubt the military will buy into what they would see as serious BS. Maybe our bosses can at least get them ready with some kind of QRF," I said.

"Yeah, I agree," Chayton said. "I'll try my best to get some military response ready, anyway. If that thing is in the water, I'm unsure how we can kill it."

I thought hard. Something was nagging at me. A thought was at the back of my head … Finally, I had it.

"Chayton. I don't think we killed the source last time," I said.

"*What?*" Chayton replied.

"Think about it. Giant explosion, and now it is back? What if it is somehow tethered to a physical thing? I mean, it is obviously not from here. So, it must have been *summoned* or something. Maybe we can kill or at least banish it if we can destroy whatever binds it to our reality."

Morris looked at me like I had gone off my meds or something, which, technically, I had. There was a long pause, and I wondered if Chayton also thought I was insane.

"I think you are right," he finally said.

"Maybe you played too much D&D as a kid, but what you said makes sense. It died in the explosion, and the other tentacle things died when it did. And we found no trace of them either. If the tentacle things are tied to the Big One's existence, it makes sense that it is also tied to something. Otherwise, it or its minions would have finished you off after the explosion."

He paused again, then said, "Look into what you think that thing is, and then let's destroy it." With that, Chayton hung up.

We had our orders. It was time to hunt—music to my ears.

Walking out to our car, we climbed in. I handed Baker his food. While he ate, we strategized.

"OK, riddle me this Batman …" I said to Morris. "We attacked a church where this Big One was hiding in the basement. It can't move far from there because it didn't chase us, so my guess is it couldn't. Now, suddenly, it can. How?"

After a pause, Baker responded from the back seat. His mouth was full of food.

"Because it had another incantation that let it?"

Morris and I turned in unison to look at him.

"Damn, all that brawn and brains too?" Morris said.

He flipped us the bird and kept eating. Damn, and I thought I ate fast. He ate like a soldier. Swallow it now and taste it later.

"He is right, you know," I said.

"Think about it. This is our first encounter with the Big One, and we're fighting all its tentacle things. Suddenly, one explosion and 'Boom'—it is no more. All its tentacle buddies, including the ones that had fallen into a dead pile before we 'killed it' (I made the air quotes with my fingers again), just disappear once it is gone. Now, it is back again. How?"

I paused to gather my thoughts.

"Because we didn't kill it, we just killed its nexus to the other place it came from. So, we need to find and destroy that new nexus again," I said.

"Thoughts?" I asked.

"Great," grumbled Morris. "Only we have zero idea of what that nexus even is."

"Well, it probably will be something weird; I doubt it's an ottoman or anything," I said.

Morris and Baker chuckled.

"An ottoman, *really*?" Baker replied.

We all laughed.

"Yeah, I don't think it is that. But I bet we'll recognize it when we see it. It must be something weird, right?"

Questioning looks came my way.

"Well, it is something to start on. Where do we go from here, James?" Morris asked.

I was dreading that question. Just because I had figured out the what, how, and why didn't mean I had a clue to the where. I thought hard.

"Let's start with that church where the three missing persons worked," I blurted out without consciously deciding.

We now had a starting point.

"Navigate to the Hope Church of Salvation in Naples," I said to the car after hitting the little speaker icon on the steering wheel.

I watched the church's address pop up in the navigation system: 5780 East Naples Plaza. I tapped the address on the screen, and it started routing us.

The Tesla made a slight whirring noise as it went into drive mode when I stepped on the brake. It was bizarre not to have an engine.

———

We arrived at the church. This time, it was not in some crazy backwoods' location owned by a cult leader. It was on Naples Island and in a dreamland location. It was Sunday afternoon. The parking lot should have had cars for an afternoon service—or at least some left from a morning service.

It was empty, though.

"What's the plan, boss?" Morris asked.

I had been assigned as team leader. Morris and Baker were my team. I had been thinking about this very question on the drive over.

"We go up and ring the bell. If we don't get a response, you pick the lock, and we go in anyway," I added with a smirk.

"Dude, you know damn well we don't have lock picks. Do you even know how to use them?" Morris said.

"Nope," I replied.

There is another myth that all police carry around lock picks and know how to use them. This is not true. Some do, but not us. We heard a jingle behind us. We both turned to look at Baker. The looks on our faces must have been comical.

He was dangling a set of lock picks.

"I'll be damned. You NMC guys never cease to amaze us," Morris said.

"What do we do though? He has to stay within twenty feet of the car," I said.

We all smiled.

"Agent Baker, as team leader, I'm giving you a direct order to accompany me to the church. Morris, you'll stay in the car. Check?" I said to them.

"Check," and "Check," in reply.

Baker and I got out while Morris stayed. We walked up to a locked and empty church. I rang the buzzer by the door. I waited. I knocked. I waited.

Then, I turned back toward the parking lot to conduct countersurveillance for anyone pulling into the lot; I nodded to Baker. He nodded back and got to work on the lock. Yes, we are breaking the law, and no, I don't care. This was a matter of life or death, and I would break the rules if it meant saving people's lives. Plus, the "fruit from the poisonous tree" legal concept that says nothing can be used in court if the officers were not legally "there" in the first place didn't matter anyway.

We wouldn't be taking them to court. We had a different plan for our enemies …

I heard a click, and the door swung open.

Damn, he was pretty good at that—these NMC guys are scary.

We went in and shut the door behind us. We waited and listened for a good minute—nothing.

F—k it, I thought.

We were already breaking and entering, so we might as well take the risk. We pulled out our badges and guns. Starting at the front, we cleared the entire church. Once again, we had already studied the schematics before going inside.

We had no idea what we were looking for—I just knew it was a church where they came from last time.

The back cloakroom was very large. It had lockers and places to sit. This is where choir members put on their robes and store their stuff in lockers. There were no locks. We went through all the lockers and found nothing to help us.

Finally, I saw it.

There were scratches and an outline where something weighty—two things, actually—once were. I took pictures of where the items had sat. I laid my credential case, which is about the size of a wallet, next to the area. That way Alan could measure the sizes back at the MCC. I sent the images to him and the rest of the task force. I waited for the captain to start asking questions about how we got in. Luckily, he was smart enough not to say anything by text or email.

We completed our search, discovered multiple laptops, and seized them.

Upon a quick review, none of the documents in the drawers appeared valuable; furthermore, it would be too heavy to carry them all back.

After finishing our pilfering, we returned to the car with a couple of hard-sided Pelican cases. I informed the task force of what we had, and Chayton told us to take the laptops to LBPD and have them accessed for information.

When we finally pulled into the LBPD parking lot, Sergeant Williams was there to meet us.

"B&E? Really?" He said to us. He was smiling, though.

"Of course not. The door was open, and there were signs of duress," I lied. "These laptops were left unattended, and we thought they should be inventoried here for safekeeping. And, due to the exigent nature of finding our missing persons, we should probably have someone look in these …"

Williams smiled and took the pelican cases, nodding.

"Anything new?" I asked him.

"Yeah, the captain is preparing to send a message to the entire task force. We, including your team members, have checked all next of kin and employers. They are all mystified. Our boat MPs (missing persons) were all church members or their families. This church is very extreme. They believe a Messenger of God will usher in the End Times. We interviewed some pretty hard-core religious types, and even they think this church is too extreme."

"Great. We have confirmation of another cult," Morris said.

We all nodded.

I called Chayton.

"Blackwell here," he answered.

"Hey, Chayton. The task force will get the memo soon, but all boat MPs were affiliated with the Hope Church of Salvation in Naples. I think a waterborne attack took out both groups. Thoughts?"

He paused. "Agreed. We were thinking the same but wanted confirmation."

"The church?" Chayton asked.

"The church was empty; no one had been there today. We seized laptops, and Alan is helping look them over now, breaking past their passwords. We both know that'll take some time … Also, Chayton, some weighty things were removed from the back room at the church. I sent Alan the pictures; it may be of consequence," I added.

There was a long delay; I knew he was considering our next move.

"OK, thanks. While we're waiting for those computers to be hacked, let's all meet at the beach where they went missing," he finally said.

"Copy that," I replied.

"It's 1605; let's meet at 1700 at the crime scene location."

"Check," I replied again. I turned to my team.

"Alright. Let's head to Bolsa Chica Beach."

CHAPTER 15
ASHTA'GOTH

Sunday—5 p.m.—Bolsa Chica Beach
Agent James

WE ALL MET in the parking lot near the fire pits, and Chayton assembled our team.

"OK. Long Beach PD has been over every inch of this beach. They sent out divers and found nothing. We are pulling at straws at this point," he said, frowning. "But let's sweep it again."

He looked at his watch. "It is 1703; we sweep and look until 1800, then we meet back here. Hopefully, someone will find something. Any thoughts or ideas, no matter how crazy, let it out. We need to brainstorm at this point. There are civvies on the beach, so no LEO stuff should be showing. Check?"

A chorus of "Checks" responded.

He talked to me next.

"James, I want you and Skaggs to go north, farther out that way, until you get to that restroom building past the restaurant." He pointed north up the beach.

"And then work your way back to here," he said.

We nodded in affirmation.

219

"Lev and Morris, you go south and start on that end …" pointing the other way down the beach, "until you get to Seapoint Street and PCH."

"Then work your way back to here," he said.

They both nodded and said, "Check."

"I'll look right here, where the college kids went missing by the fire pits."

We got to work. Some of us even had metal detectors that we borrowed from LBPD. The immediate area around the fire pits was closed, but the beaches on either side were still open to the public. It was a lovely, sunny summer day, and people walked around, played in the ocean, and enjoyed the beach. Some came over to the crime scene tape, asked the officers questions, and then wandered off to enjoy the day. It was hard to believe forty people, give or take, probably lost their lives here just yesterday.

Everything seemed fine.

We started combing the beach. I didn't think we could find anything to help; Chayton was just being thorough. Besides, we had little else to do. We had hit a brick wall on the investigation.

After about half an hour, after almost getting back to the fire pits, we found definite signs that the Big One was back. It started with a scream …

Looking out to the ocean, we saw people suddenly go underwater. And it was not in a "Help! I'm struggling to stay afloat!" way. It was in a "now you see me, now you don't" way.

Chayton did not hesitate; he keyed his police radio.

All task force members—SWAT, Police Dispatch, and the Feds—were on the same frequencies. He then sent the message out to the entire group.

"All units, enemy contact at the beach! I say again, we are in contact! The Big One is pulling people under in the water—" He broke for a moment and then continued. "X-ray Heavy, weapons free!"

We pulled out our badges and guns and yelled to everyone, "POLICE! EVERYONE OUT OF THE WATER AND OFF THE BEACH!" while motioning and pointing inland.

Most of them looked at us as though *we* were the alien creatures.

Chayton realized this and fired several shots into a safe area of the water—

BANG! BANG! BANG!

Funny thing—

A cop yells, "Get off the beach," and they stand there and look at you like you are a Sasquatch that just came down from the forest trying to communicate in sign language …

But a few gunshots was all it took—

Now, they were running for their lives.

Except for some who had run and dived into the water to save someone they knew who had been pulled under. And, boggling the mind, some were not running at all—but filming with their cell phones!

What we saw next only added to our horror.

From the shoreline, they came up out of the water. There were dozens of them—more than I could count. The tentacle things came out of the surf and onto shore with fantastic speed. Several people were ripped limb from limb.

Chayton was like a sports commentator. He was talking calmly and clearly into his radio.

"We have dozens of Tentacle Things, civilian casualties mounting currently. We need everyone and everything here now." Even as he said it, we were "tactically withdrawing."

Once again.

Our pistol rounds were almost useless against them; we fired anyway, trying to save people.

We may have dropped one of them.

Grrr-EEK!

A monster had reached Agent Skaggs, and I was the closest to him.

BANG! BANG! BANG! BANG! BANG! BANG!

We both fired, as fast as we could, into the TT that was almost on him. I had to watch as it grabbed him and ripped him into six pieces. I fired the last of my mag into it. As my weapon locked back empty, I popped the empty mag in a smooth motion that I had practiced thousands of times. Then, as it was still falling, I rammed a new one home and hit the slide release—no time for a press check. I was firing again before the empty mag even reached the sand.

I started a "rhythm drill" against it.

BANG! BANG! BANG!

In those training drills, we practiced firing at the fastest cadence possible. The trigger slack goes out just enough to reset the trigger before squeezing again. This nets about three to four bullets per second —I was right on tempo.

It turned toward me, and I knew I was about to die.

Grrr-EEK! BANG! BANG! BANG!

I had maybe a half dozen rounds left before I needed to reload again. I knew there would be no time; it could outrun me if I ran now. It was almost to me …

Grrr-EEK! GRRR-EEK!

People were screaming and running everywhere while the TTs were letting out that horrible sound they made.

WHAP, WHAP, WHAP, WHAP!

Even with all the noise, the incoming fire from the X-ray Heavy unit was deafening.

The TT closing on me disintegrated.

Wow.

Suddenly, the sound increased dramatically. Even more machine guns were firing from it now.

Further down the beach sat the Model X.

———

Bolsa Chica Beach—South End
X-ray Heavy
Agent Anthony Bachman

Marcus Clay and I sat watching the events unfolding on the beach. Each of us had screens linked to fire control systems facing our seats.

I had backed the Model X (MX) up into the corner of where the walking trail came up from the beach and met the bike path. It was the only elevated spot with the height and angle we needed to engage the targets all the way up and down the coast. I picked this spot because it could engage all the way to the restrooms that Chayton had given us for the max engagement area, although the .50 Cal could reach farther. We were south of Seapoint Street and PCH but on the beach side of PCH. We parked in the area for pedestrians only and next to the restrooms. So, we should not be parked there, on the edge of the small hill.

Unfortunately, we were well outside the taped-off crime scene area and couldn't exactly advertise why we were there or who we were. So, many people gave the MX questioning looks, and a couple of people even came up and tried to peer through the completely tinted glass. Even the windshield was opaque. They knocked on our windows, and one even yelled to us, "You can't park there!"

He was very agitated and made a point of getting on his phone to call the police.

I looked over at Marcus and gave him a nod.

He hit the lights and siren briefly and then turned them off.

WHURP!

The man jumped, startled, and dropped his phone. Cussing, he picked it up, gave us the bird, and walked off.

I thought about the many classified systems in the Model X.

The U.S. Department of Energy did not let out its capabilities, even to other agents outside the department. This was one of those systems. The MX was a mobile weapons system, not a "car." It had been designed for one or two operators to "operate the guns" and defend the convoy on missions. Especially as a "rear-end Charlie" or the rear defense vehicle of the convoy.

Each gun was an FN crew-served weapon with an integrated Defender Medium package. This gave it a state-of-the-art Remote Weapons System (allowing it to be fired from the front seats), day and night camera systems, gyroscopic stabilization, target tracking, and image stabilization, laser range finder with ballistic calculation, wide angles of operation up to 70 degrees up or 40 degrees down, burst control and round counters, and an interface with other weapon systems.

The rear tailgate went up automatically to allow the rear gun to deploy. Agent Bachman was in the driver's seat, controlling gun 2, the rear gun. The rear machine gun is an M3M medium .50-caliber machine gun that can fire 1,100 rounds per minute. This machine gun also has a casings and links collector, so they weren't all over the rear cargo area—potentially interfering with the weapon's movements. This rear machine gun has an effective 2,500-meter range, just over one and a half miles. It was rear-angle fire only because of its weight, size, and recoil, and it has five smoke grenade canisters that can be "fired" at the touch of a button to conceal the MX in dense smoke. Three of those were also CS gas—which was like a more potent tear gas that the military uses. The MX has its own "Bioweapon Defense Mode" that would be put to the test when those fired. After activating the weapons systems, it went into that mode automatically.

Agent Clay controlled guns 1 and 3, now linked to fire together. When activated, the falcon-wing doors opened automatically, allowing the right and left guns to slide out on mounts. They could rotate freely on their mounts, allowing the guns to cover each side from forward to the rear. They had casing deflectors that made sure all the bullet casing and links fell out of, and not into, the MX.

The only weak spot was above it.

But whatever threat existed had to get past the 360-degree field of fire with 70 degrees of elevation. Depending on the engagement angle, the guns would automatically fire one or both as his aim shifted. The two side machine guns were six-barrel Gatling guns—M134Ds firing 7.62mm NATO rounds at a user-controllable 2,000 to 6,000 rounds per minute each, with an effective range of one thousand meters, or about two-thirds of a mile.

There was also a heavily armored barrier wall behind the front seats, so there were effectively two compartments: the front seats with the operators, with all HVAC for just that tiny area, and the rear "bay" with the three machine guns. The vehicle was designed for heavy combat.

The suspension was the only giveaway that the MX had been modified (besides the undercover emergency lights and tinted windows). It had been modified to handle more weight, had much more under-body clearance, and had "military-style" wheels and tires.

Because we had the safety of distance, we backed up the MX to give us an ideal angle of attack. We deliberately parked to engage the beach area where the agents were; the far end was just within the maximum range of the Gatling guns.

"Gs are synched and ready—I'm up," Marcus said.

"Copy, 50 is up also," I replied.

We waited patiently as people walked on the beach and played in the ocean. Far away, colossal cargo ships sailed, and we could see oil rigs and even two manufactured "islands" that were also for oil. Far in the distance, we could see the skyline of Los Angeles.

We scanned for threats; all was quiet.

As we waited, we calibrated the guns on our screens using targeting lasers. The lasers measured angles and distances, and automatically inputted them to help with weapons tracking. Standing above the beach on stilts, the first lifeguard hut was 135 meters out. It was light blue with a large "26" on the side; the numbers went down for each consecutive hut. The jetty was 614 meters, and the fire pits where the team would meet at the end were 820 meters. Every item we input helped the computer track angles and distances for future firing solutions. We finished in a few minutes, switched to infrared view, and then waited.

Half an hour went by …

Chayton broke the radio silence. We saw several people in the ocean being pulled under.

I heard Chayton's voice again on the radio. "X-ray Heavy, weapons free!"

This made me smile. Not a happy smile, more of a rictus of stress.

The doors on the MX opened, and the guns deployed.

I hoped anyone near us would get the hint and get gone when they saw the machine guns come out—there was no time to look. With a second thought, I also activated the red and blue emergency lights.

The first TTs came ashore all over the beach. Most were past the jetty and near the fire pits where the first attack occurred. On cameras, we could easily track any of the alien creatures. The aliens have different heat signatures, much hotter than the people down on the beach.

WHAP, WHAP, WHAP, WHAP!

I couldn't help the first people, but I fired anyway—.50 Cal rounds hit both TTs and humans, breaking them into pieces. I did my best to save people, but some were already in the clutches of the monsters once I was aimed in.

At least each one I hit would never kill anyone again.

I saw my first target rip a person to shreds (everything is on thermal vision now; I can only distinguish between human and TT) and then head toward another. I could see the flame of the firearms from the two people, so it must be our agents down there—1,006 meters away.

I only had a moment to save the other agent, so I did not hesitate.

WHAP, WHAP, WHAP, WHAP!

One short burst, and the TT was gone. It looks like I didn't hit the other agent.

With no time to congratulate myself, I moved to the next target. And the next, and the next …

There were so many of them!

I could hear the intermittent roaring buzz of the Gatling guns as Marcus tore into more of the TTs. I couldn't believe how many we had killed!

Finally, the beach was mostly clear, with only a few TTs left.

"Something big and hot in the ocean," Marcus told me.

"I see it. Damn, it's huge!" I replied.

On my thermal screen, the ocean had changed to a warmer color, then a hot one, as a creature the size of a high school football stadium came ashore near the fire pits.

"Finish the TTs and then hit the Big One," I said.

"Copy," Marcus replied.

As he finished the TTs on the beach, I held the trigger down on the

Big One. Hundreds of rounds had already gone through the gun; it must be getting hot by now, but I had to keep firing. New, strange things were popping out of the giant creature and into the sky; they looked like huge, hot bats.

"Hit the new ones, too," I said to Marcus.

"Copy," he replied, as I held the trigger down on the .50 Cal—putting every round into the big one.

WHAP, WHAP, WHAP, WHAP, WHAP!

This was getting interesting.

The "bats" were heading our way.

———

Agent James

My ears hurt from the gunfire, especially now.

No one talks about just how loud warfare is. I watched in amazement as the TT before me was shredded to pieces. A hail of .50 Cal rounds left chunks of it everywhere.

Behind it were pieces of Larry Skaggs.

I hoped Lev, Greg, and Chayton were still alive. I felt a pang at the thought of Lev being hurt, especially.

Mentally thanking the NMC guys, I turned to run from the beach. Our pistols couldn't help, so I veered and grabbed an older man who was moving as fast as he could—not fast enough. I grabbed him, yelling, "Police, run!" as I took hold and sped up his run.

We reached the top of the beach—the bike path next to Pacific Coast Highway—and I turned back to the shoreline. The machine guns had ripped apart most of the TTs. Their parts were intermingled with human body parts all over the beach.

It was a bloodbath.

Sirens could be heard coming from every direction. Even the non-strike team members were told of the machine-gun fire. They were advised that the Black Model X was a federal vehicle laying down suppressive fire and was friendly, not a threat.

It had, so far, "suppressed" several dozen TTs to pieces and parts.

We made it to our vehicles and donned the ExoM suits while the NMCs guarded us. They were already in theirs. Thankfully, Chayton had us practice putting them on from the car.

Like, a million times.

We finished getting our suits on and braced ourselves to reengage. We were using our vehicles for cover—not that we were being shot at; it was just a reflex. We were looking through starlight scopes down to the beach. Some injured people were still there. Ones that had broken something trying to run or, unfortunately, been hit by friendly fire, which isn't very friendly to its victim. Some had even survived a TT attack and the bullets that killed it. Unfortunately, most of those "survivors" were also hit by machine-gun rounds. The ones still alive were screaming in pain and fear. We aimed in and sent rounds into the TTs the MX hadn't gotten to yet. Only a handful were left, and they would never cover the distance to us in time.

It looked like we were winning!

Until now …

WHHHAAAGHH!

There was a horrendous noise from the ocean, even louder than the machine guns. Bursting out of the water, seemingly everywhere, *it* came.

My jaw dropped in horror.

It was at least twice the length of a football field in all directions and "stood" over a hundred feet out of the water. It was the same unholy mass as the one Lev described, but its size now was terrifying on a whole new level. It lashed out with tentacles, some as long as construction crane arms, and cleaned the beach of body parts, TT parts, and living people (still screaming) as it flung them back toward its mass—everything.

All firing had momentarily stopped.

Everyone seeing it had been frozen in fear, combat-hardened or not. This was the End Times; this thing was the size of a God. One by one, weapons came alive again. I put the sniper rifle down and brought up the M4, firing on full auto now (that thing is hard to miss)—I was putting every round into it.

BRRRRAP!—Click!

My weapon ran dry, so I loaded another mag quickly and continued. That one also ran dry; the God monster was on the beach now. Hell, it *was* the beach now. It was moving on our position, and I could see birds over it now.

Crud. Those aren't birds.

Dozens, maybe hundreds, of these weird creatures were heading our way. I wish I still had the sniper rifle in my hands. Mentally shrugging, I dropped the FN SCAR on its sling and grabbed the M700PSS sniper rifle.

I looked through the scope at our newest addition to the monster horror show. I saw one and looked closer. It was impossible to tell the size at this distance, but it was just as horrible as the others. It flew on two long, leathery wings. Almost bat-like. A long torso with a heavily barbed tail was between those wings. The entire "head" of it was one giant maw, one big circular opening with hundreds of inward-angled teeth, like one of those worms in the *Dune* movies. I could see nothing that looked like eyes or ears. I did see a gout of purple blood, though, as it crumpled and fell from the sky—

Crack!

Once my weapon finished recoiling, I moved to another.

My next shot missed as it veered and swayed through the air. They knew they were being fired upon now and were trying to evade.

Could this day suck any more? I thought.

The thundering of hundreds of rounds per second from the MX was loud. As it hit the big one, we could see the tracers hitting it. Every fifth bullet was a tracer, making a visible line of fire going into the giant mass.

Grr-AKH, AKH, GHAA!

Thousands of mouths, and God knows what else, let out that horrible screeching, roaring sound it had made before.

I hoped it was from pain.

In a flash, I remembered the assault on the church.

"It is calling for reinforcements!" I yelled into the mic.

Sure enough, I turned back from it to look behind us. We could see dozens more TTs advancing on us—this time from every direction.

"TTs closing in from all flanks!" I said on the radio.

Spinning, I started shooting TTs coming our way from behind. Their numbers were overwhelming. Luckily, there was a fence with barbed wire on the other side of PCH, which slowed them down as they tore through it.

Cop cars were pulling up everywhere. Thankfully, dispatch had relayed that the guys in military-looking armor, bristling with guns, were the good guys. So, at least we didn't have to worry about being the victims of friendly fire. Besides, the cops, even those unaware, quickly figured out who the enemy was—

All the things that were not human.

In the movies, the police always drop their guns and run in fear when they see monsters. In reality, they shoot those monsters, even though they are still afraid. I saw cars driving around and blasts coming from them. The police, the ones that had lived through the initial attack by the TTs, had figured out a new tactic.

"All officers, stay in cars and stay mobile. Shoot from vehicles," I heard an officer call out.

"Romeo One on scene." SWAT had arrived in an armored personnel carrier, or APC. The SWAT Officers deployed out the back and started pouring heavy fire into the TTs. Several fell, but more came.

I turned back toward the shoreline. What I saw was not good.

Have you ever noticed how a big plane or ship looks like it is moving slower than a small one, even though they are both moving just as quickly? That is what I see now. Because of its size, it did not look fast. But it had already cleared the water entirely and was well on its way to the parking lot—the one we were in.

To make matters worse, I heard the MX's machine-gun fire reduce and then stop.

"X-ray Heavy, out of ammo. Falling back," they said.

Up the beach, a swarm of flying horrors was closing in on the MX.

It fired out smoke grenades and took off at a high rate of acceleration. Even as it pulled away, we could see the guns sliding back inside and the doors shutting.

It would be a miracle if they still worked after this.

We could see them glowing red from the heat, even from here. The red and blue lights, mixed with the red-hot guns, made for a strange kind of art inside the smoke.

The horrors flew in after it but quickly reversed course and flew back out toward the Big One.

A minute later, we would have smelled wisps of CS gas.

"FALL BACK!" I heard Chayton yell into the radio.

You don't have to tell me twice.

We jumped into the Tesla, and I floored the accelerator. It launched forward immediately—and a good thing it did.

WHAAP!

The three-plus tons of our loaded car bounced a little from the impact—the space our car had just been in was filled with a giant tentacle that had slammed down.

It would have crushed us flat.

The police cars that were still mobile headed for the exits.

Damn it! We just got our asses handed to us ...

I heard Chayton calling the MCC over our frequency; his voice had a tinge of despair.

"MCC, we just engaged the Big One at Bolsa Chica Beach. We lost. We are disengaging now. This thing has hundreds of TTs and some new black-winged creatures. Be advised that the Big One is on land and is at least one football field wide in every direction. Request military support. I say again, requesting military support ASAP."

"Casualties?" Alan at MCC asked.

"TBD on us, several police, dozens of civvies. Numbers are probably higher."

While all this came over the radio, I was still accelerating—pushing us hard into the seats.

The bad news is that some of the flying ones caught up to us.

The good news is that they couldn't easily grasp our rapidly accelerating car.

We could see them grabbing people, picking them up, and then dropping them to their deaths. Others were swallowed whole as they flew down and ate them with those horrible giant maws.

But what was up ahead looked even worse.

Several TTs blocked our road ahead. We were on PCH, and there was nowhere else to go besides back the way we came.

I picked one and accelerated.

BAM! Grrr-EEK!

It hit hard into the front and busted into pieces.

Luckily, our Tesla had been modified with an airbag "off" switch. We had it off right now. Otherwise, the airbags would have been deployed, and the vehicle would have come to a stop.

As it was, our car was clearly "totaled."

The bullet-resistant windshield was shattered, and pieces of the TT had come through and hit us. Thank God for armor and helmets. The inside of the car now smelled like month-old rotting fish. Purple slime and tentacle pieces were everywhere. The Tesla's front had crumpled from the crash, and the dash was filled with lit icons saying just how much our car had been messed up. There was a horrible rattling from the front, and our front left tire showed "critically low PSI."

Some light traffic was up ahead, so I hit the lights and siren.

WHAA-WHAA-whaa-whaa …

Even the sirens were messed up at this point.

The car had two motors in the back, one for each wheel and one motor for the front. According to our warnings on the dash, the front one was inoperable. Luckily, all Teslas with more than one motor were designed to run if one failed.

I can attest that is true now.

The flying creatures could hold on until about a hundred miles per hour or so. I know because I watched our speed as we accelerated away after hitting the TT. The last of the flying ones, which had managed to grab ahold of us, were being pulled off by our velocity. They disengaged and returned the way they came.

They either couldn't catch us, returned because they were called, or were too far from their mama.

Sighing, I backed off the accelerator. We had already outrun them, and I was going 120 mph as I let off. Because of all the damage, the car was loose and swerving back and forth at that speed, so I didn't dare go faster. The car was making a horrible racket, but it held together. We could see and smell smoke. The armored exterior had probably saved us in the crash.

Now, it might be our doom.

The windows were heavily armored and did not roll down anymore. So, the "Bioweapon Defense Mode" and the shattered windshield were the only things that allowed us to breathe as the car started catching fire. The smell of the TT's guts inside the car was unbearable, and we were all puking and coughing.

We just made it to the LBPD parking lot, and as we pulled up, the car went dark and rolled to a stop—it was dead. We had to use the emergency release handles to get out. By the time we did, we all were on our knees, coughing up a lung, and spent several minutes gasping for air. EMTs saw us and came to give us aid.

No one got near the Tesla, as wisps of smoke and fire were coming from under it, and the hundred-kilowatt battery was starting to go nova. I can only imagine the smell of cooking TT …

I puked one last time.

Several police cars came in over the next several minutes. Many of them were a lot worse for wear. Same with the officers who came out. They looked like ghosts. Everyone was clearly in shock over what they had just encountered.

Many of them did not return.

Some police cars had civilians with them, and ambulances, fire trucks, and paramedics were everywhere.

Then, the media started rolling in. Several police stopped them at a hasty perimeter they had set up around the station's parking lot. I had to hand it to them; they knew the press was coming and had planned for it.

There was no putting this one under the rug.

The jig was up, and we knew it. The media got a good long video of us in our ExoM suits and Teslas, especially the one we were just in, which was now a raging bonfire. Luckily, we were just one item on the filming agenda.

Civil defense air raid sirens started going off.

It was a little late, but at least they were sounding off now. Most air raid sirens in Southern California are relics of the past, rusting and inoperable on their tall poles, like the famous one in Belmont Heights. Other ones throughout Long Beach also stand silent and rusting on poles. Luckily, some Orange County coastal cities still had functional ones in case a tsunami warning was needed.

Alert Long Beach had replaced the anachronistic air raid sirens and had already sent a warning via text and email: "ALERT! Emergency situation at Bolsa Chica Beach. All residents, please stay in your homes and lock all doors. An alert will notify you when the emergency is over. DO NOT travel to Long Beach and Orange County beaches at this time."

———

Joint Forces Training Base—Los Alamitos, California
First Lieutenant Green

First Lieutenant Green, US Army National Guard, was returning with his platoon from a field training exercise when he got a message on the radio—

"Zulu One to all units. FRAGO. All units return to base for real-world missions. RTB to arm all weapons systems and receive OPORD. Expedite. Stay safe, but get here ASAP. Out."

Zulu One.

That was Lieutenant Colonel Collins, who was in charge of our battalion.

That is not good.

"GO!" I told my driver.

We ran a couple of red lights and went as fast as our Humm-V could go. Luckily, we were almost back when the call came in.

As we pulled into the depot, ordinance teams were already arming every vehicle as they came in. It looked like we were in full war footage. Everywhere, troops were readying weapons and vehicles and preparing to deploy.

Once we got into the depot, I met with my platoon sergeant, Sergeant First Class Harris. While they were loading our Mark 19 automatic grenade launcher, we received our operations order. As part of the OPORD, we set up a plan on the map for where our units would deploy, ORPs to fall back to and continue the assault, etc. Then, I briefed those present on the OPORD.

"You have to be kidding me!" said Private First Class Blaine. "Giant monster hundreds of feet wide, flying ones, tentacle ones … is this a f—ing joke, sir?"

"It better not be," I replied.

I turned to my already assembled troops, also waiting on their load-outs.

"All right, all of you here. We go as we come in. Sergeant Harris, you'll coordinate who is where and oversee load-outs," I said.

"Yes, sir," responded my platoon sergeant.

"I'm going out now with the first wave. Everyone stay frosty," I said to them all.

"Godspeed, everyone," Harris added before leaving to carry out his orders.

We had the Mk19 ready now, with over a thousand grenades. One team member also had an M60 machine gun with 2,000 extra rounds in the vehicle. The rest had M4s, pistols, and frag grenades. We were prepared for anything. I hoped this was a joke—or at least an exaggeration. However, I knew it was for real once they loaded the ordinance.

We would soon find out just how real it was.

As we cleared an underpass and made good speed toward Bolsa Chica Beach, we saw the giant creature in the distance—it was a significant lump way out there. It seemed constantly undulating, and a vast flock of birds circled over it. There were also a bunch of tiny little tumbleweed-looking blobs all around it. Luckily, military officers are trained to make decisions quickly and accurately under extreme stress.

We never "freeze."

"Driver, on the side of that hill over there, stop at ORP 7. That is our position. Everyone deploys to protect on stopping," I ordered.

"Yes, sir," the driver replied.

This ORP was our first of many. We knew of more to go to after this one. Our briefing at the base identified several of these, and we would move from one to another to confound the enemy. Plus, other fire teams would be using their ORPs as well. This would go on for however long it took to destroy the enemy.

"Nineteen gunner, kill the Big One as soon as we open fire. The Big One is your only target. Copy?"

"Wilco, sir!" Private Blaine yelled down from the turret.

We came to a stop. The Big One was about a mile away, and we deployed in an efficient military manner.

I looked out through my binoculars.

I could see the "tumbleweeds" were big blobs of tentacles, at least two meters in diameter. They were everywhere, chasing people down and ripping them limb from limb. The "birds" were horrible flying monsters.

And the big thing?

I can't describe it.

Tears were coming from my eyes, and I felt like my soul had been ripped out, but I continued giving orders methodically. It was beyond terrifying, and soon, it would be in the range of the Mk19.

My troops had deployed on stopping as ordered; Corporal Hilman braced his M60, now on its bipod, to defend the Mk19 while the rest made a perimeter to protect us all.

The M60 machine gun and the Mark 19 automatic grenade launcher started service in Vietnam. However, both are still effective today. Especially on "troops in the open."

The M60 fired 7.62mm rounds at 550-650 rpm. Its effective range was 1,100 meters for area effect and 800 meters for point targets (like people). Due to its size, it could easily hit the giant one past its effective range.

The Mk19 fired 40mm grenades at up to 1,500 meters at 325-375 rpm.

"Sweet mother of God!" yelled PFC Blaine.

He looked as white as a ghost; all the color had drained from his face. But he was resolute, and his weapon was aimed in.

"Prepare to fire!" I yelled—as I didn't want anyone to hesitate.

Considering the target size, both the M60 and Mk19 would be able to engage soon. A few moments later, it was at the edge of effective range. We didn't have to wait long …

"Weapons free!" I yelled.

The Mk19 and M60 roared to life.

————

Ashta'goth

It was enjoying itself.

The "police" had come.

Now, it could be a real battle!

The rounds from the little people on the beach did nothing to it. Suddenly, though, it sensed significant damage happening. Far up the hill, a black bug was firing nonstop, forming a red line into it. This attack was more significant, but nothing that would kill it. Maybe if it kept going for a long time?

No. It still wouldn't hurt enough.

But that was the most prominent foe so far, so it called on its minions to change course and attack it.

Crawling entirely out of the water, it "looked" out over the horizon.

Many cars were moving on a big road, over a mile away, oblivious to what was happening. Almost every vehicle and person near it, though, was running away.

Amazingly, a few people had stood their ground.

They held up little rectangular talismans between them and it, holding up the flat side. Did they think a talisman would protect them?

Silly creatures.

It smacked a tentacle on one, still holding its talisman up as it died.

Most of the "police" were now leaving. It had reached an open area where many "police" were, and it set about flattening people and cars with giant, thick tentacles.

It could sense and enjoy their terror. The flood of it now was as nourishing as the bodies were. By the time it was entirely in the open area on the beach, the black bug had stopped stinging it and was leaving.

It stopped for a moment.

The last people remaining were being killed by the Uth'raliegh tentacles and the Sharra'teth flying horrors. It wondered if more adversaries could be found inland. After all, every enemy that fell to it made it more robust and bigger.

"BOOM, BOOM, BOOM, BOOM …"

Finally! A worthy challenge!

The black bug had done the most to it so far, but the new sensation was incredible. This was the first time any real damage has happened to it. Giant gouts of purple blood, replete with big chunks of its mass, were flying off with each explosion. Partially absorbed creatures, and whole chunks of it—with alien mouths screaming and tentacles writhing—flew off it.

This was a new experience. This is the first thing that could kill it … given enough time.

US Army
First Lieutenant Green

The flying ones were the worst. Soon after the Mk19 engaged the Big One, the M60 gunner started taking out the flying ones headed our way. The other soldier and I, with our M4s, started shooting them out of the sky as they got closer as well. As good as my troops were, there were just too many.

The rolling and shambling tentacle things were also coming our way, but would take a while to get to us. We could see the flock of flying ones getting closer, though. We didn't have long …

"CEASE FIRE!" I yelled.

All firing immediately stopped.

"Load up and prepare to EVAC!" I yelled.

Everyone piled in, and the driver hit the gas.

"ORP 5, sir?" the driver asked.

"Affirmative," I replied.

Up the road, about one klick (kilometer), we got to a bend with a view down to the beach—ORP 5.

"Deploy!" I ordered as we came to a halt.

"Hoo-aahs," responded my way.

We were at our second designated ORP farther up the hill. There were more ORPs, and we would continue engaging and re-engaging until called off or until we or the enemy were destroyed.

Soldiers never just quit.

After engaging and waiting for the flying horrors to get close again, we repeated the procedure. We reached the next ORP. Just like before, we re-deployed and re-engaged. The weapons roared to life again. We continued to pour grenade and machine-gun fire on the Big One and its minions.

Grr-AKH, AKH, GHAA!

In the distance, we heard it let out a new sound—hopefully, one of pain. Other units had started arriving. We heard anti-tank rockets, recoilless rifles, machine guns, and automatic grenade launchers firing from many locations.

The M60 gunner was already on his second barrel, and it was also getting dangerously hot.

With all the units moving and engaging, it would have a hell of a time getting us all.

And more of us were coming.

Ashta'goth

That thing was quite the pest.

The little green bug was funny-looking, more like that black bug. It was shooting stuff that exploded when it hit it. Each hit reminded it of the explosion that had destroyed the altar the first time and sent it back to its plane.

But this time, things were different.

The altar was safe, guarded by the Deathwalkers it had created and the priest.

Yet, this little bug was starting to cause damage. It had called back the flying horrors when the green bug had run away. Now, more of the bugs had shown up and were also shooting it. The bugs all moved faster than the flying horrors could fly. The first bug had reappeared higher up on the hill and fired at it again.

It called for the flying horrors to attack.

It could see them being methodically shot out of the air, very accurately and efficiently. These new humans were exceptionally good at killing them.

As it waited for its flying swarm to kill the green bug, it enjoyed the sensation of being hurt, even if ever so slightly—such a strange feeling. It didn't help that more green bugs were showing up and methodically killing all the flying horrors and TTs. These new humans were fearless.

None ran away.

They would just move to new spots and continue attacking. The green bugs were starting to cause some real damage. It is concerning, but not enough to stop it yet.

Finally, a real challenge!

The TTs couldn't get to them before they moved again. These green bugs were starting to anger it, so it sent the TTs elsewhere to find other victims to rip apart—

KABOOM! BOOM! BOOM! BOOM!

The subsequent damage it felt shattered its sense of invincibility.

It hadn't experienced fear like this since it was forced to flee from an even more enormous creature. Horrific, colossal explosions erupted from it. Four massive parts of it were completely obliterated, leaving it reeling in shock and vulnerability.

It was finally changed from apex predator to prey in a brief, devastating moment.

The realization of its new, vulnerable position sent a chill through its jelly cells.

The massive explosions threw giant chunks and tons of its mass skyward in seconds—many more tons were simply vaporized in the explosions. Its entire bulk shifted directions with each of the four blasts.

Most of it was gone now.

What remained of it retreated at full speed toward the ocean. The green bugs had not stopped their assault either.

Two flying things had almost killed it, and they were far too high and fast for its flying horrors to get to. It was already in the ocean surf when it felt hundreds of new, more minor explosions laying into it. Those flying things were worthy adversaries.

It would be lucky to survive this.

US Air Force
Captain Reynolds

"Ace three, Ace four, you have permission to engage hostiles. Weapons free."

Inside his helmet, the pilot—Captain Reynolds—smiled.

The F-22 Raptor he was piloting was an excellent jet.

Our combat air patrol had scrambled out from Edwards AFB. We were a proud part of the 412th Wing of the Air Force. Each jet had eight 500-pound Joint Direct Attack Munitions (JDAMs) attached for this mission. They had loaded the GBU-39A/B-SDB 2-Focused

Lethality Munitions. These bombs use a composite casing (instead of steel) to limit fragmentation and use a focused-blast explosive called a dense inert metal explosive. They were designed to limit collateral damage for use in populated urban areas with pinpoint strikes. Plus, this variant had thermal guidance—we had ground reports that the creatures are hotter than people.

We were initially briefed to be ready to engage a large target at danger-close (close to "friendlies") range early this afternoon. We were told what the ordinance was, but we were not given information on the target.

That never happens, he thought.

So, we were beyond surprised when we found out the target was a gigantic, living creature!

Each jet also had six AIM-120 AMRAAMs (Advanced Medium-Range Air-to-Air Missile), two AIM-9 Sidewinder Missiles, and a 20mm M61A2 Vulcan Rotary Cannon with 480 rounds. The rounds currently loaded were semi-armor-piercing high-explosive incendiary rounds.

The F-22 Raptor did not need to get close for it to engage.

In the giant monster movies, the jets fly close enough for the monster to grab them. In the real world, most targets haven't even seen the plane before the missiles strike.

We rarely get close to the actual targets.

Captain Reynolds could already "see" his target on his instruments. The thermal guidance easily locked on, as this giant thing was *way* hotter than anything else in the area. It was still miles in front of him when he fired two JDAMs at it, and his partner's jet did the same. They could fire more JDAMs on subsequent passes if needed. Based on its size and proximity to civilians and buildings, the decision had been made only to fire four.

"Fox One," he said—two JDAMS sped toward it.

"Fox One," the other pilot said—two more.

Four 500-pound, precision-guided bombs were heading its way. He knew each one would hit even though he couldn't see the creature yet.

In a few seconds, the jet would be close enough to add the Vulcan cannon to the party if any part of the Big One remained.

"Wow, this is something," he said in amazement as the jet closed to cannon range. He couldn't believe what he saw now; it was horrifying. But those thousands of hours of flight training paid off.

"Fox Four," he said as he fired the Vulcan cannon.

BRRRRRRRAP!

He methodically fired 20mm rounds into it until the Vulcan clicked dry. The last of his cannon rounds hit the water it had submerged into —well, what was left of it anyway, which wasn't much.

The other pilot had done the same.

"Greetings from the United States Air Force," he heard the other pilot say as we overflew the target area.

It was nothing but sea now.

CHAPTER 16
THE HOUSE

Agent Lev

CHAYTON HAD MADE everyone respond to the beach at 1700 to look for clues. During the melee that followed, I emptied every round I had in the sniper rifle and was most of the way through my FN SCAR rounds as well. Even with my enhanced SIM reflexes, and no significant recoil because of my strength, my weapons could not fire any faster. We had piled into our car when the Big One got close, and Chayton had issued the fallback order—the empty seat where Larry Skaggs should be haunted me.

We made it back to LBPD to regroup. As we pulled into the lot and got out, there was pandemonium. People and cars were everywhere.

"Hey!"

I heard a yell and turned to see an attractive Asian woman and her cameraman behind her. Behind them was a white news van—*Crime Scene News* visible in big letters.

"I am Samantha Cox with *Crime Scene News*—will you just tell me what is happening?!"

Her features changed to one of horror as she looked at me—

"My God! What happened to you?"

I knew she was the one we had turned away while recovering at the hospital, but I was seven inches shorter, eighty pounds lighter, and my face was still wrapped in gauze back then. Now, she could see my transformation at such a short distance from me.

And she was f—ing filming it.

"Sorry, Samantha. I'm sure you can see I'm a little busy."

She said something else, but I will never know what it was—

In the distance, we heard loud explosions, much bigger than before, and the recognizable sonic boom of supersonic jets—music to my ears. We were all regrouping and figuring out how to neutralize that thing when Captain Billings came over the task force and regular PD channels—

"All units, our friends in the Air Force have made the creature retreat into the ocean—the parts that were left of it anyway," he said.

Cheers erupted.

Now, the long process of evacuating people near the shoreline, coordinating with the military, giving medical aid, and—worst of all— trying to tell the press what just happened was underway.

But not for us.

Without turning back to Samantha, I left to join my fellow agents.

Two NMCs, Agents Newburg and Phillips, were killed by the flying horrors in the parking lot, and we lost FBI Agent Skaggs on the beach. Luckily, the rest of the team made it out alive. Our job now was to regroup, rearm, and lick our wounds. All our rounds were standard issue 9mm and 7.62mm NATO. So, between the Long Beach Police Department and our new best friends, the military, we were able to top off all of our weapons—the ones not lost on the beach anyway.

It was time to go.

We had to pile into the two surviving Teslas, as the third one was now fully engulfed in flames.

There were only four of us OSTs alive now, anyway.

We stayed in our ExoM suits.

Even though bullets hadn't hit them, the other team's armor suits had admirably absorbed the glass, TT parts, and shrapnel from their

"Tesla vs. TT" crash. And we could move quicker with all our gear by being in them.

They won't keep me from getting ripped apart, however.

Chayton joined me, and we were now Alpha. Greg and James were still Bravo.

X-ray Heavy responded to Edwards AFB to resupply with PMCS for the MX's vehicle systems and guns.

Thank God for them.

I don't think we would have made it off that beach without them. When this is over, I will buy them all a drink.

Jesus, would it ever be over?

We drove the last two Teslas to the nearest place we could to make a classified report—it took us under an hour to get to the FBI Field Office in Los Angeles.

By the time we all regrouped there, night had fallen. After reporting to SAC Cho on the STU and ensuring we were ready to roll out again immediately, we cleaned up, ate delivery food, and slept. It was very late by the time we got to our beds, which were military cots the other agents had set up for us.

After the National Security Agency got the computers from the church, they got hacked a lot faster. It turned out our infamous reverend had escaped the NER church massacre and used an alias, but his movements and position at the new church helped us identify him.

One Reverend Doctor Gregory Turner, III—alias Jeremy Clark— was now public enemy number one. He was at the very top of the FBI's Most Wanted list. Although they aren't technically "ranked," everyone agreed this was the top fugitive to find right now.

There was one problem, though; we had no idea how to find him.

Well, one idea.

One car's registered owner returned to a missing person from the beach. But, unlike the other missing persons, that person's car *was* gone from the parking lot. While we were sleeping, the FBI launched a nationwide APB for the vehicle and for Reverend Turner/Clark.

The following day, we woke up very early again—

LBPD had found the BOLO vehicle.

We got in our two cars and headed to where the vehicle was found —abandoned in a Toyota dealership. That makes sense. They are closed on Sundays, and no one would think to look there until they open on Monday.

No one except highly motivated police officers, anyway.

It wasn't far and was still in Long Beach. Police units were already making the first encirclement of the area. They were positioned at every significant intersection leading out of the area, and more were making smaller encirclements within each one. We would find them if they were still in the area, and they would not get away.

After searching the area for hours, we had nothing. It was noon already, but we were still looking. As two looked, one of us tried to rest. Not exactly the best sleep, but we needed what we could get. We had already been up for a long time. It was midafternoon when I jolted awake.

"Stop the car!" I yelled.

Chayton pulled over to the side of the road and parked. He turned and looked at me.

"I can feel them," I said.

I tried not to laugh as Chayton did a perfect Spock-like one-eyebrow lift. He considered what I said for a moment, then shrugged.

"Why not? Nothing is weird at this point. Lead on Spot," he said.

The dog reference was funny but also accurate. We walked into a wooded area, but I could tell where I was going.

The warmer cooler game was in full swing.

We resembled a giant snake moving through the forest as we went one way and another, inexorably heading toward what I hoped was one of them. We eventually went through the forest and saw a house deep in the woods. It had a long driveway leading away and a solitary car parked behind it with a tarp over it. I could feel one of "them" inside.

"Bet we could have just driven here," Chayton said, shaking his head.

"Yeah, if my dog sniffer worked that way," I replied.

We both smiled.

It's somewhat funny, anyway, I thought.

Chayton had ordered a halt once we had a good view of the house. I provided security while he got on the radio.

"This is Frank One. We have reason to believe we are closing on Tango Prime," he said, then gave our location and the target's location.

"Frank three and four are en route," came over the radio.

Good, James and Greg were on the way.

We had decided on Tango Prime as the "Primary Target" for the Reverend's code name.

"I need two perimeters around this area." He gave coordinates.

"Also, send Romeo One." That was the SWAT team—the team with the APC.

Now, with new tires.

One invaluable lesson we gleaned from our After-Action Review, or AAR, received from the police station, is that the SWAT team's Armored Personnel Carrier, or APC, was impervious to tentacle things and flying terrors. CCTV footage showed dozens of them trying to get in.

The SWAT team had lost three members—KIA—and retreated into the APC. It couldn't move because the monsters had shredded its tires.

But they couldn't get in, either.

That distraction probably saved countless lives, though.

The ones busy attacking the APC weren't attacking other people. Thankfully, the Big One either didn't notice or was too busy, so it didn't flatten it.

I returned to the present when Chayton said, "OK, let's see what we have."

He raised his rifle and surveilled the house through the scope. I continued watching the forest around us.

We waited.

"Hi, Love," came out of the forest as Greg and James came over to join us.

"Advance and be recognized," I cheekily responded.

Greg and James took up positions for better 360-degree security.

"Perimeter check," Chayton keyed into the radio.

"This is Romeo One. We have established an inner perimeter."

"Adam Two, in position."

"Adam Six, in position."

Over the next few minutes, everyone else checked in.

"Sierra Two. The outer perimeter is established now. You are a go, Frank One."

Chayton turned to us. "Alright, everyone. Let's go check it out."

We made our way to the house with eight SWAT team members and the four of us. The other four members of the SWAT team had perimeter watch of the house with sniper rifles.

A feeling of deja vu washed over me.

The SWAT team stacked on the door to make entry. Using hand signals, one readied the ram. They had given me the riot-control semi-auto grenade launcher. As I had the strength to fire it accurately at full speed, I was left outside to start the attack. The team would go inside as soon as I emptied the grenade launcher.

The SWAT team leader motioned to me—it was time to start the party.

I emptied the grenade launcher through the windows on my side of the building. Though they were flash-bangs, they would affect anyone in the open. The ram took down the door as soon as the grenades went off.

"Police! Everyone down!" They yelled as they entered—immediately, there was automatic gunfire.

And it wasn't from them.

———

The SIMs

The two SIMs waited patiently inside. Both were ready. They held the weapons the Feds had left on the beach.

One of the SIMs had waited and watched while the Battle Royale was going on. When the police retreated, it moved onto the beach and retrieved the weapons. So now, both Deathwalkers had the deadly weapons systems that OST had issued.

The cameras on the house and in the woods had shown them where the intruders were, how many, and even when they stacked at the door. The SIMs wore several layers of hearing protection and had opaque visors flipped over their eyes. The windows shattered, and several grenades flew in. After they all went off, the SWAT team came through the door—

But the SIMs had already flipped up their visors immediately after the grenades went off.

Ordinary people would still have been stunned. They were not ordinary people, though—so they were ready.

BRRRRRAP! BRRRRRAP!

The first SWAT team members through the door sustained fire from both their rifles and fell. The ones behind them rushed in and opened fire.

BRRAP! BRRAP! BRRAP!

The SWAT team members were using MP-5s. A barrage of rounds hit the SIMs as they shot at the SWAT team and the OST agents. Everyone was finding cover except for the three who would not get back up.

Hundreds of rounds came their way, and many hit them, but the SIMs returned fire—with the 7.62mm rounds from the FN SCAR H-Mk2 that OST carried.

The SIMs moved to make themselves harder to hit.

Although they were not as accurate as the trained agents, they had the advantage of superhuman speed and reflexes. SWAT and OST quickly realized what they were up against. If these were ordinary people they had been shooting, they would already be dead.

———

Agent James

I knew this was bad, but I was glad Lev was not coming through that door like we did.

Nothing in my prior experiences as a FAM or soldier had

prepared me for this. We had expected spinning TTs or stunned cultists; we did not expect fully prepared SIMs using our OST-issued guns to be there in ambush. I broke to the left and dived behind a sofa.

Concealment, not cover.

BRRRRRAP!

I let out a yell as several rounds found my torso and legs through the couch. The armor must have held against some, but not all, of the bullets. I was in excruciating pain but still operational. As I came up over the top of the couch, I saw them shifting fire onto the other team members.

One saw me and turned.

The pain in my legs was horrific. Something significant was hit—I was already slipping into shock. I could feel broken bones not holding me up properly—

I have to stay in the fight!

Gritting my teeth, I lined up a SIM's head in my rifle's sights and squeezed the trigger.

BRRAP!

It dropped like a sack of bricks.

Scratch one SIM.

As more rounds tore into the last one—I shifted my aim to it as the SIM moved to engage me. I could see her—its—eyes as we started hitting each other with 7.62mm rounds at the same time.

———

Agent Lev

I could hear the gunfire from inside and knew it was too much and from too many directions. They had been ambushed! Without a second thought, I dropped the empty grenade launcher, ran, and dived through the window.

CRACK!

As a "normal" human, that would be extremely stupid. The

window was already jagged and partially blown open, but enough remained to slice me into pieces.

In real life, if you go through a window, you will be lucky to go anywhere but a hospital, much less rolling up like nothing happened. However, being a SIM-hybrid, I rolled up mostly unscathed. The acrid smell of flash-bang grenades and gun smoke was everywhere. Several team members were down. I saw the remaining SIM trying to disengage to a back room.

That is when I saw James.

He was lying on the ground in a dead heap, not moving. Blood had pooled all around him.

I could feel the rage inside me, and I lost all control.

With a low, inhuman growl, I overtook the SIM and tackled it just as it reached the door to the next room. We were going over thirty miles per hour.

As I smashed into it, we went through the drywall next to the door, taking out the supports on the edge of the door as well. While it was on the ground under me, I unlimbered one of my knives.

It tried to break out of my grasp, but I held it down.

I chopped and cut and ripped. I didn't stop. Over and over, I stabbed and slashed. Blood was everywhere. I smashed the knife over and over into the base of its skull to kill it. Long after it was dead, I was chopping pieces into smaller pieces and screaming at the top of my lungs.

I was the monster now.

When the rage left me, I didn't recognize the SIM as ever being human. Its limbs and head were severed. Its body had been ripped by hundreds of knife attacks. I looked down at the hilts of my knives. At some point, I must have drawn the other one. I had broken both while chopping the SIM to bits, and I was completely covered in dark-red blood.

I turned to my teammates, who had formed a hasty perimeter around me. I heard Chayton's voice—very calm and steady. That meant he was concerned—not about me, but about the SIM part of me.

"Are you done, Agent Levingston?" he asked.

"Not even close. I'm going to do worse to that f—ing reverend!" I responded.

I let out a low growl, and we all recognized the sound. Chayton was still looking my way.

"Are you still with us? Are you in control?" he asked calmly.

I thought for a minute. The rage had gone from a hurricane to an angry storm.

"Check, boss. In control," I replied.

"Glad to hear," he said.

"Overwatch, if it moves, it bleeds, check?" Chayton radioed to the sniper teams.

"Check," and "Check."

No one was getting out alive past us. We checked on our downed officers; I went over to James.

He looked small in death.

I gently picked him up and put him on the couch that was shredded with bullets. I could see there were many bullets in his armor, as well. The armor had stopped many of them, but some had gotten through, at least one into his torso. But then there was the one I could not help looking at.

The one through the top part of his visor.

Less than an inch.

That is the difference between glancing off his helmet and losing my favorite person in the world. I pulled off his helmet. A 7.62mm round had taken him in the skull, just above his eyes. Those beautiful green eyes, the eyes of the man I loved, now stared blankly at me.

Tears were pouring down my face, but I didn't care. I picked him up in a single motion and held him to me. The parts of his body that I could feel through his armor were already getting cold.

Sobbing, I laid him back down on the couch.

Finally, I turned to the team.

They were watching their fields of fire, but they nodded to me. I knew that meant, "We are sorry for your loss."

I nodded back—time to work.

I had a reverend to kill.

———

The Reverend

The gunfire above had stopped.

Either the Deathwalkers had won, or the police were coming down soon. Only the Deathwalkers could have picked up and moved the pedestal and altar here. The altar and platform were with him in the basement, the tome resting on top.

I heard a thunderous crash and felt the foundation above me shake. I had wondered how the battle was going until I listened to the inhuman scream of a Deathwalker. I have never heard such a sound in my life. It was deafening, and I could sense rage and sorrow as it went on … and on …

The scream pierced everything, and I must admit—

I was terrified.

There was no doubt now about the victor, and I could hear them coming down the stairs …

My *Other* had taken over my body completely, so I had the capabilities of a Deathwalker now. Holding the OST rifle, I waited, my opaque face shield down. My rifle was already aimed at the only door in or out.

This was it.

I had to stop them, or the Ascension would not happen, and all would be lost! I know I have God on my side, though. He would not allow me to fail, so I knew we would prevail!

BANG! BRRAP!

The door flew off its hinges as several flash-bang explosions and bullets tore it asunder. I flipped up my visor, ready to shoot whoever came through first.

How is this possible?

Only ten feet away from me, moving impossibly fast and covered head to toe in dark-red blood, it rushed me with that horrible sound that only Deathwalkers could make. I fired my rifle into it, but it sidestepped as it closed. Only a few of my rounds hit it.

I felt something hit my neck impossibly hard, and I flipped over backward.

———

Agent Lev

The flash-bangs and rounds took the door off its hinges. I ran through the door as the blasts went off.

I didn't care about pain or fear or anything. I was so angry I saw red.

The Reverend was in the center of the room, holding a rifle pointed my way. He was now definitely a SIM. The shock on his face was evident as he flipped up his visor, and we locked our eyes briefly—he looked scared.

He should be.

A few of his rounds sunk into my armor, and I stepped sideways as I reached him. At least one got through my armor. Strangely, it didn't hurt much; it was more of a mental registering of damage.

I put my whole body and arm into my "clothesline" to his elongated neck.

Because I had to sidestep, I struck him in the neck with my outstretched rifle instead. It hit so hard that he flipped and landed head-first. He was stunned for only a moment as he shot to his feet incredibly fast and turned on me. He had lost his rifle but had a knife in his hand and was smiling at me. My rifle had broken when I hit his neck— the barrel clearly bent and useless.

I tossed it to the side.

This is the part where I tell everyone, "Stay back! This one is mine!" and fight him *mano-a-mano.*

Well, in the movies, anyway.

I smiled back—and then dived sideways to the ground.

He looked surprised by this and started to turn back around as several MP-5s and two FN-SCARS chewed his head apart. They knew to aim for the head—and he had given them time to aim.

BRRRAP, BRRRAP!

Their combined automatic fire blew his head and neck apart, and he dropped lifeless to the ground.

"Nice shooting, fellas," I said as I got up.

Several did a nod my way.

After clearing all areas of the basement, we started our intel sweep. We rifled through the pockets of the dead SIMs, took back our OST weapons, did a thorough check for any intel to take, and then set charges on the pedestal and altar. We left the strange tome atop the altar to be destroyed as well. Then, I picked up James and carried him out.

There was no need to look behind; the other officers took the rest of our fallen.

As soon as we were far enough away, SWAT keyed the detonator.

BOOM!

The flat crack of a high explosive reached our ears as the blast wave went over our position. We got up to look. The windows were blown out, and we could already see the smoke coming from them. Explosions light things on fire.

We watched for a bit as the flames engulfed the house.

CHAPTER 17
THE END OF THE BEGINNING

Pacific Ocean
Ashta'goth

ASHTA'GOTH SEETHED WITH ANGER, its expectations shattered.

It had anticipated a worthy adversary, not a devastating defeat. The relentless assault of bombs and a barrage of a thousand cannon rounds had decimated its once formidable mass. And those infuriating green bugs had only added insult to injury.

It had recovered some of its mass from the ocean buffet, though.

Soon, it would be strong enough to attack again. This time, its desire for a challenge was fully sated.

Already, huge ships and many more flying things that had hurt it so severely were looking for it. Luckily, it had made good time and was already far into the Pacific Ocean. It would continue to hide from this "sonar" as it swam far into the deep ocean and continued to feed …

With gulp after gulp, time feed it.

It was not as big as it had been on the beach, but it was still much bigger than the tiny bit that had survived the attack, which felt good. It started to make its way inland and would come ashore in an entirely new place. Time for some revenge!

Suddenly, it felt a familiar sensation—the same one it felt at the first church—when that explosion sent it back to its parallel plane.

The humans had destroyed the new altar!

It roared in anger as it felt itself pulled back to its plane of existence.

All that was left of Ashta'goth on Earth now was a sudden, giant bubble of air—where it used to be.

The bubble quickly rose toward the surface of the ocean.

Agent Lev

We had returned to our office in Denver.

The government had given us a heroes' welcome, both for our achievement and for its own political purposes.

Still, it was nice to be treated as a hero instead of a monster.

After memorial and funeral services—far too many of them—we eventually got back to the new normal. The AARs were relentless—the government went on to analyze every shred of information on our new enemy as it could.

For those who have never been in the federal government, it is less than fully efficient. I recounted the events, all of them, dozens of times. Even though it was all in my report, every bigwig felt so important that they had to hear it firsthand from me.

Oh well, that is the job.

The TTs and flying horrors suddenly disappeared after we blew up the altar and platform. Before that, some of the bodies of the fallen monsters had been taken by the government.

And several were absconded with by civilians.

Even though the bodies "disappeared" back to wherever they came from when the altar and the tome were destroyed, there was plenty of time for the curious to document everything. Even though the other creatures died immediately, it took a few hours for all the parts of them to dissolve away into nothing. Some people had even live-streamed the attack on the beach; many of their feeds ended with a giant tentacle smashing down to end the video—along with their life. There was no hiding or covering this one up; it was just damage control.

The Big One was never seen or heard from again besides on those social media streams.

The Coast Guard, Navy, Harbor Patrol, and every news agency you could think of now scoured the ocean. The beaches were closed indefinitely, and police forensics were going over every inch.

It is safe to assume that if it were still here, it would have attacked someone by now. Confirmation also came when the TT and flying horrors died; Alan said it was an exact time match to when we blew up the altar and tome.

Thank God.

Although I was raised as a Christian, I renounced religion as an adult. Even so, I wondered what God would make such a creature as we fought. I'm sure many people were questioning the universe at this point …

I visited officers, agents, and civilians in the hospital. I filled out tons of reports.

And I cried—a lot. I am not ashamed of it. I am just glad that I can still cry. And I was relieved that my alien rage did not turn me into something utterly inhuman for good.

I decided I needed a few days off. Once management decided the worst of the damage control was over, I was granted two days. I knew where I was going.

James had no living family to contact; I would be his family. I didn't cry anymore; you eventually cry out every drop, and then it stops. I decided that he and I—well, his urn and I—would visit the destroyed church in Colorado Springs, where I was "turned." This is what led to what James and I had. I pulled up to the ruined church's parking lot.

The abandoned cars had long ago been towed to the impound lot and gone over—every inch of them.

I pulled up and parked.

I can't believe it has been over a year since it all started, I thought.

"We are here, Love. Where you and I started," I said to the urn as I walked to the imploded church.

The roof had caved in, and the outer structure, all the parts that could burn, were gone. The police tape was long gone, and signs and construction tape warned people not to enter, but I entered anyway. I could see where James was and where I was when the bomb had gone off. Forensics had determined, from looking at the data, that there were more explosives in the basement. That is why the explosion was much bigger than planned.

I was amazed.

Between surviving the explosion and the quick actions of the responding officers, we had lived.

I held back tears.

James had not lived. Not in the end—

I drew my pistol in a flash.

One of "them" was nearing; I could feel it.

Walking out of the building, I looked toward where I felt it. Nothing moved. I waited patiently, pistol steady, and aimed it at the tree line. I could feel it getting closer.

It came out of the forest.

Standing at a height of about three feet, it halted and gazed at me. Its limbs were elongated, and it likely weighed at least a hundred pounds. Its head was slightly misshapen, with large bat-like ears and striking bright blue eyes.

It ran toward me …

Taking the slack out of the trigger, I aimed for the head. When I realized what it was, I took my finger off the trigger and indexed it along the slide instead.

It was a large-sized and incredibly muscular dog!

Well, it used to be a dog—

I could see its elongated tongue flapping to one side as it "smiled" and ran straight at me. Its elongated tail was wagging behind it as it ran, and divots of earth came up behind it.

Damn, those were some mean-looking nails and teeth on that dog.

And it was running, full speed, at well over forty miles per hour.

I am unsure how, but we both knew we were friends, not enemies. I holstered my weapon and got down on one knee. The dog was letting out that weird SIM sound mixed with the happy barks of a—

What the hell kind of dog is that?

When it got to me, it tried to kill me—by licking me to death. It was happily barking and jumping into my arms. If I weren't a SIM-hybrid, it would have injured me.

The dog was incredibly muscular, and its bones were like mine. It felt like an overly excited muscle-bound brick and was clearly a SIM mix like me.

"It" was a "he" on closer inspection.

He was filthy and covered in mud and muck, and I could see dried blood around his mouth and on his body.

I laughed out loud.

Upon seeing him, I can only imagine the poor creatures of the forest thinking they had found an easy and quick meal. If he felt as hungry as I did while changing, many of his predators would end up as his snack instead.

Finally, he stopped licking, continued lying in my lap, and slept. I looked at him and the urn and smiled. I gently petted and stroked his furless but filthy body.

I guess I had a family after all.

———

After my two days off, I had to return to work and prepare for "the next OI."

Facing an extraordinary public onslaught, the government reacted as it always has: first, by trying to deny what happened and—eventually realizing they couldn't—they started blaming everyone but themselves for what happened. And, of course, blaming each other, at the highest levels of government, for an unprecedented and undetectable attack. All the talking heads and many Americans were demanding to know why we hadn't protected them from an unprecedented attack.

I shook my head in disgust.

Even with the alien bodies gone—the destruction, the dead people, and the photographic evidence still remained. Strangely, and luckily, something about the hybrids and symbiosis of all the SIMs kept them here instead of "disappearing" like the "full" monsters did when the Big One left our existence. That was good news because we could keep examining the dead SIMs, and because I did not want to go wherever they came from.

I mentally shuddered at that thought.

The other good news was that we had all the funding and support we could ever want—and then some. The bad news? All the higher-level managers who wanted to make a name for themselves are applying for command positions at OST, much like what happened after 9/11.

Most of them aren't good managers; they don't know what leadership truly is. Being in charge makes you a supervisor. Leadership involves being good at what you do, caring about the mission and your subordinates over your own comfort and safety, and inspiring them to follow you and your orders—not out of fear but out of earned respect.

Oh well. I scratched Frank's ears.

Frank.

I looked down at Frank and giggled. He looked up at me with the silliest, cutest open-mouth smile you could ask for.

It turned out he still had a microchip.

When I took him to the vet, we found out who his owners were—a family with the surname "Scott." Their son, also presumed dead, was named Timothy Scott.

I also found out he is a "Mexican hairless," or the formal name of "Xoloitzcuintle" or "Xolo." I'm glad I can just say "Show-Low" for short.

This one was *much* bigger and more fearsome than the "standard" version of its breed.

I had to have the veterinarian sign a nondisclosure agreement. Although my dog seemed healthy, it was apparent that it had followed me in the "it's not natural" department. The veterinarian was ashen-faced when he talked with me.

For some reason, my dog and I made him nervous.

Maybe it was all the tentacles on Frank's X-rays and MRIs?

Frank was a hit at the office, too.

By the end of his first day at the office, he had been petted by everyone there, and many even received a lick from his foot-long tongue. However, despite all the affection, the SAC initially said "no pets" until I managed to reason with him.

I asked if that included SIMs.

After asking what I meant, I told him we would soon have weapons that are illegal for police, already had a SIM/human mutant in the office, and were now fighting the occult for the survival of the entire world. Did we really need to enforce a "no pets except for service animals" rule simply because it is a government building? I asked.

Robert got my point.

Plus, I told him I would quit on the spot if he said no. I *do* have to take care of Frank now, after all. No Frank—no me, I told him. Robert reluctantly agreed.

I then had to list Frank as a service animal.

Government people are weird.

———

Finally, after two more weeks, the FBI granted me two more days of leave; I took Frank and headed for the mountains—specifically, Boulder, Colorado.

I had booked a hotel in the heart of Pearl Street, the "main drag" of Boulder, with many shops and restaurants on a pedestrian-only outdoor street.

The Hotel Boulderado.

My Jeep stopped at the valet.

A young man, probably all of twenty, came to my door and opened it.

At least chivalry is not dead, I thought.

"Here you go, ma'am," he said as he opened my door.

He clearly was trying not to ogle me; I was still beautiful.

His features did a comical 180 when my face turned, and I got out. He had seen the left side, obviously. When he saw the scarred right side of my face, it was like the Phantom of the Opera. And when I stretched to my full height and Frank "smiled" at him, he nearly fainted.

"H-h-here you go, ma'am." He handed me a valet slip.

"Thank you," I replied with a half-smile.

I went around and got Frank out.

The young man had gone around back.

"Do you want me to call a bellhop for you, er … for your luggage?"

I looked at the two large and heavy, fully loaded suitcases.

This will be fun to watch …

"Nah, I got it," I said.

Then I grabbed both handles and picked them up in one hand, holding Frank's leash in the other.

He went pale again and scurried off.

I went into the lobby and heard conversations go quiet, one by one, as people saw me and Frank. I am not sure which of us scared them more. I waited my turn and checked in.

"I see you booked for one night. How many keys would you like?" the pretty young woman asked me. I don't know if she was hyper-professional or just didn't mind, but she treated me like …

Like a person.

"Two, please," I responded with a genuine smile.

She returned my smile and leaned over the counter to look down at Frank.

"Aww—he is cute!" she said. "Does he need anything?"

She reached down, and Frank licked her hand. She smiled and looked back at me.

"No, I have everything I need, thank you."

"Then have a nice stay, Miss Levingston."

I waved goodbye.

It was so nice to just have a "normal" conversation for once.

We walked to the elevator and then to our room. Other staff and guests gave us the hairy eyeball when they saw Frank's "Service Animal—Do Not Pet" vest but said nothing. If they had, I would have said he was for PTSD and to keep me from getting angry. All true.

After settling in, I took Frank for a walk so he could relieve himself.

We went downstairs and took a walk on Spruce Street, which runs parallel to Pearl Street, the "main street" most people were on.

Pearl Street was fantastic. Couples and kids strolled and played, and it was usually filled with people to be around. Right now, though, I wasn't in the mood to be stared at in fear. So, Frank and I took the road less traveled …

It was a pleasant summer evening; we could smell the flowers and enjoyed the lush trees giving us shade as we walked. Frank was excited to see people but didn't understand why they were reluctant to come over and say hi now. He found an exciting lawn area to sniff, then spun a few times and relieved himself.

I picked up his poop in a baggie I had brought.

Judging by the bag's weight in my hand, his appetite had clearly not diminished. We disposed of the bag and went to eat at a Sushi place on Spruce Street, near the hotel. It had outdoor seating, and once the hostess seated us, we took a seat at a table.

Other people tried not to stare.

I looked up and saw a nervous couple with a child looking my way. The boy was about twelve years old. I could hear them talking in low tones with him. Finally, they seemed to come to an understanding. The man turned to me and said, "Excuse me, ma'am, I know your dog is in training, but may my son pet him? Is he—" He paused, clearly nervous at the idea "—friendly?"

"Of course," I replied.

I held Frank by the collar—so he wouldn't get too excited and accidentally hurt the kid.

Frank was a brilliant dog, and I think he understood.

Quivering with excitement, his whole muscular body shaking, he calmly let himself be petted and then licked the young boy's hand and arm with a massive, elongated tongue. His parents blanched at the "indog" tongue. I guess that's what you call it—since it's called "inhuman" for us.

But the boy just laughed happily!

"Is a tongue like that normal?" he asked me, with wonder in his eyes.

"No, but Frank here is *special*. He also really likes you!" I glanced up at his worried parents.

"Thank you for visiting us, but you should probably get back to your parents," I told the young boy.

They shot me a relieved "thank you" look.

We finished our dinner in peace, and the boy's parents started to relax.

The boy giggled every time I held up a piece of sushi.

I was playing the "magic game" with him: I would put a piece of sushi on my leg, cover it with my linen napkin, and make Frank wait to eat it. Then, I would say "OK" to Frank, and with a flourish of my linen napkin, he would snap it off my leg like lightning. The same thing happened to anything I dropped; it would never reach the ground. His speed made the sushi seem to "vanish."

Even his parents were smiling at us.

Finally, bellies full, we headed up to our room. After getting ready for bed, I placed Frank's bed over by the gas fireplace. I climbed into bed for what I hoped would be a good night's sleep.

I was almost ready to try to sleep when I felt eyes on me—

Frank was just standing there, staring at me. He let out a little whimper and wagged his tail once.

"No, Frank," I said.

He whimpered and wagged his tail once again.

Dammit. He is going to do this all night until I give up.

"Fine," I said reluctantly, tapping the bed beside me.

Insanely fast, there was a dog beside me in the bed. His tail wagging madly, he went to lick me.

"Unh-uh!" I said, holding him back with one arm.

Damn, we are going to need to train him; his actions will accidentally hurt a normal person.

I clicked my fingers and pointed at the bottom of the bed. He obliged and went to the foot of the bed. With a contented sigh, he lay down and looked at me. I turned off the light, and we went to sleep ...

The next morning, we got up and went down to breakfast.

I was preparing to return to the office again tomorrow—duty called. I smiled and looked up at the beautiful blue sky with fluffy clouds.

What a great day!

After finishing breakfast and a morning constitutional, we got in our Jeep and returned to my condo in the Denver Tech Center.

It was a nice break, but I started thinking of work more now as a cause than as a job. After those things had killed James, I sincerely wanted to kill them all. I knew they were out there and wanted me—and all of humanity—dead. Well good, because I felt the same about them! So, at least I was getting paid to go after them.

Speaking of pay, the good news is that I have racked up quite a bit of overtime. We usually don't get overtime as agents because that is what our extra "availability" pay is for. But we get extra pay when they cancel our days off or schedule us for overtime, and I have gotten a lot of "extra" lately.

CHAPTER 18
AARS

OST DENFO
Agent Lev

WE HAD RETURNED to regular duty, and it had been three months since the Occult Incident was over. We have developed a rotation now for QRF. Each team took a week. The rest of the time, we trained. With every agency and group you could think of. No training was disallowed.

I was finally slated to take the FBI course the other OSTs already had. After that, I was slated for SEAL school in Coronado. There are no women Navy SEALs, but there have also never been any women who were human/SIM-hybrids who attended training there.

So, I may be the first of both.

Everyone knew I was inhumanly strong, but inhuman stamina and will are what every SEAL has. That is why we were all curious to see how I would do. I am sure the government was more than just curious —they would surely study everything I did.

Heck, we even got slots to train Frank in K-9 schools while I was in SEAL training.

Frank and I were in MWR when Greg Morris walked in. He came over and sat next to us.

"Hey, Lev. I need to talk to you," Morris said.

I looked at him questioningly. He never started talking that way, without any preamble—something was up.

"Alright, what's up, Greg?" I said, leaning back in my chair; it groaned under my weight.

"This is classified, and I can get in a lot of trouble, to say the least —" he started.

"Is it a plan to bore me to death by not getting to the point?" I said testily.

He looked at me strangely and *calmly*. I did not like where this was going. I deliberately was short with him to see how serious it was. The fact that he didn't get testy back meant it was important.

"James is alive," he said.

How f—ing dare you! I thought.

I was so angry that I almost struck him, which would have been *very* bad.

"That is the most insensitive and horrible thing you could say to me! What is wrong with you?!" I yelled. Well, not a yell, but not quiet either.

I still had James's ashes in an urn in my condo, and I had gone to his funeral to say goodbye.

This was the least funny "joke"—ever!

Frank got up and looked a bit evil. He could sense my anger and was ready to defend me. Greg made the *shut-up* motion with his hand.

A man named Harold Palmer, one of the NMC guys, came over, drawn by the sudden commotion.

"Everything OK?" he asked.

"Yeah, we are OK," Morris said.

"We are just having a spirited debate," I added.

Harold shrugged and walked away, and Morris turned back to me.

"They lied to you, to all of us. The ashes are not from him. They are studying him now to figure out how he is alive," Morris said.

"You better not be messing with me," I growled.

It had that alien sound when I was genuinely upset.

"I am not. No one is supposed to know. But you know how well the FBI can keep a secret from its own FBI agents … He is in what doctors can only describe as an alien-induced coma."

That's not terrifying or anything, I thought.

I was conflicted because now I thought I had saved James by infecting him, but God knows what he would become. It didn't matter why he was alive, though. I loved him, so come hell or high water, I would see him.

"When I go to see him, and you knew I would, how do I keep the source of the leak secret?" I asked.

He laughed.

"Hell, I'm surprised you hadn't heard it already. Just go."

———

I walked into SSA Blackwell's office without any preamble.

"Chayton, I need a few days of leave," I said.

He looked up at my brusque demand. "No problem. When did you want them?"

I just stared at him—He could see I was pissed.

He sighed.

"Now, I got it. I'm sorry I could not tell you, although someone must have. I'll book a flight to Quantico for you," he said.

I nodded and left. I was going to see James, and I was taking the first flight I could get.

I left Frank at OST DENFO.

In my mood, he might bite someone I was mad at …

The first flight was early the following day, and I landed later that morning in Quantico, Virginia, and went straight to the FBI Headquarters.

"Good morning, I'm here to see Doctor Jeffries," I said.

The receptionist looked up at me and my visitor badge.

"May I tell him the nature of your visit?" she asked.

"Sure. Tell him I'm here to see James," I replied.

She went pale.

Jesus, did everyone but me know?

A short while later, an older, tall, skinny man came in and … waved at me.

"Agent Levingston, good to finally meet you," he said.

We started walking to the hospital wing. I was glad he knew all about me, as he could see the anger in my eyes.

"Please don't kill me. And I mean that," he said, clearly scared. "We had to keep this under wraps. Obviously, that didn't work, but it is still classified and need to know. I'm sure you understand," he said nervously.

"Domestic … f—ing … partner," I growled; the alien menace in my voice was terrifying—even to me. I was getting furious, and he knew it. He looked genuinely frightened.

"You're right, you're right! We should have told you as soon as we knew. I'm s-sorry," he stammered.

Damn straight you are, I thought.

I curtly nodded.

We walked to the ICU and then into a private room. On the outside door, a placard read "ISOLATION PROTOCOLS."

James was in a bed now, but I knew he came from the cold metal table of the morgue.

He was dead on arrival.

And not like the "I saw the light and could see people around me from above, and then came back three minutes later" type of dead. He had multiple GSWs: a 7.62mm round through his brain, another through the left lung, and numerous ones to both legs. And no EEG/ECG activity.

He was *dead* dead.

I tried not to, but I started crying uncontrollably when I saw him lying there in that hospital bed. There were all the usual IVs and monitors, plus *way* too many other monitors I didn't recognize …

My bosses and I will have to have a serious talk about HIPAA.

I was not sobbing. I was beyond that; crying a steady stream of anguished tears. His wounds were horrible, more so because you could see where the surgeries and wounds were already healing, surely causing scars, as I well know. Now, there were signs of life—I watched his chest's slow rise and fall. At least the doctor had shut his eyelids, and I could see them moving in REM.

I was terrified; I knew the only thing that could have saved him.

I had heard the crass term "Marine by injection" when some of the guys at my work (former Marines, obviously) talked about their wives or girlfriends. Well, he was probably alive because I infected him—with the world's first alien sexually transmitted disease. I was terrified about what he would become. Would he still be human?

Would he remember me, us? Would he start to have trouble with his temper?

Doctor Jeffries broke my trance.

"So, they brought him here in a body bag that was shipped to Quantico. I have to tell you—he damn near gave Doctor Mandela, the coroner, a heart attack. You can imagine the doctor's surprise when he realized James had started breathing," he said, pausing briefly.

"The doctor doing the autopsy did not expect to see his chest subtly rising and falling. He immediately took his pulse and watched his respirations. His pulse was 10 bpm, and his respiration was seven breaths per minute. Taking his blood pressure next, he saw it was also very low—thirty over twenty. He should not be alive. So, alarms were raised to his supervisor, which is me. I then sent it to my supervisors and so on. His "survival" was immediately classified and became need to know at the highest levels. Naturally, it immediately got out to almost everyone in the FBI—our internal security is atrocious."

I also felt they had messed up royally.

Since when does a domestic partner not have a need to know?!

I calmed myself and took a good look at the man I loved. He lay utterly still except for the unnaturally slow rise and fall of his chest. I could see where the tissue was already healing and worse …

I could sense him.

He was one of *them*. Or I should say now, one of *us*.

Doctor Jeffries spoke again. "We have already taken blood

samples; they all have alien cells. The best we can tell, it's like the opposite of AIDS."

AARS—Acquired Alien Rejuvenation Syndrome? I thought to myself.

I stared silently at James for a long time.

I don't care how he comes back; I love him.

"You'll keep me advised with *complete* daily reports on his condition," I told the doctor.

It was not a question.

"Yes, Ma'am," he replied, with a nervous gulp.

I turned silently away and walked off. I had to leave; I was in agony. I had saved James's life—

But what had I done to him?

Deep in my heart, I knew this whole nightmare would never be a one-off.

EPILOGUE

Two Years Later—the Start of the School Year—Late August
Tonto National Forest—Tempe, Arizona
Dorothy

DOROTHY SCRANTON'S heart raced with the thrill of what would come.

Beta Zeta Sigma had a new pledge, Amanda Collins, a young woman who had quickly become like a sister to her. The anticipation for Amanda's initiation ritual, scheduled for tomorrow night, was building up in Dorothy. She couldn't wait to see Amanda's reaction and witness what was about to take place.

She was going to get the scare of her life.

The idea came to us while having dinner at the Top of the Rock Restaurant, where we often gathered to discuss our plans, usually every Friday at different—and always expensive—restaurants. It was Claressa's turn to pay, and she also had no idea what paying off her credit cards looked like. We all came from affluent families, a fact that often led to our reckless spending habits.

Speaking of extreme spending, my diligent personal assistant,

Peter, had scoured the state to find what I desired. I had explicitly asked for a book that emanated an "occult" aura, one that was large and contained summoning rituals, a book that held secrets from a forgotten time. And it should be costly.

He scored big time.

This was no ordinary book; it was a portal to a world of mystery and intrigue. An occult bookstore in Sacramento had it. It wasn't even on the shelf, and he had to work hard to convince the owner to part with it—for a hefty sum. So much so that Peter had to use one of my credit cards, the Mastercard Black Card. I didn't ask how much it cost or the balance on my card, and I didn't care. Dad covered the bill.

After dinner, we all left. I couldn't believe it was almost time!

Tomorrow night was going to be awesome!

———

Late the next night, Saturday, we went deep into Tonto National Forest. We had already scouted the perfect spot the weekend before.

The girls from Beta Zeta Sigma sorority assembled atop the hill. They decided that the initiation of their newest member called for a good scare.

They had all agreed to perform the "Summoning of the Damned."

As the sorority president, I made the decisions—and I picked the creepy spot high on a hilltop, perfect for isolation and privacy.

There were ten of us, including Amanda.

Under the shimmering light of the full moon, the other sorority sisters and I gathered. We had meticulously planned a Wiccan-style summoning at the stroke of midnight, a surprise awaiting Amanda at the end of our ritual. This surprise was not just a simple initiation or a life-altering experience that would leave Amanda in awe, we all felt the thrill of the unknown in the air.

"OK, ladies. It is time," I said.

Everyone started disrobing except for Amanda, who looked shocked. We all smiled. Of course, we had not told her that the summoning would be done in the nude! All of her actions, even disrobing, looked awkward.

This was going to be fun!

It was quiet at almost midnight. There was no wind, the moon shone brightly, and a pronounced chill was in the air. The "chill" in the air was a cool seventy-six degrees.

Cool compared to the hundred-plus-degree days, anyway.

Once everyone, including Amanda, was naked, we circled the book. We had placed it on a stone about three feet in diameter, and it was open to the incantation of some nebulous demon creature.

I didn't care what the demon was.

The book warned us of this creature's power but then told us precisely how to summon it. As if a book would warn you about something and then tell you how to do it anyway …

I always thought the D&D stuff was just for boys who wanted to stay virgins eternally. I only cared because it gave me something to read aloud while the other girls chanted.

They made Amanda sit on a rock next to the book, and she was in the position the book called for to be "the sacrifice."

We lit candles all around to provide light. Although the clear sky and full moon made them unnecessary, they added ambiance. I had otherwise carefully followed all the instructions in the book.

This was going to be my best initiation ever!

The other women started chanting as instructed by the book. At the appropriate spot, I added the words of the chant to bring forth the most potent "demon" in the book.

"Othra'fla, Hellious, Shara'goth …"

I kept saying all these nonsensical words until the "summoning" was complete. As I finished, a low, plaintive moaning came from the woods, and an unnatural mist formed on the ground around us. It seemed to just come up from the ground all around us, a grey blanket that shouldn't be swirling at our feet—but it was.

We decided the moaning from a phone recording we found would come from a little speaker we had brought. As Amanda got scared, we would all scream in fear and run away—

That was the plan, anyway.

When Laura had hit the remote control, which she did near the end of the summoning, the recording of the low, menacing moaning began. There was a problem, though. Right after she started playing the recording, I finished the summoning words—

That was when the mist had started.

None of the girls were running away now—because they couldn't. Somehow, I was frozen in place, as was everyone. They all looked as terrified as I felt!

The mist was not something we had planned on.

Beyond the recorded wail of the damned we were playing, a creature slowly coalesced from the mist.

———

The Mist

The rift was slight, almost invisible, but it was there. Just as the chants that allowed Ashta'goth to pass to this plane had not gone unnoticed, this Earth had not gone unnoticed.

Nor unfelt.

Even now, the most formidable and attuned beings are relentlessly scouring for ways to break the divide. The easy-prey buffet was irresistible to them.

It had relentlessly sought a way into this new world for countless eons. Now, in a brazen act of reckless desperation, some unwitting humans had dared to summon it, unknowingly sealing their doom.

It came to this new world, this new reality, as a giant area of mist. The cultists had done an excellent job summoning it. As decreed in the ancient tome, it coalesced from the mist into its proper form. The sight was more than any human mind could handle and stay sane. It could see their terror and now—madness—and it was delicious!

It attacked and then permeated into its living sacrifice. After subsuming its prey, it smiled at the others assembled around it. Amanda's inhuman smile split her face almost in half, revealing hundreds of long, razor-sharp teeth.

The feast, culminating in their insatiable hunger, was on the brink of commencing …

ACKNOWLEDGMENTS

I am deeply grateful to all the individuals and experiences that have influenced and shaped my books.

First, I want to express my profound gratitude for the influence of Mark Everett Stone's BSI series of books. His series was a guiding light and profoundly influenced my narrative and character development. I highly recommend exploring his works.

Also, HP Lovecraft and his Cthulhu monsters, GURPS Horror, physicists everywhere for the parallel universe concept, and evil cultists who want to bring about the end of the world.

And, of course, my beta readers and development team at My Word Publishing for all their help in creating a quality product for you—my reader.

Last, but certainly not least, my experiences with the federal government: as an enlisted soldier and officer in the military, a uniformed and undercover law enforcement officer, and an instructor.

I hope you enjoy the adventure—and the horror—of the Occult Strike Team.

ABOUT THE AUTHOR

———

RK Jack is a retired government agent with over thirty years of experience in federal law enforcement and the military. He has been on SRT and VIPR teams and worked in uniformed and undercover positions, including twenty years as a federal air marshal (FAM).

He deployed for OP Desert Storm as an enlisted soldier and later became a US Army National Guard lieutenant.

Now, he is busily writing books to portray the military and police not as stoic, unfeeling superheroes—but as real people with real feelings and fears. Those fallible men and women show their heroism by facing those fears to protect others when duty calls.

He hopes you find the realistic portrayal of these people, as they go up against the supernatural for the first time, to be delightfully unique.

This book is the first of the Occult Strike Team series, with more to come …

CONNECT WITH THE AUTHOR

I hope you enjoyed reading my book!

If you would like to leave an honest review, it is always appreciated.

This is just the first book in the Occult Strike Team series, with sequels already on the way…

If you would like to have me visit your book club or group, I live in Denver, Colorado, and am available upon request. I can be reached anytime at my website at rkjackauthor.com

Thank you for your patronage!

GLOSSARY

AAR After-Action Review

AFB Air Force Base

APC Armored Personnel Carrier

BATFE Bureau of Alcohol, Tobacco, Firearms and Explosives

BB Battle Buddy (military)

CAP Close Air Patrol

CCTV Closed-Circuit Television

CS CS gas (military)

D&D Dungeons and Dragons (a role-playing game)

DENFO Denver Field Office

DL Driver's License

DM Defensive Measures (hand-to-hand fight training)

DOE Department of Energy

EDIP Explain, Demonstrate, Imitate, and Practice

EDP Emotionally Disturbed Person

EOD Explosives Ordnance Disposal (military)

EVAC Evacuate

FAM(S) Federal Air Marshal (Service)

FFL Federal Firearms License

FLETC Federal Law Enforcement Training Center

FN FN Herstal (company that makes firearms)
FRAGO Fragmentary Order (military)
FTX Field Training Exercise (military)
GOV Government-Owned Vehicle
GSW Gunshot Wound
GURPS Generic Universal Role-Playing System
HIPAA Health Insurance Portability and Accountability Act
HIT High-Intensity Training gear
HVAC Heating, Ventilation, and Air Conditioning
IR Infrared
JTTF Joint Terrorism Task Force
KIA Killed in Action
KST Known or Suspected Terrorist
LEO Law Enforcement Officer
MCC Mission Control Center
MMA Mixed Martial Arts
MX Tesla Model X SUV (modified for combat)
MWR Morale, Welfare, and Recreation (military)
NATO North Atlantic Treaty Organization
NER Church of the New Era Revivalists
NMC Nuclear Materials Couriers
NSC National Security Council
NVG Night Vision Goggles
OCC Office of Chief Counsel
OI Occult Incident
OPORD Operations Order (military)
ORP Organized Rally Point (military)
OST Overwatch Surveillance Team (Occult Strike Team)
Overwatch Watching over a person taking direct action
PA Public Address (system)
PAX Passenger(s) (airline)
PMCS Preventive Maintenance, Checks, and Services
POV Personally Owned Vehicle
PT Physical Training
PTSD Posttraumatic Stress Disorder

REM Rapid Eye Movement

RON Remain Overnight (airline term)

QRF Quick Reaction Force

RDO Regular Day Off (airline)

RFID Radio-Frequency Identification

RO Registered Owner (of a vehicle)

RTB Return to Base

SA Special Agent

SAC Special Agent in Charge

SATCOM Satellite Communications

SEAL Sea, Air, and Land (SPEC OPS for US Navy)

SFB Space Force Base

SIM Simulant, or Simulant Infected Monster

SITREP Situation Report (military)

SMG Submachine Gun

SOP Standard Operating Procedure

SSA Supervisory Special Agent

STU-III Secure Terminal Equipment (model 3)

SWAT Special Weapons and Tactics

TT Tentacle Thing

VIPR Visual Intermodal Protection and Response

WOG Wrath of God